*Raves for Dianne Day and Fremont Jones*

## DEATH TRAIN TO BOSTON

"Fremont Jones is a laudable and attractive heroine. . . . Ms. Day has done her research and readers who relish being transported to another time will find this an extremely appealing book. Every facet of the novel—the writing, the characterizations, the suspense, the history—provides knowledge and just plain good storytelling."
—*The Book Report*

## EMPEROR NORTON'S GHOST

"Fremont is a spirited young woman ahead of her time and her adventures make enthralling reading."
—*The Purloined Letter*

"[An] appealing portrait of a spirited, irrepressible heroine."
—*Publishers Weekly*

"Fremont is . . . [a] delightful, feisty, independent adventurer . . . [who] exhibits a wry sense of humor."
—*Southbridge Evening News* (Southbridge, Mass.)

## THE BOHEMIAN MURDERS

"Thrill to the third in this exciting series featuring the liberated Fremont at her bravest. . . . This knockout setting draws you in like no other. *The Bohemian Murders* conjures up the murkiest mystery—you can just hear the waves and smell the fog. Bravo."
—*Mystery Lovers Bookshop News*

"Delightful." —*San Francisco Chronicle*

"A plucky heroine, a darkly handsome suitor in the wings, and a glimpse back into history all add to the charms this series has to offer."
—*Alfred Hitchcock Mystery Magazine*

"Light, entertaining, and ever-so-slightly racy, *The Bohemian Murders* is perfect summer reading."
—*Wisconsin State Journal*

"An attractive and involving historical."
—*Library Journal*

"Fast-paced machinations keep the reader turning page after page with anticipation." —*The Carmel Pine Cone*

"By the third book in a new series, most new sleuths tend to flounder. Not that plucky Bostonian Caroline Fremont Jones . . . The strong-minded Fremont surrenders neither her independence nor her intelligence. . . . This liberated woman has come too far ever to go back."
—*The New York Times Book Review*

### FIRE AND FOG

"A winner." —*Monterey County Herald*

"Day's decorous, spirited heroine is as charming as ever as she picks her way through a world of rubble where every acquaintance could be a killer." —*Kirkus Reviews*

"The strong-willed, intelligent Jones shines, whether she's helping her friend, fending off suitors, or fleeing the clutches of ninja smugglers." —*Publishers Weekly*

"One of the best books of 1996 . . . showcases Dianne Day's incredible storytelling abilities." —*Mostly Murder*

"Great fun." —*Nashville Banner*

"An attention catcher . . . you won't put the book down in a hurry." —*The Times & Democrat*

"A distinctive and appealing voice." —*Library Journal*

"A delightful period mystery." —*Booklist*

"Excellent, involving tale." —*Bookwatch*

## THE STRANGE FILES OF FREMONT JONES
### Macavity Award Winner for Best First Mystery Novel

# Death Train to Boston

*A Fremont Jones Mystery*

## DIANNE DAY

**BANTAM BOOKS**
*New York Toronto London Sydney Auckland*

DEATH TRAIN TO BOSTON

A Bantam Book/published by arrangement with Doubleday.

PUBLISHING HISTORY
Doubleday hardcover edition published October 1999
Bantam mass market edition / July 2000

ISBN 0-553-58055-8

Published simultaneously in the United States and Canada

Bantam Books are published by Bantam Books, a division of Random
House, Inc. Its trademark, consisting of the words "Bantam Books"
and the portrayal of a rooster, is Registered in U.S. Patent and Trademark Office and in other countries. Marca Registrada. Bantam
Books, 1540 Broadway, New York, New York 10036.

PRINTED IN THE UNITED STATES OF AMERICA

OPM     10  9  8  7  6  5  4  3  2

## ACKNOWLEDGMENTS

Thanks are due to Robert Rosenblum, for the basic concept that evolved into this book; and to Robert Irvine, for sharing his extensive knowledge of Utah geography and matters Mormon.

# Death Train to Boston

# 1

THIS MUST BE how it feels to come back from the dead, I thought as I struggled to open my eyes. Every inch of my body, especially my uncooperative eyelids, felt heavy as lead. I heard a sound, a plaintive moan, and only when another voice spoke did I realize the moan had come from me.

The other voice said, "Awake, unfortunate woman!"

That voice and its biblical-sounding manner of command were unfamiliar, so alien to my ears in both language and tone that fear coursed coldly through me and broke my leaden bonds. I opened my eyes.

Immediately I wished I had not. I was lying stark naked in a strange bed, in a strange room, with a man I had never seen before in my life standing over me. I had not the slightest idea in the world how I'd come to be here.

Whatever this was, whatever I had done now, whatever horrible mistake I'd made, I couldn't face it. I closed my eyes and turned my head away. That is, I *tried* to turn my head, I meant to turn it—but the pain

was so severe, and my head was so heavy, that I doubt I
moved at all. Instead I was sinking. Everything went
black, and I was glad of it.

———

Goddammit!" Michael Kossoff swore aloud, adding
several more obscene words under his breath for good
measure. As the sky stopped spinning overhead, he began to assess himself and the situation.

His collarbone was broken on the left side. He was
certain of that much, due to the pain that ensued when
he tried to move his left arm, and where the pain was
located. He lifted his right hand and felt his face, which
appeared to be intact, beard included, though he had
the very devil of a headache. Without looking down he
moved first one leg and then the other. Flexed his ankles; wiggled his toes inside his shoes. Everything
seemed in working order except for the shoulder, and
that damned throbbing in his head.

He supposed he could have been unconscious for a
while; in fact, on further thought he believed he must
have been, because of the initial dizziness combined
with a certain sluggishness of mind. He wasn't yet entirely sure what had happened. He did know he was in
no way ready to sit up, so he closed his eyes and put his
ears to work.

Michael heard—and felt—a vast silence around him;
the unnerving sort of silence that one notices when for
days there has been steady sound in the background,
then suddenly the reassurance of that steady sound is
gone. Yes: The comforting, lulling hum and clack of the
train moving swiftly over its tracks was now missing.
He listened harder: Within the disturbing hush there
were people crying, moaning, sobbing—and for one ter-
rifying, irrational moment Michael wondered if he had
finally died and gone to hell.

"Where I belong, several times over," he muttered,

aware even as he did so that Fremont would not agree with this last point.

Fremont. . . .

Along with her name, her face filled Michael's mind: the murky depths of her green eyes that always made him wonder what she was thinking; the quirk of her mouth; that dark reddish hair as stubbornly straight as her narrow, uncorseted backbone.

Michael lay for a moment not caring where he was, just contemplating, with an aching pleasure that was quite different from the other aches in his body, how much he loved Fremont Jones. Even better—indeed the cause of a sudden, revivifying warmth that coursed through his whole body—was knowing that she also loved him.

But then, in the blink of an eye, all pleasure vanished as he cried aloud, "Oh, my God! Fremont!"

———

Someone kept poking and prodding at me, when all I wanted was to sleep. If I moved, it would hurt—that was my one thought. Yet this poking about on my person had to stop.

As forcefully as I could, I said, "Stop that!" And then, with the greatest reluctance, I opened my eyes.

"Just what do you think you're doing?" I asked the strange man who was examining my anatomy as minutely as if I had been a specimen for dissection in a laboratory. Perhaps I was. Perhaps I had died, or some ill-informed person had thought I was dead and shipped my body off. Dimly I recalled knowing a woman that same thing had happened to. . . .

But no, on second thought that was not likely, for most definitely I lay not on some cold, scientific-looking metal trolley but in a bed, on a mattress that might have been comfortable had I not, overall, hurt so much.

"I am examining you to determine the nature and

extent of your injuries," the man said gruffly. He may have intended to smile, but obviously he did it so seldom that his face had forgotten the corners of the mouth were supposed to turn up.

"I will thank you to desist and give me back my clothes," I said, injecting a note of outrage into my voice as best I could. Then I crossed my arms over my breasts with great difficulty. I would have drawn up my legs, but I could not; they refused to cooperate with me. Nor could I raise my head. I said, "You are a doctor, I presume?"

"No," he replied, making no move whatever to cover my nakedness, "I am not a doctor. I am your savior."

More biblical language. "A likely story. Savior, my foot!" I scoffed, but without conviction. Perhaps I really *was* dead.

My mind refused to work with its usual efficiency. I wanted very much to escape back into unconsciousness, where my body might rest and my thoughts attain oblivion. Yet my brain, which is undoubtedly my most reliable organ, argued against that. For one thing, judging by his odd vocabulary this man could be a dangerous fanatic; certainly he was no savior. Second, around fanatics one had better stay awake—therefore I would.

I strained my peripheral vision in an attempt to ascertain if there might be someone else in the room who could assist me. Preferably another woman. But I couldn't see around my fanatical savior. He was a large man, standing so close that he completely filled my visual field.

"You should be grateful," he said. "I could have left you there to die."

"A likely story," I said again. But I wondered, *Left me where?*

"You have a serious head wound and were bleeding profusely."

"Do you always completely undress people who have wounds upon their *heads*?" I inquired, emphasizing the final word. Speaking at all required tremendous effort. I was trying hard to be my usual insouciant self, but I was a long way from hitting the mark.

He turned his back without response and moved away from the bed. I forced my head to roll to one side, intending to scan the room, and immediately became nauseous beyond my ability to control. I vomited all in one horrid projectile gush.

What a humiliating performance! I was afraid of the man, yet I wanted—needed!—him to come back. Obviously I could not take care of myself.

He did come back, with a clean white sheet, which he draped over my body, and a wet washcloth with which he bathed my face.

I murmured, "Thank you."

"Hunh," he said, a gruff acknowledgment, as he moved from cleaning me to cleaning up the floor. At least I'd managed to miss the mattress and bedcovers beneath me. I watched him work, forcing myself to make note of every detail of his appearance, though I was not at all sure what compelled me to do so.

He was ash-blond and big-boned. His hair was thick and straight, too long for fashion, cut bluntly at the level of his equally blunt jaw, and tucked behind his ears. His skin had a reddish cast, such as happens to fair-skinned folk who spend much time outdoors. He had no freckles. His eyes were quite a brilliant blue. And rather chilly, I thought, as he looked up and caught me staring at him.

Again he attempted that odd smile. He sat back on his haunches, which put him on a level with me. "Can you tell me your name?" he asked.

For a split second my mind went blank. But then, like an obedient if exhausted child, it offered up my name. I opened my mouth and deliberately said, "Caroline."

"Caroline what?"

"What's *your* name?" I countered. "And what have you done with my clothes?"

"I am called Melancthon," he said. An important-sounding name, which he pronounced in a self-important tone of voice.

*Hmm,* I thought. I persisted: "Melancthon what?"

But the effort was costing me, and my throat hurt from heaving. *Courage, Fremont,* I counseled myself, *be strong!*

"You are gravely injured, yet spirited as a filly," he said, rubbing his chin again. "You must come of good stock. My full name is Melancthon Pratt. And yours is . . . ?"

Ignoring his unfortunate livestock metaphor, I responded, "Caroline, ah, *James.* From— Oh, never mind, what business is it of yours anyway!"

The truth was, at the moment I could not quite remember where I was from. It was most distressing.

Melancthon Pratt gave me a look such as one gives a child on the edge of reprimand.

I summoned up one last surge of determination and said firmly, "Delighted to make your acquaintance, Mr. Pratt, I'm sure. Now give me back my clothes and as soon as I've rested, I shall trouble you no longer."

"Likewise," he said. "However, I cannot return your clothing, nor would you want it until your things have been washed and mended."

He bent over me, took the edge of the sheet in his large hands, and as he did so the flat blue of his eyes deepened and his pupils flared. *Egad!* I thought as I recognized the sexual intent behind the expression. Would he ravish an injured woman?

Apparently not. To my relief, Melancthon merely

tucked the sheet close under my chin, then straightened himself up and moved away from the bed.

Warily I watched him go. The man had to be over six feet tall, though I supposed my prone position would have made any standing man look like a giant. He was dressed for farming or some similar activity, in blue denim trousers that were made—hmm, how odd— someplace I knew well and could recall if my mind were working better. He also wore a cotton flannel shirt of blue and white checks. His hands, I'd noticed, were very clean. In fact, it occurred to me that his whole person, and the room, the bed, everything around me, were spotless. Yet somehow this very cleanliness was not so encouraging as it might have been. For one thing, a farmer should have callused hands, and there should have been other signs. . . .

"You cannot remember anything of what happened, I take it," he said from on high, "yet you can remember your name. That is a good sign. The rest will come, or not, no matter."

"It matters to me! Please, tell me what happened." A plaintive note sounded in my voice; I disliked begging intensely, but there it was.

"Not yet. You should rest first."

"Nonsense. I need to know where I am, and how I came to be here, and—" I stopped abruptly, consumed by the enormity of all I must have forgotten.

"You'll be here for quite a while," Melancthon said. "There's plenty of time for that."

"A head wound," I scoffed. "It's not much. A matter of a few days, that's all, I shall be right as rain."

He leaned over the bed, lifted the sheet, and com- manded, "Move your legs."

I did. That is, my mind gave the order, and perhaps my knees bent, but that was all. Excruciating pain brought tears to my eyes. I dared not move my head, or

# 8 Dianne Day

the sheet, enough to look down and see what might be the trouble.

A flicker of satisfaction—for surely it was not sympathy—passed through Melancthon's observant eyes. Eyes of so beautiful a blue, yet pale-lashed and oh so cold. "You will not be going anywhere anytime soon," he said, "because both your legs are seriously injured. You were pinned beneath a good deal of wreckage. I will go for a doctor. The trip is two days' ride, one there and one back. Meanwhile, my wives will take care of you. Now go to sleep."

*Wreckage? What wreckage?*

I wanted to scream at him; yet at the same time something deep inside me did not any longer want to know the whole truth, not yet, it would indeed be too much. I closed my eyes and let myself tumble into that warm, quiet, black place again. At the very last moment before surrendering to sleep, I wondered if he'd really said what I thought he had: *wives*. Plural.

---

Fear: an unfamiliar feeling, characterized by clamminess of the skin, sickness in the pit of the stomach, a sense of uncertainty, hesitancy, intimations of dread and consequent paralysis of the will to act. He had not often personally encountered this cluster of feelings during the forty-five years of his life, but now Michael Kossoff identified them in himself one by one and knew he was afraid. Afraid for Fremont, because he could not find her anywhere. Afraid for himself, because of what his life would be without her. Not to find her, not to have her with him again . . . unthinkable! Impossible!

He sat down on the ground right where he was, rather abruptly, because his muscles weren't cooperating. He shivered and felt his face all wet with involuntary tears, which he wiped away with the back of his hand. He supposed he must be going into shock, if he wasn't in shock already, but there wasn't a damn thing he could do about it.

The relatively unharmed passengers had begun to help those more seriously injured; Michael was not sure which category he fell into. For the moment he felt paralyzed. Yet still his eyes played over the wreckage both human and mechanical, searching again, still, always, for Fremont Jones.

He had no problem recalling how she'd been dressed. An image of her as he'd last seen her was burned forever in his brain. She'd been, in a word, magnificent—in a dress bought new for this trip. The dress was a deep purple color, almost black; a color that had special meaning for Michael because she'd had a cape that same shade, which she had worn a lot the year he grew to love her. Aubergine, that shade of purple was called—and in this narrow aubergine dress with a teasing hint of bustle at the back, Fremont had left their table in the dining car and walked up the aisle with her back to him, tall and straight as an arrow. At the door she paused to wait while the porter opened it for her, and Michael waited too, to see if she would turn her head, sending an invitation to him with her eyes.

They were traveling incognito to Chicago on a job for the railroad, living in separate compartments in different cars of the train. From Chicago, with the investigation presumably done, they'd continue on to Boston for a visit with Fremont's father. Establishing the undercover ruse, they'd pretended to meet for the first time in the club car just the other side of Sacramento, and had begun a flirtation that excited Michael anew. Fremont too, he'd thought; yet she had not turned, did not so much as cast a glance over her shoulder, but had gone directly through the door.

So Michael had sat there at war with himself, hardening with desire for her, yet bound by the rules of their game not to go to her until she let him know, in one of the many little ways women have of doing such things, that she wanted him. Just as if they really had met for the first time in the club car outside of Sacramento. No matter that for almost a year they'd been living together as if they were truly man and wife; no matter that he hadn't been in her bed, or she in his, since the train pulled out of San Francisco—what was it, two days and nights ago? It seemed longer. Much longer.

Michael Kossoff had been thinking how much he desired Fremont Jones when, without warning, the train exploded.

---

I needed to use the bathroom. I opened my eyes, but then it took some time for them to focus. I was sick, very sick, sicker than I had ever been in my whole life. And I was completely lost. This room was strange to me, sparsely furnished, filled with shadows and a strange, reddish light.

I groaned and moved my head to one side, seeking a window, worried that the reddish light might mean fire. Through the one window I could see the humped line of a mountaintop, and behind it a blazing sunset. No fire, then. But I was alone, lost, sick, and the sun was going down.

I needed to relieve myself so badly I could hardly bear it. I tried to get up, but the pain was too great. I called out, "Is anyone there? Can someone help me?"

But no one came.

I shuddered, first hot, then cold, then hot again. Finally I could stand it no more. I wet myself and the bed.

After that, I did not so much go to sleep as give myself over to oblivion. In my head I whispered to the God I'd never quite believed in: *Please take care of me.*

# 2

THE SUN was going down behind the high mountains of Utah when Michael struggled to his feet again. Before darkness fell he wanted to have a look at the other side of the train tracks, to see if any passengers had been tossed off in that direction, though the damaged cars themselves had derailed on the side where he was standing.

He turned his head and squinted into the low red ball of the declining sun. Its angle gave him more of an idea where they'd been when the explosion occurred: east of Salt Lake City, on the way to Denver, well into a range of mountains called the Wasatch. Michael was unfamiliar with the area, but as always when he traveled, he had studied and memorized the route. Now he called up a map of the railroad in his mind: The tracks took a dip toward the south soon after Salt Lake, so that what lay to the right-hand side of the train was no longer true south but, rather, southwest. Now from that direction spilled the blood-red light of sunset, dyeing deeper the reddish soil of these mountains. *Appro-*

*priate,* he thought. A rather routine investigatory job had suddenly become a serious, bloody business. Perhaps even deadly. He hoped not.

Michael scanned the surroundings, looking dispassionately past people and debris as if they were not even there, committing the contours of the mountainous terrain to memory. He might have to find this place again, and once the broken track had been repaired that might not be as easy to do as one would now think. How many miles from Salt Lake City had the train traveled before the explosion? He recalled passing through a station at Provo. After that, he was afraid he'd been focused on the pleasure of trying to seduce his business partner; how many hamlets they may have passed through after Provo, he had no idea. They were high up in the mountains, no doubt about that—the air was thin, crisp, and quite cold for early October. And while there were trees and other vegetation, their growth in terms of height and thickness seemed lackluster, which suggested a struggle to survive at altitude.

Michael walked slowly along parallel to the tracks, up toward the break. He moved in a kind of trance, focused on his search for only one face among the many, the dark purple of a narrow dress, particularly alert for a certain shade of auburn hair. Vaguely as he passed, he noticed that panic had subsided, and people were caring for their own injuries or the injuries of others, either murmuring or mutely.

A new sight broke through his concentration: At some distance, beneath some trees, a volunteer brigade of men were lining up the dead in a neat row, one by one. So, the worst had happened. No more bothersome if not too costly accidents—now it was a matter of multiple murder.

Michael turned his head away and marched determinedly forward. He would investigate these crimes, but not right now. And he might have to take his turn looking for Fremont in that neat row of the dead, but not just yet. Never, if God was merciful.

*You have a job to do,* said a voice inside his head.

"Bother that!" Michael responded aloud, under his breath.

*That's not what she would say,* the voice commented.

He took a few more steps, realizing it was true: Fremont would say that while he was looking for her, he might as well be making observations as to the cause of the train wreck at the same time. Because the explosion might have a direct relationship to the job for which the Southern and Union Pacific Railroads had hired the J&K Agency.

*Two birds with one stone,* said the voice, this time sounding rather self-satisfied, and quite a bit like Fremont Jones.

Michael's spirits picked up and his mind felt sharper, which was all to the good. Various details began to register: There was smoke in the air, he could smell it, and somewhere nearby, plaintive and weak, a baby cried. A conductor, his voice full of crisp authority, issued orders to galley cooks, whose aprons were no longer white but streaked with blood and soot.

Michael stopped to watch them. Incredible as it seemed, a meal was in the making, with food being salvaged from the overturned galley car. He considered approaching the conductor, whose mind was apparently in good working order, and who, to judge by the state of his uniform, had not been harmed in the blast. Questioning would have to begin sometime, somewhere. But—

Frowning, Michael fumbled with his good hand at his inside jacket pocket; but even as his fingers touched the flat wallet, he remembered that the identification he carried was false. The business cards that identified him as the Kossoff half of the J&K Agency, Discreet Inquiries (Fremont Jones being the other half), were in his train compartment, inside the lining of his suitcase. Other, more important identification papers, linking him to both United States and Russian secret service agencies, were locked away in San Francisco—in an office safe at the house he and Fremont owned on Divisadero Street.

With a sinking sensation in his stomach and instant dryness of his mouth, Michael realized that Fremont most likely carried no identification at all. She routinely disdained reticules and other small purses, preferring instead a rather large leather bag she slung over her shoulder in most unladylike fashion. But on this train trip she was playing the part of an indulged, wealthy woman, a coquette, a fashion plate; clearly the leather bag did not suit the picture. So for the most part, as she moved about the train, Fremont had been going without whatever it was most women felt compelled to carry around with them, handkerchiefs and the like. Had she brought any kind of purse with her to the luncheon table? Michael thought not.

He did think it more than likely that she'd been thrown from the train, as he'd been, when the explosion occurred. He could only pray she hadn't been too near the actual blast point. He tried to keep the terrible images out of his mind, but he could not. He knew how dynamite could blow off arms and legs, slash a torso to bits, and scatter those bits over the ground in a roughly circular pattern that a knowledgeable person could read to determine the center of the blast. . . .

Michael Kossoff was such a knowledgeable person. He was more familiar than he wanted to be with the various forms of violence and destruction that human beings could visit upon one another. He sighed heavily, wishing again that his life had been different, that he might have been a peaceful man.

Michael had made his way now through people and debris to the break in the tracks where the explosion had occurred. *Of course,* he thought, *I should have known.* . . .

The tracks broke off, and then continued again on the other side of a narrow gorge or canyon. They—whoever *they* were—had blown up a railroad bridge. The front half of the train had crossed over to the other side, where it had stopped with the engine almost out of sight, at the point where the rails curved around the mountain. Broken tracks dangled down into the gorge like a toy torn to pieces by a gigantic, bad-tempered boy.

Michael tried in vain to moisten his lips—his mouth had gone utterly dry with apprehension. He counted the cars still connected to the engine, and tried to remember in exactly which one Fremont's compartment had been. But he wasn't sure. Moving forward through the train from car to car, of course he could find it, for she had been in the car just before his own. But counting, looking . . . no, no, he couldn't, he didn't know, couldn't tell, it was impossible.

*Delayed explosion,* his mind commented, and filed away the observation whether he wanted it at the moment or not. The engine had tripped a triggering mechanism as it crossed the bridge, then seconds had ticked by before actual detonation. This information would remain in his head, he knew, until he needed and called upon it. Such was the power of the human mind to behave in accordance with strict training, even—perhaps especially—under the most severe kinds of stress. Automatically he continued his observations.

On this side of the gorge all the cars had been derailed and lay tumbled and broken on their sides: two passenger cars, the dining car, the galley kitchen, two baggage cars, and the caboose. But that was not all—a part of the train was missing.

Michael smelled smoke again . . . and this time it stung his eyes. The smoke rose up out of the gorge,

thick and black, billowing and curling in on itself. The
nearer the edge he approached, the more acrid the odor
became. *Sulphur and brimstone,* he thought, *the fires of
hell and damnation.*

Michael's eyes watered. The toes of his black boots
protruded over the edge of the gorge. He wavered,
looking down, thinking, *Hellfire.* . . .

A hand grasped his arm, the left, which he held close
to his body so as not to jar the broken collarbone; and a
male voice said, "Don't stand there, sir, it's dangerous."

"I have to see," Michael said gruffly, twisting his
whole body violently to throw off that restraining
hand. A pain shot through him, white-hot; the shock of
it served to make him more alert. He was indeed peril-
ously near the edge. He moved back, and then looked
down again . . . a long, long way down.

The explosives must have been placed on the timbers
that supported the bridge. Those timbers no longer existed, they'd been blown to bits. But it was not the
bridge that was burning. No. Rather, two train cars lay
sprawled and broken in the bottom of the gorge, both
spewing fire and billowing black smoke.

Michael forced himself to look hard and long. A few
scattered bodies had been tossed from the wreckage.
Not one moved, not one called for help.

The angle of the setting sun could not penetrate the
shadows in those depths. He couldn't tell if any of the
bodies wore a dark purple dress—with such a lack of
light, it was almost impossible even to tell the females
from the males.

"I have to get down there," Michael said.

------

Eons passed, or so it seemed, before I regained full consciousness. Much of this time I couldn't tell if I was
awake or asleep; in either state I was miserable. I was

continually either shivering with cold or drenched with sweat. I had terrible, violent dreams, full of screeching, tearing noises, screams and fire and blood.

In my better moments I saw faces I had never seen before, and heard voices I'd never heard before. I was afraid, and angry with myself for being afraid, but too weak and sick even to stay angry. I called for Michael, called and called, but he did not come. I called for Father too, and a man did come—but he was not my father.

At last I gave up wanting and calling. I stopped fighting the strangers. Fortunately, or so I must suppose, they did not stop taking care of me. And so, I did not die.

A time came, finally, when I opened my eyes and saw clearly the woman who sat by my bed. She was a stranger, yet not a stranger; I knew somehow that she had sat in that chair many a time in the past days . . . not only that, she had done a great deal more than sit with me. By now the poor dear must have known my body as well as I knew it myself. At least on the outside of my skin.

She was mending or sewing, with her head slightly bent, and had not yet noticed that I was awake. I lay perfectly still while committing her features to memory, for I had a sense that she was kind and that I might not have survived without her. She was certainly several years older than I, perhaps even approaching forty; her skin had a weathered look, full of tiny criss-crossing lines. Her hair, of an indeterminate color, neither brown nor blond nor yet quite gray, was skinned back into a knot or a bun or a braid, I couldn't tell face-on. She had large hands with big-knuckled fingers, possibly arthritic, but they were nimble enough as she plied her needle, working some kind of garment by hand. I could not see her nether limbs, of course, but she appeared to be a large woman. Not fat, just big. Her manner of dress was simple and countrified: a plain gray dress covered by a pinafore apron, white with narrow pink stripes running vertically.

As her fingers flew, she hummed tunelessly under her breath. Did I detect a slight tremor in her hands? Was she nervous? Or just worn out with looking after me? My heart went out to her.

"Hello," I said, or rather tried to say. I had to clear my throat and try again: "Hello."

Her head jerked up suddenly, and she jumped as if I'd come up behind her in the dead of night and whispered *Boo!* She pricked her finger with her needle—I saw a drop of blood fall, not on her sewing but on the pinafore.

"Saints be praised!" she said. "You're awake, and talkin' sense!"

I smiled, weakly no doubt, but sincerely. "Thank you for taking care of me. I know I've been very ill, but"—I frowned—"I'm afraid that's about all I know."

"Don't you fret." She put aside her sewing, sucked on her finger for a minute, frowned at it, then rose and came to the bedside. "No need for thanks, neither. Takin' care of sick folks is our bounden duty." The woman laid the palm of her hand against my forehead and nodded in satisfaction. "Fever's gone." Her fingers explored my scalp, lighting upon an exceedingly tender spot.

I winced, and raised my own hand to touch what I deduced from its sensitivity must be a healing wound, on top of my head and to the right, in line with the outer edge of my right eyebrow. Where there should have been hair, my fingers felt instead a bunch of prickles and coarse puckers. "It feels so odd," I said.

"That's where the doctor shaved your head to put in the stitches."

"He *shaved my head?* Oh dear!"

"Not your whole head, just where the cut and the

blood was, where all the hair was matted up. He had to, so's we could keep it clean, but the wound got ugly anyways. Festered some. You had a high fever." She bent over me while pushing down gently on my chin with her hand, so as to see the top of my head better. I cooperated, listening with relief to her clucks and um-hms.

"The festering, I suppose that was what made me so sick," I mused. "You've taken good care of me, and I do appreciate it. You probably saved my life. Thank you—" I stopped abruptly, once more caught up short by ignorance. "I don't even know your name."

"It's Verla. Verla Pratt. I'll say you're welcome just because it's mannerly, but it wasn't me saved your life. 'Twas Father who did that. You'da died if he hadn'ta brought you home, he said so himself."

"Thank you, Verla. This is your house, then? You live here with your father?" The name Pratt was dimly familiar to me, but I couldn't for the moment call up its association.

"You might put it that way, yes. You thirsty? Like a drink of water, Carrie?"

Yes, I was thirsty. Verla helped me to sit up, helped me to hold the glass because when I tried, my hand shook so badly I would have spilled water all over the bed and all over the soft, worn flannel nightgown I was wearing. It was a few sizes too big for me. I wondered what had happened to my own clothes.

Then, belatedly, I took note of what she'd called me: Carrie, a shortened form of the name Caroline. My mother had particularly hated to hear anyone shorten my name to Carrie, though I'd rather liked it myself. Certainly I'd preferred it to Caroline.

As I slowly sipped, getting the hang of it and taking the glass on my own, I thought how odd it was to be called either Carrie or Caroline. Mother was dead, I knew that. Surely I had gone by my middle name, Fremont, for years now?

A rudiment of memory rushed forcefully back, and I blurted, "Where is Michael?"

Verla gave me a stern look, took the glass from my hand, and set it on the washstand beside the bed. She didn't answer me right away, but went to a dresser against the opposite wall and took up the pitcher from which she'd poured the water. At the foot of the bed she paused. "You were askin' for him before. We don't know who he is. Father didn't bring anybody else home but you. Now you're awake, in your right mind and all, you'd best fergit all about that Michael and not speak his name no more. It makes Father angry. You remember that."

"But—"

Verla ignored my protest as if I hadn't spoken. "I'll go for Father right now. He wanted to know the minute you came to your senses. And while I'm gone, I'll fix you something to eat. You lay back now, wait for Father."

I sank back on the pillows, noting an emptiness in my stomach that I very much feared had nothing to do with hunger.

But Verla did not leave the room immediately. Instead she thought better of it, put the pitcher down again, picked up something else from the dresser, and came back to the bed.

"Here," she said, pushing a hand mirror and a wide-toothed comb at me, "with Father coming, you'd best tidy yerself up as best you can. If you think you can manage."

My eyebrows went up; my new-found friend, the only one I had in this place—so far as I knew, which was not far at all—seemed suddenly rather irritated with me. "I can manage," I said; then, as I felt my weakness assert itself, I amended, "that is, I'll try."

"Best a body can do sometimes is try," Verla muttered, turning back to the door. This time she left, taking up the pitcher on her way out.

I struggled up higher against the bed pillows, and raised the mirror before my face. "Oh *no!*" I said in a hoarse whisper, appalled.

I had always been on the thin side, but the face in the mirror was thin beyond belief. Not much more than a skull with green eyes.

How long had I been here? What had happened to me? Why couldn't I remember?

---

FROM MICHAEL KOSSOFF
HOTEL MORONI
SALT LAKE CITY UTAH
TO MRS EDNA STEPHENSON MR ALOYSIUS STEPHENSON
J&K AGENCY DIVISADERO STREET
SAN FRANCISCO CALIFORNIA

RETURNING TO SAN FRANCISCO STOP WHEREABOUTS OF
FREMONT JONES UNKNOWN STOP PLEASE LOCATE IN PALO
ALTO MISS MEILING LI STOP SAY HER ASSISTANCE IS
NEEDED STOP ASCERTAIN IF SHE CAN BE AVAILABLE STOP
ARRIVE TUESDAY STOP KINDEST REGARDS STOP
MICHAEL

---

I conquered my distaste for my appearance by the simple expedient of putting the mirror aside. I did not need a mirror to comb my hair. Odd Verla hadn't braided it, I thought, as it should have been much easier to take care of in a braid.

But as soon as I began to comb it, I understood why: tangles. Masses of them. Not to mention that my hair—indeed my whole self—was badly in need of a washing. I combed straight back as best I could, by fits and starts, wishing all the while for a hair ribbon. Though I had always detested fuss and frills, even as a child, it did occur to me that a well-placed bow might hide that awful gap on the side of my head.

More composed on account of knowing what to expect, I took up the mirror again and ventured another look. It was bad, no two ways about it, but hair grows back. And weight can be gained if one eats enough and doesn't go around running one's food all off, which was what my mother always used to say I did when I remained a young, skinny, flat-chested thing long after all my friends had begun to have interesting little buds beneath their bodices. Young girls are such lemmings, and I hadn't been much different then, I'd wanted breasts too.

Eventually I'd grown them, after a fashion, but by then my mother was dead. . . .

I turned my head to gaze out the window at nothing, for there was nothing out there but reddish brown hills with a few trees. Not thickly forested, not farm land either, not much of interest in the visible landscape. But I wasn't looking at the scenery anyhow, for I had begun to remember . . . many things. Things that included the name of this place with the reddish soil: Utah.

I remembered being on a train. Eating luncheon with Michael Archer Kossoff in the dining car. I was wearing my new aubergine dress and had looked quite wonderful in it, if I did say so myself; purple and green being my best colors, though Michael also likes me in blue. For lunch I'd had creamed tiny shrimp with peas in a puff pastry shell, and a salad of orange segments tossed with butter lettuce in a sweet dressing, plus a light, fruity white wine to drink, and coffee after, no dessert for me. Michael had had lemon meringue pie.

I remembered telling him, over the food, about my distant relation John C. Fremont's maps of this area, which he had made long ago, before the Civil War.

About the incredible hardships he and his men had gone through on their surveying expedition, how they'd followed riverbeds that dried up and vanished underground, how their Indian guides had deserted them one by one, how the food had run out. I'd told Michael how everyone, Cousin Fremont included, had believed there was only one great mountain range between the Mississippi and the Sierra Nevada—but this had not proved to be the truth. No, the land of the high Western plateau was all folded, range upon range of mountains pushed up with valleys and even a vast desert in between. So over and over again, Fremont and his starving men had climbed to the top expecting to see the blue waters of the Pacific in the distance, only to have their hopes dashed. All that lay ahead was more desert and another range of mountains. No wonder many of Cousin Fremont's party had given up hope and gone insane.

I had told Michael all that, bit by bit, spinning out the grim tale deliciously slowly, while he had done his best to get me thinking, if not talking, on another track entirely. I knew what he wanted, of course, I knew that look in his eye. . . .

How very odd! I remembered putting my napkin beside my plate, properly draped not folded, and then walking up the aisle between the tables with Michael's gaze burning into my back. He'd wanted me to turn around, to give him the matching look of desire that would bring him into my compartment, and into my arms. Oh, and I would, but not . . . then, not . . . just yet . . . and as I passed through the door a uniformed porter held open for me, I'd been wondering how long I could hold out against Michael's seductiveness. . . . And that was all.

I frowned. There was more, just a bit more, I could almost, *almost* grasp it. . . .

But no, not quite. The pictures in my head wouldn't

come together. Only a noise, a terrible, ear-splitting
sound, an . . . explosion!

Yes, that was it, an explosion!

I touched my head. I lifted the covers and looked at
my legs, heavily bandaged and immobile. I tried to
move them, which proved not to be a good idea. Far
too painful.

The enormity of what had happened overwhelmed
me. I let the covers fall and closed my eyes, but still two
tears slipped out from beneath my eyelids.

*So somebody blew up the train,* I thought. The good
people here saved me. But I couldn't have been the only
survivor, surely not? Where were all the rest? Where
was Michael? WHERE *IS* MICHAEL??

I heard the latch pop on the door to my room, and I
opened my eyes. A very large, rather handsome man
came in first, then Verla behind him, and four more
women behind her. The women fanned out behind the
man in a semicircle, like the chorus in a Greek drama.
Verla took one step forward and said her line: "Carrie,
here is Father."

I looked at the large man and said the one thing that
was foremost in my mind, even though it was the one
thing I'd been told not to say.

"Where is Michael?"

# 3

WELL, I NEVER!" said Edna Stephenson, tossing her head with such a jerk that her tightly wound curls bounced. She was a tiny woman who stood not much higher than the waist of the very tall son beside her. "It's not *nize,* that's all there is to that."

A hint of a smile flickered across Michael's lips at Edna's consternation, which was as typical as her putting a "z" in the word "nice." But he immediately suppressed any hint of amusement, which in the circumstances was not hard to do.

"What Mama means—" Wish began.

"I don't need an interpreter, Aloysius," Edna interrupted, glaring up at him, then turning her small but piercing eyes on Michael. "Mr. Kossoff knows just ezzactly what I mean. Right? Right."

"Let's continue this conversation in the kitchen," Michael suggested, "over a cup of coffee."

"I didn't make it yet," said Edna with a hint of satisfaction in her voice.

Michael deduced that their secretary and office manager was quite angry with him. But he suspected her anger was the kind a parent displays when a child, lost through his own adventurousness, finds his way back home. He said, gesturing with his good arm, "In that case, I expect I can manage a coffeepot one-handed. It will be good practice. After you, Edna. You too, Wish."

Darting one last glare Michael's way, Edna took off in her tottery gait, aiming for the archway that led from the J&K Agency's front office into the conference room, which had once been a dining room, and on into the kitchen.

Wish—as he was called by everyone except his mother—rolled his eyes at Michael, then turned to follow her. Wish was by nature a quiet, thoughtful man of great integrity. He made an excellent private investigator due to his police training and his passion for justice. Michael and Fremont had been quick to snap him up and add him to their team at J&K. Yet Wish's temperament also worked against him; there was always the question, at least in Michael's mind, of whether experience would toughen Wish or break him. The young man had been through one of those make-or-break experiences over the summer, and as Michael followed him through the archway, he thought the verdict was not yet in. Wish had survived, but he still seemed a bit tender, perhaps fragile. In the present situation Michael knew he'd best bear that in mind.

Michael fixed his face in the expression that Fremont described as "enigmatic." He did not want either Edna or Wish to know how worried he really was, or how physically debilitated he felt. His shoulder ached. His eyes burned as if he had not slept at all the previous night, his first back in this house that he and Fremont shared on San Francisco's Divisadero Street.

It was a large, double house, in the Italianate Victorian style. He owned one side and Fremont the other—hers was the side that had the J&K Agency's offices on the first floor; her own living quarters were on the second and third floors. Therefore he now paid her rent corresponding to his half-ownership in the business. Their financial arrangements had become rather complex since, on her twenty-fifth birthday a few months back, Fremont's father had given her a large part of the estate she'd expected to inherit only on his death. And most particularly since she would not marry Michael—which would have greatly simplified everything. At least to his way of thinking, though Fremont vehemently disagreed.

Michael sighed. Their not being married bothered him now more than ever. Yet perhaps she was right. Perhaps it did not really matter and he was only being a hidebound traditionalist. If they had boarded that fateful train as man and wife, would it have changed a single thing? Anything at all?

*No,* he admitted to himself as he sat down at the kitchen table, forgetting he'd said he would make the coffee, *probably not.* They would still have been working together as partners, as equals, each with an aspect of the investigation to conduct. They would have been traveling incognito, would have gone through the same charade, played the same enticing game of pretending to be strangers who'd met in the club car. Fremont would still be missing.

Michael sighed, unconsciously, as once again the vivid picture of Fremont as he'd last seen her flooded his mind. A piece of paper and a wedding ring—on this trip she would have worn it on a ribbon around her neck rather than on her finger—would not have made Fremont turn around that last time he'd seen her and, with her eyes, invite him to follow. That was the only thing that could have made a difference: If he had been walking right behind her at the very moment of the explosion, most likely they would have been thrown off the train together. Only that, having her by his side no matter what happened, could have prevented this never-ending pain in his heart, this cold fear in his gut that he might never see her again.

"Michael," said Edna in a voice so soft she did not sound like herself at all, "I'm sorry. You're not the one I should be mad at. I wasn't thinking. Just . . . it's easier to be mad than sad, y'know?"

"What?" He emerged from his thoughts to realize the corners of his eyes were wet. He squeezed the bridge of his nose with his fingertips and leaned his head back, as if his eyes were only tired, but Michael doubted he was fooling Edna. The woman was not much bigger than a child, and had certain mannerisms that were child-like, but in truth she was both wily and wise. And incredibly efficient.

"What I'm sayin' *izzz*"—she drew out the "z" sound —"the railroad's gotta be held accountable for every single person as was on that train. *They* gotta satisfy *you*, not the other way around. We'll make 'em find Fremont!"

"Mama," Wish said from the long drainboard next to the sink, where he was doing the task that Michael forgot, "I'm sure Michael has thought this all through. I for one would like to hear the whole story of what happened, from the time of the explosion ten days ago to when he decided to return to San Francisco and got on the train in Salt Lake." Wish put the coffeepot on the gas stove and turned on a burner, which he lit with a long sulphur-headed match. Then he turned to join them at the table.

Michael sighed again, this time caught himself at it, then nodded and cleared his throat. In the hope that a relaxed posture might lead to a more relaxed mind-set, he crossed his right leg over the left and slouched as best he could, considering his tautly bandaged left side, which he needed to keep immobile for the sake of the mending collarbone. Then he began:

"The force of the explosion threw the back half of the train off the tracks. That's where I was, still in the dining car. Fremont and I had finished the midday meal only minutes before. I was debating between going to the club car for a smoke and going back to my compartment to read, when it happened."

He paused, his mind going again over territory it had covered a million times by now, or so it seemed. "I cannot be sure exactly how many minutes passed from the time Fremont left the dining car to when the explosion occurred. Also, it's not possible to know whether she was delayed along the way, for example by someone temporarily blocking the corridor; or if she might have stopped to admire a pet, such as the silky little terrier belonging to that woman. . . ."

Michael's voice trailed off as he became lost in the memory of Fremont so foolishly and atypically taken with the tiny dog—what had it been?—a Maltese terrier. The only sounds in the kitchen were the measured tick of the Regulator wall clock and the hiss of the coffeepot coming to a boil. After a moment he gave his head a quick shake and resumed: "At any rate, the exact timing is impossible to know, and essential if we're to determine Fremont's fate with any hope of accuracy. We do know, it has been established, that one of the two train cars that fell to the bottom of the gorge and burned was the one in which Fremont's compartment was located. The other, directly in front of it, contained my compartment. Both these cars had burned completely by the time anyone was able to get down into the gorge and begin a rescue."

Again a silence fell, as Michael deliberately paused before speaking all that was in his mind. He had a suspicion that seemed bizarre, yet he could not let go of it: that those two train cars might have been targeted; that someone had wanted not only to blow up the train but also to do it in such a way as to maximize the chances of harming him and Fremont. Yet who had known, aside from the Director of the Southern Pacific, who had hired J&K, that they would be on the train?

The coffee began to perk, and Wish got up to adjust the flame under the pot. Michael waited for him to return to the table, then focused his eyes on the younger man's lean, sensitive face, as if by directly addressing Wish, the pain of what he had to say might become easier to bear.

"The trainmen—conductors they're called—who had put themselves in charge of things, wouldn't allow me to go down there. I had no identification to prove that I was working for Southern Pacific in the capacity of private investigator, nothing to suggest I might have any authority or any special skills to contribute. So I was forced, along with the other ambulatory survivors, to get onto the rescue train that was sent along up the tracks—I don't know how much later. I lost track of the time. They took us to Provo for medical attention and booked us into hotels. Fremont was not on that rescue train. She was not booked into any of the hotels. She was not kept in the infirmary at Provo or sent on to the big hospital in Salt Lake City. Her body was not among the dead."

Here Michael's voice cracked. "At least, not the visually identifiable dead."

"Oh!" Edna exclaimed, and her hand flew up to cover her mouth. She'd made the sound involuntarily.

Wish frowned and blinked. He said, "My God."

Michael nodded gravely. "Yes. Many bodies were burned beyond recognition. Hers may have been among them. We can only know through dental records, and so one thing we must do is to send Fremont's dental records to the morgue in Salt Lake without delay. However, here is where the timing becomes so important: If Fremont had not yet reached her compartment at the moment of the blast, it's far more likely that she would have been thrown from the train. The people who burned to death were trapped inside the cars."

"But," said Wish, still frowning, "in that case, she would have been among those rescued, as you were. Wouldn't she?"

Michael winced, then raised his right hand to run it hard through his hair—a habit of his when distressed.

"Now, now, son," Edna said, recognizing the significance of the gesture and nodding, "you let the man go on tellin' this his own way. He knows where he's goin' with it. You go on, Michael."

"Thank you, Edna. But yes, Wish, that's a logical assumption and I'm getting to that very point. I stayed on in Provo until all the bodies and all the bones from the charred wreckage were brought out. They did a head count. At least one person was missing."

Edna and Wish looked at each other. Then they both looked back at Michael.

"I think Fremont survived. I think she was hurt and confused, and wandered away into the wilderness. Head injuries will do that to a person. It may be days or weeks or months, or maybe never, before someone with that kind of injury regains knowledge of who she is, where she is, what has happened."

Just then the coffeepot began to perk vigorously, as if in affirmation.

"I believe Fremont is alive," Michael said, getting up with a sudden surge of strength and striding over to adjust the flame beneath the bubbling coffee. "She may even find her own way home. Or, there is another possibility: Meiling and I will find her."

———

As soon as the words were out of my mouth I regretted them.

"I beg your pardon, sir," I said nervously, one hand splayed at the throat of that too-large nightdress, "I should have begun by thanking you for saving my life. Thank you very much indeed." I bowed my head deferentially, thinking, *But where is Michael?*

"I was directed to you," said the man called Father, advancing toward the bed and growing bigger with every step—or so it seemed. "I do not know who Michael is, but I was not directed to him. Only to you."

Now I remembered him, though his name did not immediately come to me: the religious fanatic. The *dangerous* religious fanatic, who had hovered over my naked body, it seemed like a century ago.

"I am very sorry to hear that," I said.

"Who is this Michael? You have called for him loud and long."

"He is . . . my business partner." That was true enough, but somehow the lie on the tip of my tongue felt more like the truth. I wanted to say *He is my husband,* but then I thought better of it. Further explanation seemed required, so I said, "We were traveling together on business. On the train that blew up."

Now the religious fanatic stood at my bedside. The five women had advanced along with him and fanned their semicircle out around the foot of my bed.

"So you've remembered," he said.

"I remember some things, yes. I do not recall your coming to my rescue, or very much since I've been here —it's all a jumble, I'm afraid." I looked at the women and smiled. I had not smiled for the man, nor did I want to; there was something about him I did not like at all, although I was not quite sure what. To the women I said, "I don't know how many of you took care of me, aside from Verla"—I found her eyes with mine and nodded—"but to all who did, I give my most sincere thanks. When I'm home again I'll want to see that you're all rewarded."

"You *are* home," the man said. "This is your home now."

Verla came to the other side of the bed and took my hand, saying, "You're one of us now."

I snatched my hand back, too shocked by what they'd said to care about rudeness. I exclaimed, "I beg your pardon!"

No sooner had I reclaimed one hand from Verla than the man took hold of my other—so firmly that I quite got the point: He did not intend to give it up.

"Carrie," he said in a low voice that might have been rather thrilling under different circumstances, "do you not recall the promises I have made you?"

"I can honestly say, sir, I do not even recall your name."

He dropped my hand, straightened up to his full height, and with a severe expression said to Verla, "Set this right, wife."

"Yes, Father," Verla replied.

He turned his back and walked away, rather dramatically I thought, to stand at the window all alone while the women came closer still and huddled around the bed. They seemed curious as kittens. Well, so was I. If Verla—who looked as if she might be a few years older than the man, or perhaps she was just worn out—was the mother and he the father in this household, then these other females should be the daughters. I scanned their faces; only one of the remaining four appeared young enough to be their child.

"Carrie, we are the wives of Melancthon Pratt. I am first wife. Next to me here is Sarah, she came second." Verla was introducing them counterclockwise around the bed. "Norma is third wife, then Tabitha is number four, and this is our youngest and most recent, Selene. Selene, like you, came from far off."

Selene was the young one, probably about fifteen years old. She was very fair, with hair like cornsilk, so thin and fine, and great watery blue eyes. She bobbed her head and said, "Pleased to meet you, Carrie. Welcome to Deseret, and welcome to our home." The others did the same, murmuring and bobbing.

"Five?" I whispered in disbelief. "Five wives?" Deseret I took to be the name of their farm—of course in that I was mistaken, as I would soon find out.

"Father rode out twelve days ago because he had a vision in which an angel told him to go to a certain place, and there he was to find something we've all been praying for. Three days later he came back, with you."

I ignored the business about the angel and the vision —that was all too absurd and only proved my guess that the man, Melancthon Pratt, was a religious fanatic. I remarked instead upon the practical, altogether obvious fact: "It is against the law to have more than one wife."

"We are Mormons," Verla said. "It is not against our laws, or the laws of the Prophets, or the laws of the True Faith. We Mormons are called to bring into the world as many souls as possible. To this end, a man needs more than one wife. Our men are also priests; they know the laws of God, which are far more important than the laws of man. It is not for us women, or for people of other faiths, to question the word of a Mormon man."

*Poppycock,* I thought. But I did not say anything. The language in which Verla had given her "We are Mormons" speech sounded a great deal like an Episcopalian reciting the Catechism. No use trying to argue with that. Besides, they all agreed with her—they were nodding, all those women. I was seriously outnumbered. But no, wait, not all. Young Selene wasn't nodding, she just stared at me with her huge, pale eyes.

"You said," I addressed Verla, but kept track of the others from the corners of my eyes, "that Father rode out looking for something you'd been praying for. You think I have some connection to this, this . . . whatever it was?"

Verla glanced at Father, who still stood at the window with his back to us, then turned back to me. "Yes. The angel led him to you, Carrie. You yourself are the answer to our prayers."

---

Yes, what is it, Wish?" Michael asked, looking up from his desk to the younger man, who stood in the doorway of Michael's small study, just off the conference room. It had once been a butler's pantry.

"I want to come with you to look for Fremont. I'm offering my services."

"I would prefer that you stay here, keep the investigations of J&K going. I expect you need the income, and of course any cases you take while we're both gone would be entirely yours, you'd keep one hundred percent of the fees involved. Edna will pay herself the usual salary from our account."

"I don't need the money that much. Look, may I come in while we discuss this?"

"Of course." Michael gestured. "Do come in." It had been rude of him to keep Wish standing in the doorway, but he was too exhausted to think straight. "Have a seat."

Wish closed the study door before taking the one other chair the room's size allowed. "I'd rather Mama didn't hear us," he explained. "She's already pretty upset about, you know, Meiling."

"I don't understand." Michael picked up a pencil and began to slowly spin it end over end in his long fingers, touching first the eraser, then the lead tip to the desk blotter, over and over again.

"Well"—Wish pulled at his ear, crossed his legs, looked over Michael's left shoulder with all the awkwardness that had once claimed his every hour—"you know you wired us to get in touch with her. With Meiling. And so, Mama did it. Mama's the one who found her, talked to her on the telephone, and all that."

"So?" Michael's black eyebrows arched upward.

"So, well, Meiling's Chinese."

"Of course she is. She is also one of Fremont's best friends, and one of my oldest and dearest friends. I have known Meiling since she was a child. She comes from one of San Francisco's oldest families."

"Oldest *Chinese* families," said Wish, crossing his legs the other way.

"Don't tell me Edna is prejudiced! Edna? I find that hard to believe!" The pencil came to a rest, jabbed point down into the green desk blotter with some force.

"Only against the Chinese," Wish declared earnestly. "The Italians, the Irish, the Spanish, the Negroes, even the Indians don't bother her at all."

Michael pulled a half-smile with one side of his mouth; it was the best he could do. "I see. What a pity she's chosen our largest minority to be bothered by. I suppose there's no talking her out of it? No chance she'll change her mind once she meets Meiling?"

"I really don't think so. Anyway, there's a couple of other things you don't know yet. I mean, you just got back last night after we'd already left for the day; there hasn't been time to tell you."

"Go on," Michael said. He turned and turned the pencil.

"Meiling's not at Stanford anymore, and she's not living at the address Fremont had for her in the address book. Got a different telephone number too."

"Hmm. I don't suppose you know why she left her studies. Don't suppose she told your mother in whatever conversation they had?"

"No, afraid not. Meiling'll see you, though, and she wants to talk to you right away. We've got the new address and the new telephone number—she's still in Palo Alto. Mama didn't tell her Fremont was missing or anything like that, she just told her you needed some help with something if she were free to do it. That's how we know she doesn't take classes anymore. She laughed, Mama reported, and said she was free as a bird to come and go any way she wanted."

"I suppose that sounded altogether too irresponsible for Edna." This time Michael did smile.

"Well, yeah," Wish said, "especially considering Meiling's, you know—"

"Chinese."

"Yeah," Wish said, nodding his head rather miserably. With his shoulders hunched, he cocked his head and looked sideways at Michael. "Don't you think it would be more, well, appropriate if you took me with you instead of Meiling? I mean, she's not just Chinese, she's a woman."

Michael set the pencil down carefully, lining it up precisely with the edge of the blotter's leather keeper. "Wish, it's because of her gender that I want Meiling with me. You know, as an investigator, how useful it can be to have a woman for a partner. She can go into places where you or I cannot. Also in Meiling's case, she is actually far better able to defend herself than our friend Miss Jones. Meiling is skilled in the martial arts. And she has other skills as well."

"Oh. Martial arts, fancy that. What other skills?"

"Knowledge of the workings of various drugs and poisons, that kind of thing. Meiling was the only child in the youngest generation of the Li family, much beloved by her grandfather, who gave her unusual privileges because of her being his sole heir. And she was trained by her grandmother, who was an unusual woman in her own right."

"Still," Wish protested, "it would just look a whole lot better—"

"Next you'll be telling me that it looks improper

when I travel and work with Fremont. After all, she too is a young unmarried woman."

"Awww—"

"Wish"—Michael stood up to indicate their talk was over, because exhaustion was making him short-tempered—"tell your mother, if you please, that I need you both to stay here and keep the business going. It's what Fremont would want as well. And that's an end to it."

Wish lumbered to his feet. Whether it was his concern for Fremont, dislike of having to deal with his mother's disapproval, or whatever, something had caused him to revert to all the awkwardness and uncertainty that had characterized him when he was a rookie in the San Francisco Police Department. Michael was sorry, but he couldn't handle Wish Stephenson's problems. He had big enough problems of his own.

———

Melancthon Pratt turned from the window and came back to the bed. His wives scurried around to the other side so that he could have one all to himself. He looked down at me, not unkindly, but rather with a burning concupiscence that was bad enough. "You are no doubt hungry," he stated.

"Yes," I agreed.

"Norma, you will bring a meal, something appropriate for a convalescent. You will all leave now so that Carrie can rest. I will stay while she rests. When she has rested and eaten, I will begin her instruction. That is all. You may go."

Each of the wives said goodbye to me, a series of soft "Goodbye, Carrie"'s. I wanted to call them back, but I did not have the strength. And besides, it was perfectly clear that it would do no good. Melancthon's word was law here, not one of them would go against him.

When the door closed behind Selene, the last to go,

Melancthon said to me, "You must be tired. It will take at least half an hour for Norma to bring you food. Close your eyes and rest. I will sit here beside you."

I said nothing, but watched through lowered lids as he took the chair where Verla, his first wife, had formerly sat. When seated, he folded his hands and bowed his head as if in prayer. Only then did I close my eyes. I put away my thoughts and all my questions and most of my fears. I wasn't going anywhere—my legs wouldn't let me. I still had a lot of questions, and Melancthon—Father—could answer them better than anyone else. For now, it was obviously best to play along, whatever the game might be.

A sigh escaped my lips as I thought, *I must not despair!* Even though being where I was, in the condition I was, seemed a lot like being in prison.

# 4

_____

I WAS SO WEAKENED by my recent trauma that I sank immediately into a state of being neither awake nor asleep, but somewhere in between. No question but that I would have slept had I been alone; however, Melancthon's pervasive presence kept me from letting go entirely. Still, I did not think but rather drifted, farther and farther toward the Land of Nod.

In this oddly restful state I began to feel that someone, some wise female person (for surely these were a woman's thoughts), was counseling me; and such was my detachment that it did not seem so strange to me that this person should be invisible. Perhaps she was a spirit, or a guardian angel. That in my everyday waking state I did not believe in, or at least questioned, the existence of such entities did not for the moment seem important. What did seem important was the quality of the counsel, which impressed me with its wisdom—a type of wisdom I certainly should never have arrived at myself, for the things suggested were so alien to me:

_Be docile and submissive in manner; keep differing_

*opinions to yourself; try not to show your keen mind. Your body needs time to heal itself. Carrie James is a role you must play meanwhile, until you can be Fremont Jones again.*

This advice made eminently good sense, no matter where it had come from. I committed it to memory by allowing the words to sound over and over again as I spiraled closer and closer to true sleep. Especially those first two. *Be docile, be docile, be docile. . . .*

———

Michael had apprised Meiling of the basic facts of Fremont's disappearance over the telephone. This was possible because of the newly installed long-distance telephone lines that connected San Francisco to the villages of the lower peninsula, all the way to San Jose. He had Edna to thank for keeping them up to date in such matters; anything new-fangled, preferably mechanical, excited Edna Stephenson beyond the ability to control herself. She pounced on anything that even vaguely smelled of progress.

*Next,* Michael thought as he downshifted the Maxwell preparatory to turning left off the old El Camino Real, which was still the main road down the peninsula, *she will be wanting me to teach her to drive. God forbid!* But his grin belied the thought.

He made a left turn in front of the gates to Stanford's Farm, as the university campus had once been, and sometimes was still, called. The sandstone pillars of the gates had tumbled down during the Great Earthquake two years earlier, along with even more substantial structures around the Quad, but now all had been rebuilt, as Michael knew from previous visits. He did not enter the campus, but rather went the opposite way, into the town proper.

He was looking for a street named Bryant, and soon found it, then proceeded south. The day was beautiful, warm and sunny. Fall in California was generally warmer and more pleasant than either summer, with its fogs, or the rainy winter. Having been born in the state, Michael had grown up knowing that when the distant hills were golden brown, the season was fall; but in spring, after the winter's rains, those same hills would be covered with emerald-green grass. Here and there among their gently rolling contours, groves of live oaks stood in clusters of deep, dark green. Along either side of Bryant Street the same type of trees, occasionally interspersed with shaggy, fragrant eucalyptus, cast their shadows. Compared to San Francisco, Palo Alto—which in Spanish means "tall stick"—was a small town with a decidedly rural atmosphere.

The Maxwell motored along in its reliable fashion, causing a few little children to look up from their play in yards along the way, their mothers to glance out of windows. So tiny, those children . . . but of course they were the very young ones, Michael thought, the older ones would be in school; and then he reflected that he was not very good with children. He had never thought he would have any, yet as he looked at those little heads—some tousled, some shaggy, only one tidy with a bow on top, that one a girl of course—he suddenly realized all he was missing. He felt it like a blow to his heart.

Meiling had told him to look for a house with wind chimes hanging in a laurel tree, and colored streamers beside the door. Michael found it easily—the scarlet, yellow, green, and purple streamers would have been hard to miss.

*Very Chinese*, he thought as he parked the Maxwell on the side of the street a few feet from the laurel tree. A breeze stirred, running through the wind chimes like cascading silver bells, lifting the streamers in twisting lines of color. He walked up a slate path to the front door. Aside from Meiling's additions, the small house was unremarkable, a wooden box with windows and a door, not a single architectural ornament except for shutters, and those were false.

Answering his knock, Meiling opened the door and said, "Hello, Michael."

His black eyebrows rose as he stared, then hastily said her name: "Meiling."

She bowed her head slightly. Her long black hair swung forward with the motion. "Welcome into my home," she greeted him formally in Mandarin, which Michael understood.

After a moment's hesitation he bowed too, and responded, also in Mandarin: "I am honored to be your guest." He untied first one shoe and then the other, and left them at the door, donning soft black slippers from an assortment of sizes that Meiling had placed there for guests. Only then did he enter the room, which was just as well, because he needed a few moments to decide what to say.

The last time Michael had seen Meiling, she'd been wearing the latest American fashion, complete with corset (which Fremont refused to wear, ever) and hat (likewise, at least most of the time). When Meiling had left San Francisco after the Great Earthquake, moving to Palo Alto to attend Stanford as a special student, she had declared her intention to be simply an American woman who happened to have a Chinese name and a Chinese face. In every other way she was determined to be no different from any other female on the campus, whether student or faculty. But now . . .

Meiling stood a few feet inside the living room of her plain little house, which might once have belonged to a worker on a rancho in the Spanish period, or to a laborer on the railroads decades later. In other words, the room was unpretentious, not the least exotic. By contrast, Meiling herself would not have been out of place had she stood a few feet from the gilded gates of the

Forbidden City. She wore long, straight black trousers in a heavy fabric with the faint sheen of silk, and over them a long-sleeved tunic of black brocade trimmed in emerald-green satin piping. Her shoes were also satin, emerald-green, curving slightly upward at the tips of the toes. Her hair was unbound and hung to her waist like a shimmering curtain of ebony.

"I see I have surprised you," she said. Meiling was taller than most Chinese women, and her voice was deeper. Deeper, in fact, than Fremont's mellow alto, darker and richer than Michael had remembered. Certainly of a richer texture than it had seemed over the telephone only last night.

"Yes," Michael admitted as he came into the living room, "but it is a happy surprise. I'm glad to see you wearing the garb of your ancestors."

"I have had a change of heart, a revision of plans," Meiling said, and then smiled, a mischievous glint in her dark eyes. "But I have acquired a taste for coffee. Come, we will go sit in the kitchen, where the sun comes through the windows this time of morning. And we will talk of what to do for my friend, your partner and your lover, Fremont Jones."

---

The smell of soup brought me fully awake. I was using my elbows to work myself into a sitting position against the pillows, dragging my useless legs, before my eyes were even open. My stomach rumbled; I felt thoroughly starved.

"Oh my goodness, that smells wonderful!" I exclaimed, with the most enthusiasm I'd had for anything in quite a while. There is nothing like a serious illness, I was discovering, to teach a person what is truly important in life, and that is sleeping and eating. The rest, such as love and sex and all that, is just the frosting on the cake, very nice and certainly delicious, but possible to live without. "Thank you," I repeated. "Is it Norma? Have I got your name right?"

"Yes, Carrie. I'm Norma."

She darted a quick glance at Father, as I supposed she would call him, while with one hand she steadied a tray beside me, and with the other helped to plump up the pillows behind my back. That male personage—I certainly wasn't going to call him Father—sat there like a useless lump, not bothering to offer his assistance. No, he was entirely occupied, it seemed, with staring off into the middle distance. Where perhaps, if it ever suited his purposes, he might someday claim he had seen another angelic vision. The ability to see and converse with invisible beings is no doubt a useful talent, if one is not overly concerned about mendacity.

I turned my attention back to Norma, who made a more rewarding subject. Number three wife, I recalled; she was younger than Verla, the number one wife, and prettier than either Verla or Sarah, the number two, though Norma and Sarah might well be of an age. I guessed they'd be perhaps thirty, a few years older than I. Norma had hair so black it glinted blue, like a raven's wing, where she had pulled it tight against her skull. Her eyes were almost black too—but instead of the limpid, innocent, baby-animal appeal that many dark eyes have, hers were hard as marbles. Her complexion was of a golden rather than a pinkish cast, the type of skin that browns easily in the sun. She was a small woman yet not dainty; decisive in her movements; and her hands, like Verla's, had known hard work.

"I am so hungry!" I said avidly as Norma spread a napkin over my lap, then placed the tray there.

"Just don't eat too fast," she cautioned. "Can you manage alone?"

"Yes, I think so, and thanks again. You may be sure my gratitude is in direct proportion to my hunger," I said, picking up the soup spoon.

Norma folded her hands at her waist and addressed the man on the other side of my bed: "Shall I stay, Father?"

From the corner of my eye I saw his head jerk up. I was already too occupied with the delicious repast in front of me to care about anything else. The soup was a thick broth, laced through with shreds of beef, grains of rice, chopped onions and celery, and some green herbs for seasoning.

"No need to stay, thank you, Norma." He raised one hand, either in blessing or dismissal or both—it was an odd, formal gesture that I did not understand between husband and wife.

*Perhaps,* I mused, breaking off a piece of soft roll and dipping it most inelegantly into the soup, *when a man has that many wives he finds it necessary to devise hand signals, like a traffic cop.*

"Then may I bring you anything?"

This was interesting. She did not accept dismissal so easily. I dunked another bit of roll and watched Norma surreptitiously. I like a woman who does not immediately comply with what is expected of her, but takes her own time to at least think about it.

"No," he said quite firmly, "I do not require anything at this time."

To my utter amazement, Norma pouted. Her lips were nicely shaped, and even as I watched, her lower lip grew fuller. Slowly she turned away from my bed and walked toward the door; halfway there she looked back over her shoulder with those dark eyes glinting and asked, "Father, will we all be at table together for supper tonight?"

Melancthon Pratt let a pause gather in the air before he replied. I stopped chewing and swallowing because even I could feel the sudden, subtle charge in the atmosphere. "Nnoo," he said slowly, drawing out the word, as if making his decision as he spoke, "I think not. I think you may lay a table for two in front of the large window. And tell the others they may go ahead and eat when they've a mind to."

*Hmm,* I thought, *very interesting.*

And then, because that was precisely what *he* would have said, I felt most dreadfully the pang of missing Michael.

Missing Michael did not, however, stop me from finishing the soup and bread. There was a sweet pudding for dessert. I tasted it, and decided to have it later. For my first real meal in a while, I'd already had enough.

Now that I was done with the food, something that had been bothering me asserted itself. As I folded my napkin and pulled it through the napkin ring that had come on my tray, I asked in a tone both casual and sincere, "Do you enjoy watching people eat, Mr. Pratt?"

He did not reply. His face took on a rather odd expression, as if my question had somehow hit him right between the eyes.

This pleased me quite a bit, so I decided to needle him a little more. Opening my hands in a helpless gesture, I looked down at my lap and then back up at him. "Would you take this tray? Eating has quite exhausted me and I cannot lift it. Please, if you'd be so kind."

"Humph," he said, but he rose to his feet, covered the space between the chair and the bed in two long strides, and snatched up the tray, which he then went to place on the dresser against the far wall. But that necessitated moving the pitcher to one side, which in turn meant he had to balance the tray on one hand, and that almost proved too much for the big man. The tray's contents slid . . . and slid . . . until at the last possible moment he righted it and set it down on the dresser.

"Thank you so much," I said, sagging back against

the pillows with unaffected languor. Certain sensations reminded me that I would have to take care of the necessary bodily functions before too long, and I wondered how much longer he intended to stay.

"Humph," the big man said. This syllable seemed to serve all purposes for him save exposition.

I fixed my mouth in a neutrally pleasant expression, adjusted first one shoulder and then the other against the pillows, ignored an itch that had begun on my left leg, and waited while he brought the chair right up next to the bed. He took my hand.

The voice I had internalized said, *Be docile.* I clenched my teeth and let him have the hand, although just that one contact, that seeming act of possession, made me feel even more entrapped than reason told me I already, truly was.

"Caroline James," said Melancthon Pratt, "the wives have taken to calling you Carrie. I prefer Caroline."

*You would,* I thought, but I forced the corners of my mouth to curve up a little higher. "As you wish," I said. Then seizing the opportunity, I added, "I shall call you Mr. Pratt."

"It would please me if you would call me, as they do, Father."

"But I cannot do that, can I? First, because I already have a father. He lives in Boston, and as soon as possible I must let him know what has happened to me. Second, because it would be inappropriate for me to call you Father, as we have no children between us, which would be the only other reason I can think of for giving you that appellation."

"Ah," Melancthon Pratt said, smiling, "that is how I shall begin, then. I will tell you about the angelic vision that led me to you, and the many children that were promised me in that vision. Through you, Caroline. Through you."

Meiling Li's kitchen was a perfect blend of East and West; the black cast-iron cooking stove served as a good example. The body of the stove had been fitted with pipes and rings to convert it from wood-burning to gas. On the top burners a beautifully blackened wok occupied one side, while a percolator of some shiny, polished silvery metal occupied the other. The room smelled of coffee and spices; sun poured through the windows; flowers were everywhere, some in vases and some growing in pots.

"I am glad to see you, Michael," Meiling said, placing a large porcelain cup and saucer before him, "but I regret the circumstances."

"No more than I do, you may be sure." He gazed at the cup, which remained empty for the moment, and recognized the pattern, although at the moment he could not name it. The cup and saucer were very old, certainly valuable, possibly priceless.

"I am sure," Meiling said, returning with the coffee which she had poured into a serving pot whose handle and spout were intricately shaped and painted to resemble the curving neck, head, and tail of a red-gold dragon that had twined himself around a cobalt-blue ball. She set the pot on the table.

Michael watched mutely while Meiling, equally silent, moved about her kitchen. She took a plate from a shelf, opened a pot shaped like a large ginger jar, and stuck her hand inside. The cookies she brought out were shaped like stars; one by one she put them on the plate. Michael felt thoroughly shaken. He wondered how it could be that he had held up relatively well until now, not giving in to his grief or his fears, constructing the wall of reasoned faith in Fremont's survival that gave him hope. Suddenly he wanted nothing more than to let it all out, cry, yell, scream, or at the very least get stinking drunk—with Meiling, of all people. Why? How could he be feeling this way? It was despicable. He loathed himself.

Meiling brought the plate of star-shaped cookies to the table and silently placed them by the dragon-pot. She went away again. Michael clenched his jaw, ran his hand through his hair first one way and then the other, messing it up, smoothing it back again.

"You must be very upset," said Meiling. Her back was to him; she did not turn around. He didn't know what she was doing, but he was glad of it, because he didn't want to have to face her just yet.

"Hm," Michael said noncommittally. He uncrossed his legs and turned in his chair so that he could see out the window. Meiling had placed a temple-like structure on a pole in her back yard. It was filled with tiny birds of several different colors—yellow, pale green, purple, deep pink.

"They are finches," she said. He had not heard her return to the table. Now she too had a cup and saucer; she poured coffee into his first, then hers. "I recall you do not require either cream or sugar, but take your coffee black," she said.

"Yes."

"So do I."

The finches had a pert, twittery little chirp that was just audible through the glass. Michael liked Meiling's ability to sit in quiet companionship. Fremont was like that, he thought, she had been like that from the beginning. Such a remarkable woman.

And then he understood why being with Meiling had nearly undone him. "You and she are very much alike, you know," he said.

"I know."

"It doesn't really matter that you are Chinese born in San Francisco, and she is an American born in Boston."

Meiling smiled. "That is because Fremont's soul was

born in San Francisco too, or someplace very like it. But I know exactly what you mean, Michael. She is the sister of my heart."

"And the woman of mine." Tears welled in his eyes.

Meiling turned her head so that her profile was to him, while she deliberately looked away. "Let me tell you something about me that you do not know. It is a thing that separates me from Fremont, and from you, and from all who have been educated in the West. It is the means by which I can tell you I am certain Fremont is still alive, a means that may help us to find her."

"Yes, tell me," Michael said. The tears flowed down his cheeks, unchecked.

# 5

"YOU HAVE probably heard," Meiling said, her profile still to Michael, "at some time in your long acquaintance with my family, that some people thought my grandmother was—as they say in English—a witch."

"Yes," Michael said, managing just the one word. He could not control his voice, his facial muscles, or his tears; he hid behind an upraised hand while Meiling continued to speak.

"She was a wise woman, as powerful in her own way as my grandfather was in his. My grandmother left me a legacy that I knew nothing about until a few months ago. Remember, Michael, that when I left San Francisco the year before last, I did so in great haste immediately after my grandmother's death. If I had stayed even long enough to attend her funeral ceremony, I would have been forced into marriage with one of the Li cousins, because certain family members would not accept a female heir to the main line of the House of Li."

Meiling paused and sent a swift glance Michael's

way. Elbow on the table, he continued to shield his face with one hand. She turned away again and went on: "That Li cousin has been sent back to China now. He was not of a very strong character, as I had feared, though many thought him handsome and, what is the word . . . charming. He gambled and got into trouble with a money-lender, and so his family sent him far away, where perhaps he will learn a few lessons, and perhaps not. I myself think he will not, but what I think is neither here nor there."

She tossed her head and with a flick of her wrist sent a wide swath of her hair flying back over her shoulder. Michael stirred and cleared his throat, but Meiling went on: "Of course I have cast myself out of the family by running away as I did, but since my judgment proved accurate in the matter of the man I did not wish to marry, some unknown family members apparently took pity on me. At least, enough to send to me a certain old chest my grandmother always said I should have when she died. I do not know how they found me, but they did."

He had himself under control now. Her story had captured his interest. He had wiped his face with his handkerchief and was sipping the coffee, which was still warm enough to be bracing.

"What was in the chest?" Michael asked.

Meiling turned to him now, with a small, mysterious smile. "Magic. Chinese magic."

---

If anyone had told me, at any point in the past that I can even dimly recollect, that the day would come when I should be heartily glad to have both legs broken, I would have called that person totally mad. Yet such a day had come; verily (to use a Prattish turn of phrase) it was upon me.

I could hardly be expected to bear, much less to conceive, or God forbid to practice at the conception of, Melancthon Pratt's children as long as my legs had not yet healed. When my legs could not take my own weight, the poor limbs certainly could not be expected to accept his as well. Or any other attentions in which the legs might possibly be kept out of the way but still might have to become involved. Oh dear, such things did not bear thinking about.

Yet they were often thought about in this strange Mormon household. They were all, Melancthon and the five wives, completely obsessed with having children, and therefore also with the process by which one conceives them. Not to put too fine a point on it, they were obsessed with sex.

It is redundant, surely, to call a household both Mormon and strange? Perhaps not. For the sake of most Mormons, who after all built Salt Lake City, which is quite an achievement, one must hope that Pratt and his wives were not typical of the entire breed. Isolated as we were, I had no way to judge.

I had lain in my fever, Verla told me, for about ten days. Once I began to eat and drink again, I made rapid progress. The fourth day of my true convalescence— which I calculated must have been exactly two weeks after the train wreck—I was able to get out of bed and sit in a chair by the window. Of course I did not accomplish this feat alone. I had the help of both Norma and Tabitha, wives three and four respectively. Having shifted me from bed to chair, Norma was impatient to be on her way, but Tabitha stayed behind and began to tidy the room by remaking the bed.

I felt as if the weight of the world were upon me. Being able to sit up in a chair was encouraging, but looking out of that window was not. The view only emphasized the extreme remoteness of our surroundings.

Better, then, to watch Tabitha. Perhaps I could draw

her into conversation. I did not want the wives to see me as a rival, but I feared they already did. Or rather three of them did. Verla's attitude seemed completely neutral, I supposed because she was first wife; and Selene was so young that she did not seem to me anything like a wife at all, but more like a younger sister.

Tabitha had a soothing, quiet presence. She did not bustle about, but rather her motions were both deliberate and graceful.

Impulsively I asked, "Is dancing against your religion?"

She looked up, wide-eyed, as if amazed that I would speak to her. "No," she replied. That was all; she did not inquire as to why I'd asked, or volunteer any information of her own, but returned to tucking the top sheet under the mattress at the foot of the bed.

Tabitha was quite attractive in her own quiet way. She was of average height and build, with regular features, neither pretty nor plain but somewhere in between. Her hair was light brown and had a tendency to curl around her face, though she had arranged it in a figure-eight bun on the nape of her neck. She wore a brown woolen dress with buttons all down the front, to which she had added a white collar and cuffs trimmed with tatted lace. *Lace, no apron—pretty fancy for a Pratt woman,* I thought. Perhaps she was going into town?

"I asked," I said, venturing further, "about the dancing because you have such a graceful way of moving. I thought perhaps you might dance, yourself."

"Oh, my goodness, no." Surprised, Tabitha paused in the act of shaking out one of the feather pillows. A smile curved her faintly pink lips, and suddenly I saw what Melancthon must have seen when he'd chosen her to be wife number four: a gentle sweetness that was quite appealing. She gave the pillow a final shake and put it down in place, smoothing the pillowcase with her

hand as she rather shyly admitted, "I do know how,
though. When I was a child in town, we danced some.
But, well, I suppose Father isn't much of a one for dancing."

"No, I suppose not."

She went around the bed to repeat the process with
the pillow on the other side, while I returned my gaze to
the view out the window.

"We appear to be hemmed in by mountains on all
sides," I remarked.

The reticent Tabitha did not respond.

"Of course," I went on, "the view from other parts
of the house may be different. I have no frame of reference here beyond this very room. I am beginning to feel
positively claustrophobic."

"I don't know that word." Tabitha had finished with
the bed now, and moved over to dust the dresser and
the chest of drawers, picking up objects and putting
them down again so carefully that she made not a single
sound.

"Claustrophobic?" I glanced swiftly her way, not
wanting to appear too eager to involve her in conversation, for fear that she would bolt. She had that doe-like
quality about her. I explained, "It means a fear of being
confined in a small or tight space. It is a word of Latin
origin, used by doctors of psychiatry and people of that
sort, who study the workings of the mind. I'm very
interested in such things," I said with a shrug, a gesture
I meant to imply my understanding that most people
were not. And then I looked out the window again, as if
I did not care a bit whether she continued talking to me.

"You are well educated, then. I thought so. I said to
the others, just last night, that I thought from the way
you speak you must have spent a lot of years in
school."

"I did, yes, that is true."

"But you were not a schoolteacher." Tabitha came

over to the window and leaned against the window sill. Sunlight shone behind wisps of her soft brown hair, surrounding her head in a golden halo.

"No. How do you know that?"

"By the dress you were wearing when Father brought you here. It's very fine—I mended it myself. I've never seen a dress like that, with such a narrow skirt, and such pencil-thin pleats and tucks on the bodice; and that high lace collar on the dickey has little, thin boning in it, to make it stand up. Teachers do not have such clothes."

I smiled. "I think some teachers in San Francisco might. Though they probably would not wear them for teaching."

"San Francisco!"

"That is where I am from." *And where I must return, as soon as I possibly can.* I knew better than to say that aloud.

Tabitha frowned. "Once we're here, we're not to talk about where we were before. Especially you."

"Why is that?" As soon as the direct question was out of my mouth, I regretted it. All my instincts told me that the only way to learn anything about this household was by stealth and indirection.

But Tabitha surprised me. "If I tell you, may I stay and sit with you awhile?"

"Of course," I said. "I should be glad of the company."

"Father says we are not to tire you." She brought over the other straight-backed chair.

I said, "I appreciate that. But on another hand, it can be tiring in a different way to have no distractions or diversions, especially as I cannot move about and I have no books to read. Except, of course," I hastened to add, "for *The Book of Mormon,* which Mr. Pratt gave me." And which I did not intend to read; I consider it my duty to resist indoctrination of any sort. Otherwise I should be untrue to myself, and then where would I be?

"Very well." Tabitha sat at a slight angle to me, arranging her skirt so that only the tips of the toes of her leather shoes were visible. "I would like to talk with you more, but you must tell me, Carrie, if you start to get too tired."

"I will. Now, you said you would tell me why it is you're not—*we're* not—supposed to talk about where we come from? Surely one's origins are important?"

"The people, our families, are certainly important. We must bring them all into the fold of the True Religion, and that can be done only in the Temple."

From Pratt's instruction I had already learned that when a Mormon said "the Temple," it meant the temple in Salt Lake City. Rather in the same fashion as, to the Jews, there was only one "Temple," and that was in Jerusalem. Exactly what might reside in such a sacred precinct would be most interesting to see. Though I supposed one would be struck blind after. Highly religious experiences tend to be tedious that way.

"But," Tabitha continued, folding her long-fingered hands in her lap, "the places themselves where we have lived are not so important, especially to Father. He is very devout, you know. He takes his priesthood so seriously."

Tabitha broke off, biting her lower lip and looking a little troubled. "He can explain this much better than I."

Although I was listening attentively, another part of my mind was equally occupied with making the kind of observations for which I had been trained as a private investigator. I had completely recovered my memory. Among other things, I knew perfectly well what Michael and I had been doing on that ill-fated train. But I'd chosen not to let the others, particularly Melancthon Pratt, know much at all about me; they believed I still suffered from some memory impairment. It was a ruse, which I intended to maintain as long as it proved useful to me.

"Pray continue," I said by way of encouragement.

Continuing my observations, I noted that Tabitha's hands did not appear to be so accustomed to hard work as Verla's, or even Norma's. How interesting.

Tabitha said, "I really am not sure I understand it all very well myself. But you probably know that we are, well, different."

"I am not familiar enough with Mormonism to make any comparisons," I said, while thinking that Sarah, whom I had seldom seen, bore a physical resemblance to Tabitha. Further, I wondered if Sarah's hands also might be less work-worn, as Tabitha's were. I tried to mentally picture Selene's hands, and could not, but no matter—she was so young I could not really think of her as one of Pratt's wives. In fact, I hoped she might still be in school somewhere.

"I didn't mean Mormons are different—although of course that's true, and is the whole reason Prophet Joseph Smith started our religion. What I meant was, we —that is, Father and the families in the area who follow him—are different from the rest of the Mormons. We adhere more closely to the true spirit of the teachings of Joseph Smith. Father has recovered this purity in the same manner that Joseph himself achieved it: through communication with an angel."

"Um-hm," I said, "fascinating."

"Father says we are the True Saints."

I raised my eyebrows, but could think of no way to remark upon this extraordinary notion. As I had my own suspicions about Pratt and his angel, not to mention his possible sainthood, I decided to change the subject. "Tabitha, it has just occurred to me that Sarah bears a considerable resemblance to you."

Tabitha blushed. "It's the other way around. *I* resemble *her*. We're sisters. She is three years older than I."

"Oh, I see." And both married to the same man. How bizarre.

To keep my thoughts from continuing along that line, I doggedly pursued my alternate train of thought: "May I hazard a guess? In the division of housework, you're in charge of the sewing. And Sarah, does she do the same?"

"Well, yes," she replied, cocking her head to one side. "How could you tell?"

I said, "Your hands are smooth, which suggests to me that they are not often in hot, harsh water. Therefore you do not wash clothes or dishes, or scrub floors. Or do much work outside, as in a garden, raising vegetables or flowers. Furthermore, in the bright sunlight I see tiny prick-marks on the fingers of your left hand, which I think should be from a needle. And a slight indentation at the tip of the middle finger of your right hand, as if you often wear a thimble on it."

"Goodness, how clever! I must go get Sarah, she must hear this." Tabitha jumped up out of the chair excitedly. "I'm sure you got so clever by spending all those years in school. We both wanted to go longer to school, you see, but then, well . . ." She blushed. The high color in her face was most becoming.

I smiled and said nothing, as I could not think of anything to say.

"I'll be right back. And I'll, I'll—well, Sarah and I will have something to show you. You'll be pleased, I think, to see how right you are."

"All right," I said, still smiling, and now curious too.

But as soon as Tabitha had closed the door behind her and I was completely alone, gloom descended upon me.

I have never been very fond of mountains; given the choice of a trip to the mountains or to the seashore, I would always choose the sea. So, to have those mountains as the only view available to me was exceedingly oppressive. More oppressive still was the sense of hopelessness that continually threatened to take me over. In a way, I might have been happier if I hadn't recovered my memory.

"No, no," I muttered aloud, "I mustn't think like that."

Silently I recited; *I am Fremont Jones. I live in San Francisco. Michael Kossoff is my partner, in life and in work. We are the J&K Agency, private investigators. Our telephone number is 3263.*

The Pratts had no telephone. I had inquired, of course, on the second day after regaining my senses. I'd asked Verla, who had frowned at me and said, "What a notion!"

Being unwilling to give up so easily, I'd approached Norma, who came in later that day to sit with me for a while. I had asked her if she would send a telegram for me the next time she was in town. I needed to let my business partner know that I was all right, I said. She had replied, "You don't have any business anywhere anymore except right here, so I reckon there won't be any telegrams sent. If God wants you here, who are you to argue that? And we know God wants you here, because Father says so."

*Hm,* I'd thought, *God may want me here, but you do not.* That was as plain to me as the nose on her saucy face. Then I'd filed that observation away in my mind, along with all the others I was accumulating.

Someday, surely, all these observations would be of use.

I sighed. What was taking Tabitha so long to return with Sarah? Why couldn't I hear footsteps in the hallway outside my door when people came and went? Surely there was a hallway outside the door, and in a simple farmhouse, no more than a cabin really, it would not be carpeted. . . .

Suddenly I could not get my breath, my heart began to pound, and my hands dripped cold sweat. Down to the very marrow of my bones I understood the origin of the phrase "scared to death," because I was. Surely one could not live long and feel this way?

Oh, dear God, I was trapped in this one room! Trapped, without knowing where I really was, knowing nothing of the layout of the house, in or near what town it was situated, knowing nothing at all except these four walls and the view from this one window. I could not bear it! My heart fluttered like a bird in the cage of my ribs.

When I was a child in Boston, one of my mother's friends had kept canaries in her house around the corner from us, in Louisburg Square. She had a whole room full of the tiny little yellow birds, each in its single, separate cage. I couldn't say how many cages, because I'd been too young to count them, but the day had come when I couldn't stand anymore to see those caged birds singing their pretty little hearts out. I had opened the doors of all the cages; and then I'd run away myself. I hadn't stayed to watch and see if they would fly away or not, but I knew what I would have done if I had been a bird. . . .

I shifted in the chair to get my legs right under me. The chair had no arms, but I braced my hands against the seat. Did I dare to let my legs take my weight? Were they really broken and mending? I had only Pratt's word for it. I didn't remember the doctor's visit. What if my broken legs were as much a construction of Pratt's grandiose imagination as his angelic visions? What if my injuries were far less severe than he'd led me to believe?

*Oh please,* I thought, *I must get away. . . .*

I slowly lifted myself from the chair, keeping most of my weight on my hands. I felt pain; beads of moisture popped out on my forehead. My breath came in shallow bursts and I was dizzy, but the cold dread of absolute terror passed, because *now I was doing something.* The pain was not so bad . . . until I tried to straighten my knees.

———

So early in the morning that the sky was still dark, Michael waited on the platform of San Francisco's train station for Meiling to arrive from Palo Alto. He had engaged an auto-taxi for the trip from the station to the Ferry Building; there they would cross the Bay to Oakland, and from Oakland their main journey eastward would begin.

He was alone on the platform. Two porters in their red-capped uniforms leaned against the walls, perhaps catching forty winks. If they had been on duty all night, and they probably had, Michael did not begrudge the hard-working men their sleep. He preferred to be alone anyway.

Michael's footsteps clicked on the cement platform as he walked back and forth, back and forth. He took off his bowler hat and ran his hand through his hair once, twice; then put the hat back on again. He didn't like to admit it, but Edna Stephenson had shaken his confidence. Was he doing the right thing by involving Meiling?

She'd changed. *Well, people do that, especially when they're young, they change,* he thought. The thing was, though: Meiling had changed so much, and in ways that Michael did not understand. Ways that would have been mysterious to most Chinese, and were incomprehensible to him. Her grandmother's magic, she'd said, had changed her.

Meiling had gone to Stanford with the goal of studying geology, or, as she herself had called it, "the science of the earth." But after receiving the gift of her grandmother's chest, her eyes had been opened to much, much more. Meiling now claimed to understand more about the earth than science alone could teach. She talked of *chi,* the life force that runs through all living things, and through the earth and sky as well. She talked of maintaining a healthful balance, of the ways good energy moves, and of things that block the movement of energy. Her wind chimes and the colored banners outside the tiny house in Palo Alto had something to do with all this. So did the colors that accented her clothing, and so many other things it made Michael's head spin.

Also in that chest, Meiling's grandmother had left a very old book, full of secret teachings and recipes for magic, a kind of Chinese *grimoire.* Bells, incense, combs and mirrors, silk ribbons and satin ropes, bones and beads and shells—all that and more came from the chest. With the book and her recollection of lessons from childhood, Meiling was teaching herself to be a Chinese magician.

This would have been fine with Michael if not for two things. First, she had abandoned her studies at Stanford in order to follow this questionable pursuit; and second, Meiling had begun to talk of demons and malevolent spirits. Michael did not believe in demons and malevolent spirits, he believed that man was evil enough already and did not require any help from the spirit world.

From away in the darkness the train's locomotive gave its haunting whistle. Michael stopped pacing to stand near the edge of the platform and look down the tracks. He could see the lamps on either side of the engine glowing like eyes in the dark. His imagination, fired by thoughts of Meiling and her magic, could easily turn the train into a dragon belching steam.

*Dragons are good luck to the Chinese,* he thought, forcing the corners of his mouth into a grim smile. *And Meiling and I will need all the good luck we can gather for the time ahead.*

# 6

WHEN I LET my legs take most of my weight, something both quite remarkable and perfectly awful happened: My body simply would not support me. With a painful protest, it gave way all at once. Being woefully without medical knowledge, I could not have said whether it was the musculature of the legs that would not perform, whether the bones beneath those muscles were fractured, whether my blood had simply grown too thin, or what. Add to that the shortness of breath that had me gasping once I'd collapsed back into the chair, and altogether it made for a genuinely bad experience. As I have seldom been sick in my life, I did not know what to think of this—other than to try not to let it make me feel too much worse than I already did.

I was thinking how much I should like the doctor to come back and see me again, now that I was in my right mind and could question him, when Tabitha returned with her sister Sarah. Once again I did not hear them approach—it was Tabitha's light knock followed by the opening of the latch that alerted me to their imminent appearance.

"Come in, please," I called out, very glad of the distraction.

"I'm back," Tabitha announced excitedly and unnecessarily. "Here's Sarah too, and we've brought some of our things to show you!"

The sisters did indeed look much alike, though seeing them side by side I thought Sarah seemed more than just the three years older that Tabitha had mentioned. Sarah's dress was blue-gray rather than brown, and her collar and cuffs bore delicate cutwork instead of lace. There were other differences as well: Sarah lacked her younger sister's gentleness. In fact, it was very interesting to see how their similar features had been influenced, molded one was tempted to say, by their individual personalities.

Sarah was just a little taller, a bit thinner. Her hair was the same light brown, and she wore it the same way, parted in the middle and pulled back into a bun shaped like a figure eight turned sideways. Also, from the tiny new hairs she had above her ears as we all do, I could tell that Sarah's hair had that charming tendency to curl—a tendency I always notice and envy in others, on account of mine being so utterly straight. But Sarah's hair was not escaping from its arrangement, no indeed; she had pulled it back so tightly that the corners of her eyes turned up. I winced inwardly to look at her.

Yet, hard as Sarah seemed (if that hairdo was any indication) to be on herself, she was easy with others. The smile she bestowed on me had the same sweetness as her sister Tabitha's, and that went a long, long way.

"Carrie," Sarah said, "I'm so glad Tabitha suggested I come along to see you. I've brought some of the things she and I are currently working on. I thought we could talk while we sew. Tabitha and I, I mean; we don't expect *you* to sew! We have a quota to meet but we can certainly talk at the same time. That is, if you aren't too tired."

"Not at all," I agreed heartily, "but what is this about a quota? I certainly wouldn't want to distract you from meeting it."

The two sisters glanced at each other, as if deciding which one of them should answer. Tabitha spoke up: "We sew for the family, of course, but we also make things for sale. These are, well, rather special. We promise delivery times and so on."

"I cannot wait to see! But before we proceed, either we shall need an additional chair from the next room, or I must get back in bed so that one of you may have this one."

Sarah put down the large basket she was carrying. "Since there is no 'next room,' I expect we'd best help you back to bed."

"By all means," I agreed, after a slight hesitation due to the fact that I knew I'd soon need to relieve myself, and so was thinking of asking for their help. But no, I would not; the procedure under my present circumstances was so laborious—and rather humiliating—that I preferred to postpone it as long as I could. I smiled at each of the sisters in turn and said, "I'm ready when you are."

Tabitha and Sarah each draped one of my arms over their shoulders and linked their hands behind my back. "I'll count three," Tabitha said. "One, two, three!"

On "three" they lifted me by their linked hands until my toes barely skimmed the floor, and the first thing I knew I was back in bed. I thanked them both, and submitted to a lot of quilt-smoothing and pillow-plumping before they pronounced themselves satisfied that I could be as comfortable as I claimed.

"Now then," I said, glancing from one to the other of their similar yet different faces, "which one of you will tell me what you meant when you said there was no room next door. For surely in a household this size, there must be more rooms on one side or the other?"

Sarah did not look up from her unpacking of the basket, which she balanced on one knee while her lap received its contents. I did not pay much attention, being far more interested in this opportunity to learn what, exactly, lay beyond my always-closed door. It was again Tabitha who answered me.

"I suppose no one has told you. We forget you haven't had the freedom to look around. Um, er—" she darted a sidewise glance at her sister, whose head was studiously bent over the basket, as if she had discovered some new species in there. Not gaining any help from that quarter, Tabitha bit her bottom lip briefly and then said, "Father is the only one who *lives* in the Big House. And actually, the truth is it really isn't all that big, not compared to some I've seen. In Provo, for instance."

"Mmm, that's true," Sarah commented. She steadied the basket on her knee with one hand while the other rested atop a small pile of folded cloth, most of it bleached white, but some left a natural ivory color. "Still, for here it's large."

I frowned, the questions in my mind showing, I should imagine, on my face.

Tabitha said, "Each wife has her own cabin. This one that you are in is for guests. When you're well, Father will build you one of your own. You'll get to choose your own furnishings, what color curtains, and so on. You might even get a rug. Oh, and best of all, a ride to town to pick them out yourself!"

"Really," I said dryly. I thought, *How extraordinary!*

"We do not spend all that much time in our cabins, which is why they're so small," Sarah said somewhat apologetically. She set the basket carefully on the floor and resettled the pile of cloth in her lap with her hands on both sides, holding it like some sort of precious gift.

"Our cabins are primarily for sleeping. That is, when we sleep alone."

Tabitha chimed in hastily, "There are lovely rooms in the main house for all of us to use during the day, and of course there's the big dining room."

*Um-hm,* I thought, *I am beginning to perceive the order of things.*

"Who does the cooking?" I inquired, interested in the arrangement. I could actually rather see the point, division of labor, many hands make light work, and all that.

"Verla and Norma take turns. They're teaching Selene, but she's not a very apt pupil," Tabitha replied.

"Too dreamy," Sarah commented.

Her sister nodded. "She forgets things all the time. And she's always in a hurry. Her creamed potatoes and mashed turnips always have lumps."

I reflected that my creamed potatoes and mashed turnips would have lumps too if I were forced into this duty, and feeling like a kindred soul, I leapt to the youngest wife's defense. "Selene is still a child. I'm sure she'll learn."

At the same time the sisters both said the same thing: "Perhaps." Then they looked at each other and laughed. Laughing, they blushed, and I had an impression that would later prove to be accurate: Laughter was not a common occurrence in the Pratt household.

As if to make up for the frivolity and merriment, Sarah straightened both her face and her backbone, and proceeded to show me one by one the articles she had folded on her lap. After she had displayed each one and told me about it, Tabitha—who by now had also sobered up—took each in turn and carefully refolded it, then placed it back in the basket, which now sat on the floor between their chairs. They handled these clothes reverently, as I supposed was befitting since they called them "temple garments." The final two temple garments were not yet completed, and so remained on the sisters' laps while they threaded their needles, adjusted their chairs so as to make maximum use of the light from the window, and set themselves to sewing.

"I don't like to betray my ignorance," I admitted, "but I have never seen, or heard of, a temple garment before. I suppose from the name there is some religious significance?"

"Your instruction has not gone that far yet?" Sarah asked. She cocked her head to one side, in the same motion I'd seen from her sister an hour or so earlier.

"If you mean the instruction Father, I mean Mr. Pratt, has been giving me"—they both nodded, paying rapt attention to my every word without missing a stitch—"so far he has been telling me the extraordinary story of how Joseph Smith was given the Tablets of Gold by the Angel Moroni, and how the tablets were all covered with writing purported to be hieroglyphics. How Mr. Smith could not read them, because the hieroglyphics were not in any known system of language decipherable by any means, including the Rosetta Stone. And so on." I dismissed the rest with a wave of my hand that I hoped was not too cavalier.

But Tabitha said, greatly excited, "Did you get to the part yet about Urim and Thummim?"

I resisted the urge to roll my eyes. Only the previous evening, Melancthon Pratt had told me a story I'd thought preposterous, about how, along with the Tablets of Gold, the Angel Moroni had given Joseph Smith two magical stones called the Urim and the Thummim. Hebrew words, supposedly. And supposedly these stones had enabled Smith to translate the tablets—which after the translation the angel most conveniently took away again, so that the truth of all this could never be either proved or disproved. I wondered what had become of the stones, for Pratt had not said that

the angel took them away too . . . but I certainly was
not going to ask him. Nor these two sisters.

Cautiously I replied, "He told me last night about
the magical stones."

Not looking at me, concentrating on the symbol she
was embroidering with thread that exactly matched the
cloth, Sarah muttered a significant remark: "I wonder if
it could possibly be that Carrie finds that whole business about Joseph Smith doing his translations with his
face in his hat as ridiculous as I do."

*Hmm*, I thought. Another observation to file for
later.

But Tabitha did not ignore it. "Sarah!" she chided.
"It's just as well for you to say such things to me, since
I've known you my whole life, you are my big sister,
and I'd die for you. But what will Carrie think?"

"I think," I said, smiling, "that a good deal of the
Christian Bible seems equally ridiculous to me. A
prophet is a prophet, no matter how he arrives at his
prophecies, whether that may be on top of a mountain
or with his—what was that you said, Sarah?"

She looked at me levelly, with clear, calm eyes. "His
face in a hat."

"Mr. Pratt's recounting did not go into that detail," I
said.

"Well, I think Carrie has just exactly the right attitude," Tabitha said, nodding her head decisively and
taking up her own sewing. "She understands that you
just have to take it on faith. And really, Sarah, even if
you are my sister and I'd never tell on you, I do think
you could have more faith!"

I smiled across at Sarah. "I won't tell on you either."

"If I'd thought you would, I'd have kept my
thoughts to myself," Sarah said, returning my smile. I
felt like a conspirator, and so decided to return to a
safer subject.

"I'd still like to know about these temple garments.

Are they worn in the Temple?" I was getting a very odd mental picture of men and women walking around in rather scanty outfits. Perhaps they performed their worship around a large fire. That would fit with another thing Pratt had told me: that the Mormons of today and the American Indians had common ancestors who had been the brothers Nephi and Lamaan. These brothers fought; Nephi was the "good" one and Lamaan was the "bad" one. In addition to being somewhat unscrupulous, Lamaan was a better fighter, so he won and wiped out the Nephites. The last survivor of the Nephites was Moroni—yes, that very same Moroni who came as an angel to Joseph Smith—whose last act had been to bury the golden tablets on which the good Nephites had recorded their beliefs. Today's Indians were supposed to be descended from the Lamaanites.

Sarah and Tabitha both giggled. Tabitha said, "Yes, temple garments are worn in the Temple. Also for shopping, and for travel—not that we get to do much traveling—for gardening, for . . . hmm, for sleeping—"

"And don't forget bathing," Sarah interrupted. Then they both broke out in polite peals of laughter.

"You mean—" I began, but suddenly I too was laughing, though it was not really quite so funny as all that.

"Yes," Tabitha gasped between peals, "we never take them off. Never!"

"Not even, not even—" Sarah began, but she was laughing too hard to finish.

She didn't have to. I knew what she was going to say, so I said it aloud myself: "For sex."

"Carrieeeee!" Tabitha squealed, beside herself with laughter. Sarah and I were not much better.

At that inopportune moment the door was pushed inward with such force that it hit the wall, and I feared for the safety of the hinges. Then Melancthon Pratt's glowering face appeared, and I feared for the safety of us three.

———

I am not much concerned about what people think," Meiling said. "If we need to speak privately, then it makes no difference to me whether we do so in your space or in mine."

That was what Michael had expected her to say, but somehow being alone with Meiling in her train compartment seemed much different from being alone with her in her small house. Different too from being with her in the apartment house where she had lived when she'd first moved from San Francisco to Palo Alto. He was uncomfortable, and supposed the train's compactness had something to do with his discomfort. So he did not venture farther into the little room, nor did he close the door. Instead he stood leaning in the entry, knee and hip holding the door open, and said, "If we hold our discussion in my compartment, you'll have the assurance of knowing you can leave any time you like. Whereas if I stay here and you become uncomfortable, you'll have to ask me to leave. You might be concerned that I would refuse."

Meiling's long, straight hair swayed with the motion of the train. The clackety-clack of the wheels on the track was both soothing and a constant reminder of where they were, what they had to do.

With that perfect seriousness Chinese and Japanese people seem able to achieve, while Europeans can only hope for something approximate, Meiling said, "There will be no reason for me to ask you to leave. You are wasting time. I know there is much you have not yet told me, so come in and sit down, and let us begin."

Michael took a deep breath, stepped forward into the compartment, and allowed the door to close behind him. She had burned a stick of incense; the air had that clean, spicy fragrance he remembered from her house a couple of days earlier.

"Do sit down," Meiling said. She was smiling slightly. Perhaps his nervousness amused her. That wouldn't be too surprising, considering that he had known her since her infancy; Meiling's father, before he was killed in the Tong Wars, had been Michael's good friend.

"Thank you." Michael sat on the bench seat opposite Meiling. He looked for a moment through the small window, set off by sharply pleated curtains of starched lace. Intrigued, he reached out a finger and touched one of the pleats, as if to see whether or not its sharp edge might cut his fingertip.

"If you took them down and put them on the floor, do you think they would stand up by themselves?" Meiling asked, tipping her head to one side.

"What?"

"The curtains. They are so heavily starched I thought they might stand alone. It was a nonsensical question." Meiling leaned back against the cushion and crossed her legs at the knee. She was wearing a split skirt, and for an instant as she moved, Michael saw a pale flash of skin. "But then I can see that you are not ready to talk about whatever it is we must begin with. And so"—she shrugged—"one bit of nonsense is as good as another to pass the time."

"How did you become so wise?" Michael placed one ankle atop the other knee, unbuttoned his suit coat, and breathed out through his nose, a long breath, in an attempt to relax.

"My grandmother. The things in the trunk."

The question had been rhetorical, yet she'd answered him. "Tell me more about that. No, first tell me"—he gestured with one hand—"how you arrived at the sort of costume you are wearing. It seems to be, well, a sort of compromise."

"Very astute, for a male of the species," said Meiling with a little bow of acknowledgment.

"I'm nothing if not observant, including of women's clothes." His traveling companion wore a long duster coat. Her divided skirt was of silk in a weave that had the heaviness of cotton twill, yet a luxuriousness that cotton could not match; a glow that came perhaps from the depth of color the fabric could absorb—in this case the shade of autumn leaves. Michael knew the silk must feel like heaven to the skin. The duster was loosely fitted and the whole outfit appeared to have been put together more for comfort and ease of movement than for fashion, yet it was so striking that Michael would not have been surprised to see Meiling start a whole new fashion. That is, if she had not been Chinese.

"My clothing is related to my grandmother's teachings," Meiling said, dipping her head in respect as she mentioned her grandmother. "It is of my own design. The skirt is divided, as some women now wear for riding horses astride, which is most sensible. Yet it looks much like the usual kind of skirt when one is not moving about, and so it is, as you said, a compromise. The coat"—she extended her arms in demonstration—"'is cut loosely enough that I have freedom of movement throughout my upper body, and at the waist. This is very important, so as not to restrict the movement of *chi*."

"And what is *chi*?"

"You are not a good pupil, Michael." Meiling wagged her finger, smiling.

"No, wait, I remember. *Chi* is the life force that moves through all living things."

"That is correct. Our friend Fremont Jones is wise to refuse to wear a corset. Likewise—but in a converse manner—when the not-so-honorable ancestors of my people wished to subjugate and to enslave their wives, they bound up their feet. Any kind of tight, restrictive, binding clothing is not healthy. What may be equally important to our purposes on this journey, I could not defend myself if the necessity should arise, dressed the way American women dress. Yet I should call far too much attention to myself if I were to walk through the train in the silk trousers and tunic I prefer to wear. Does this answer your question?"

"Yes. Thank you." Michael looked out of the window. It was nighttime, their first night out, a clear night by whose bright moonlight he could see the tall black shapes of trees flash by. The train tracks wound their way up onto the western slopes of the Sierra Nevada, following a path slashed into primeval forest lands. He said a silent prayer and turned back to Meiling.

"What," he asked, "does your *chi* tell you about our main task?"

"You mean finding Fremont?"

"Yes."

"She is alive," Meiling said, "that is all I can tell you. I feel her energy here, in this dimension of our existence. She has not migrated to another plane."

Michael frowned. "You talk like a Spiritualist." He'd had enough of Spiritualism a few months back, though Fremont had deplored his negative attitude.

"Taoism is a spiritual practice. It is a kind of religion. I was taught as a child to follow the way of the Tao. All that I'm learning from my grandmother's notebooks simply enlarges upon those spiritual principles."

"And the magic?"

Meiling smiled enigmatically. "Perhaps the magic is a joke."

Michael said, "Or perhaps not."

She bowed her head. "Precisely."

# 7

"CAN YOU SEE into the future with your magic?" Michael asked Meiling half-seriously.

"No," she replied, "for that you would need someone who is skilled at interpretation of the *I Ching*. This I have not studied and do not intend to. It would be the work of a lifetime and my focus is elsewhere."

"Hmm," said Michael, gazing out the window again. He felt oddly reluctant to deal with the reality of any of this—Meiling grown up and turned wise, Fremont gone missing—it was all too much, and so he made his mind a blank and simply gazed. Beyond his own dark reflection in the small square of glass he could see very little, for trees crowded up against the track and blotted out the moon and sky. He felt as if the train were speeding through an uninhabited land, a void. . . .

Meiling's voice came to his ears as if from far away: "My skill is in working with energy—sensing, moving, following. I can perhaps alter or influence the course of events. I can find that which has been lost. I have done this, though so far in a small way only, many times."

"Hum," said Michael again, a brief sound from deep in the back of his throat. Then he roused himself as the meaning behind her words pierced the darkness of his reverie. "I won't ask how you do it. I'm just glad to hear that you believe you can."

"It is as well you do not ask," Meiling said, nodding. "I am not sure I could explain to your satisfaction. Now, suppose you explain to *me* how you intend that we should proceed."

————

Norma said there was a disturbance in the guest quarters," Pratt announced as his glowering expression dissolved, being replaced—most amazingly—by a slowly spreading smile, "but she didn't say what kind of disturbance. I see the two sisters are amusing the newest member of my house."

*My* house, not *our* house: Another observation went into my mental bag, which was becoming positively stuffed chock-full of them.

"You don't mind a little frivolity, I hope," I said.

"Of course not," he said, now positively beaming. "Good afternoon, my dears."

Like well-trained children we all replied, "Good afternoon, Father." Except I did not say the word "Father."

As I looked at that big man standing a few feet from my bed, his legs spread wide apart in a stance that just a moment before had been belligerent, I suddenly pictured him in one of the garments Tabitha and Sarah were sewing. I fancied they might be picturing him the same—which doubtless they could do with far more accuracy than I—because when I turned and looked at them, I saw that they too were sucking their cheeks in to keep back the laughter.

The effort proved too much for all three of us. They were facing Pratt, and covered their mouths with their hands, but with the back of my head turned to him I rolled my eyes as the irrepressible laughter came spewing out. Of course I was slightly hysterical, but it was the most fun I'd had in a very long time and so I did not care.

"Perhaps one of you would be good enough to share the joke with me." Pratt sat on the end of my bed, placing his big hands on his knees.

"Oh! Uh—" Tabitha began. She was always ready to please, but in this case she did not get any further than this abrupt start before words failed her. Sarah didn't even try—she appeared to have been struck dumb.

It was up to me. "We really can't," I said, in the midst of another torrent of giggles, "it's a, a female sort of thing. You couldn't possibly understand."

"And as a female matter," said Sarah, the first to recover her composure, "it is inferior and beneath your attention anyway. Sir." She seemed to add the last word as a sort of placation.

"Yes, well, that may be." The smile now gone, Pratt rubbed his chin thoughtfully. Those too-blue eyes roamed over us, each in turn. Such hard eyes, so brilliant and so cold, yet such a gorgeous shade of blue. No matter how long I should have to stay here, or what I might have to do in order to get away and resume my life again, in that very moment I knew I would never forget those eyes. As I was chilled by the realization, all remaining traces of my own amusement fled.

Sarah tied off her thread, reached into her pocket for some tiny scissors and snipped. Then she folded the item she'd been sewing, but not until she had tucked her needle neatly into the cloth to mark the place where she'd left off and should begin again. Then she fixed a level gaze on her husband and inquired, "Do you wish to be alone with Carrie, Father?"

Tabitha also was putting her work away. I felt dismayed. I wanted them to stay. And especially not to leave me alone with him. Yet I knew what he would say, and what they would say, and what they would then do. It was all so inevitable. And indeed it did all come to pass, one remark following upon the other exactly as predicted, sure as night follows day.

I sighed and surrendered to my fate, asking Pratt to wait outside for a few minutes while I took care of a "personal necessity." To his credit he agreed without question.

"I hope you will both come again soon," I said quietly to Sarah and Tabitha as we finished handling the tricky task that a simple physiological process had become for me.

"Of course we will," Tabitha assured me. She washed her hands in a basin at the washstand. Whatever else Mormons might be, they were very clean and neat in their habits, which of itself was encouraging. Though of course I was grasping at straws. I wondered if the big house, Father's house, had indoor plumbing. Out here in the wilds I rather doubted it.

Sarah looked, I thought, as if she wanted to say something but the cat had got her tongue.

"Sarah?" I asked, searching her eyes, wishing I could reach into her and physically draw out whatever it was.

She blinked. For a moment I thought she would speak what was in her mind, but the moment passed, her expression changed, and she asked only, "Is there anything you'd like us to bring you?"

"Books," I replied without hesitation, "magazines. Something, anything to read besides—in addition to, I mean—*The Book of Mormon*. Not that I don't think *The Book of Mormon* is simply splendid, fascinating, and edifying, but that a little variety would be so much the better."

Sarah smiled. "Leave it to me. I'll see what I can do. I

am allowed to go into town for fabric and thread. I do believe I feel a need for more ivory thread coming on, and who knows but what I may find some reading materials along the way."

She kissed me on the cheek, as if I too were now her sister, and so did Tabitha. And even though Pratt brought his overwhelming presence into the room as soon as they left, I felt more comforted than I had at any time since the accident.

*No, not an accident. . . . Deliberate, malicious destruction.*

I wished I had not had that thought, because it made me miss Michael so much I could hardly bear it.

Though it was the last thing I felt like doing, I smiled, for it would not do to show sadness or weakness to Melancthon Pratt. He smiled too—the second time in an afternoon, what a surprise. Up to now I had not been at all sure he knew how. But apparently he had his lighter side, his better moods, and was still in one. I was determined to take advantage of it, to wring from him every consideration possible. How I should accomplish this I had not the slightest idea.

"Sarah and Tabitha have been telling me many fine things about you, Mr. Pratt," I said. "I'm much impressed. Do I understand correctly that you are a leader of the religious community here? What is it called, the True Saints?"

He nodded his large head. "Correct on both accounts. But as I've told you before, I prefer that you also address me as Father. As my wives do, since you will soon be one of them."

*That is a problem!* The words leapt in my mind but I did not allow them to pass my lips, because something deep inside me warned against it. I wanted, I longed to lie, to tell him I was already married, or promised to be married—which of course was not far from the truth, or that I had some dreadful disease that made touching me worse than death itself. . . .

"I'm honored," I said, "but I feel I cannot call you Father until, er—" I felt a blush arise and for once was glad of it. I expected he would like to see me blush. More evidence of how sex-obsessed they all were, how the slightest hint in that direction titillated any and all of them, Pratt himself most of all.

"Er," I resumed, "until we have our own children. Which brings to mind: I appreciate that you must have asked your wives to keep the children away until now, in order to speed my recovery. But I'm so much better, and sadly in need of occupation. I'd like very much to meet the little ones. How many do you have?"

Pratt turned to stone. Or as good as. Obviously I had said the wrong thing, but I could not understand how, or why. He himself had explained to me the Mormon belief in "spirit children," which exist in some other place (where, exactly, that might be was not a part of the story), and that it is the duty of mortal men and women to bring as many of these spirit children into human existence as possible, by conceiving and giving birth to them. Of course if the man and the woman who have the babies are Mormons, members of God's Elect, then so much the better for all those children, as they've been born into the right place—so to speak. Therefore I assumed Pratt must have a slew of children.

"I do not yet have any children," Pratt said in a sepulchral voice. "The first five wives are barren, even to the youngest. But you, Caroline, will be fruitful. It is promised by the angel that led me to you."

---

The train rolled into the night, on tracks climbing ever higher into the Sierra Nevada. In the prevailing silence of Pullman cars long since made up for sleeping, Michael could hear occasionally the train's long, moaning whistle; and if he listened intently, the chuffing of the locomotive working hard to move a great weight up and up, in defiance of the laws of gravity.

He couldn't sleep. He lay in the bunk created by folding down the bench seat in his private compartment, and thought about the plans he'd laid out for Meiling. In the dark Michael grimaced with knowing how much he'd wanted to hear Meiling say, *Yes, of course that will work, that is the best plan, you have done well, we will find her.* But Meiling was too smart for that, and too honest to make false promises. She had inclined her head in a slight gesture of assent, and that was all—the only approval he was going to get. It wasn't enough, but it would have to do.

Michael grunted, turned onto his uninjured side, got up on that elbow, pounded the pillow a few times, then put his head down again. Of course mauling the pillow about had not helped—the discomfort that kept him awake was internal. A thin line of light from the outer corridor showed beneath the door, enough to illuminate the shapes of his shoes on the floor and his bathrobe hanging on a hook, swaying with the train's motion like a bodiless wraith. His mind felt as dark and constricted as the tiny room, consumed by the unanswerable question: *Where are you?*

Michael began to go through his plans again, reciting them like a litany to keep fear away: He and Meiling would leave the train at Provo, Utah. There they would hire horses and a guide. They'd have to be satisfied with whatever they could get, even if that meant substituting mules for horses. Such elements of uncertainty were maddening, for Michael was a meticulous planner; he believed in spending weeks, months if necessary, making sure all the pieces were in place before moving a muscle or even a finger. But there had not been time. Then too, writing or wiring ahead for horses or reservations of any sort might possibly alert the wrong people

—they were out there, even if he didn't know who they were.

It was frustrating as hell, not knowing what or who was behind that explosion, and whether the goal had been simple destruction or destruction for a particular purpose, and if so, what that purpose might have been. Robbery-gone-wrong was still a possibility. The dynamite could have gone off a minute too soon—perhaps it had been intended to send the two baggage cars rather than two passenger cars to the bottom of the canyon. Another possibility: disruption of the train's route for the weeks it would take to rebuild the bridge across the canyon. Now on its temporary route the train switched onto a secondary rail line at Provo, and from there went due south, to a junction at a place called Nephi. From there, the Southern Pacific Railway was providing wagons to transport passengers overland to the undamaged portion of track, from which they would continue on east. Michael hadn't paid much attention to those details, since he knew he would not be going that far, not this time. Not unless he found Fremont, and probably not even then.

This time he and Meiling would part company with the train at Provo. On their own they would ride into the mountains. He aimed to start at the scene of the wreckage, at the bottom of that gorge he had since learned was called Fretts Canyon; he intended to go at last where his lack of identification had prevented him from going before. So long after the explosion, he had little hope of finding anything. It was a place to start, that was all, a place from which to begin and work outward in an ever-widening circle.

Ostensibly Michael and Meiling would be continuing the work for which the J&K Agency had been hired: to ascertain if any one person or group could be held responsible for an escalating series of accidents on both the Union and Southern Pacific Railroads in recent months. Pinkerton, the railroads' usual detective agency, had been unsuccessful at putting a stop to the accidents, which in fact only continued to increase in number and severity. So J&K had been secretly called in, not to replace the Pinkertons but to supplement them.

Had the explosion been a part of that pattern? The culmination of it, perhaps? No, Michael didn't think so. It wasn't accidental, for one thing; for another . . . well, Michael admitted to himself, as he lay in his bunk with all these thoughts crowding his mind, he didn't *have* another reason. He had only a hunch. A strong hunch, even if wildly improbable. He wished he could discuss it with Fremont—she was so good at providing reasons for his hunches. She could go into his thought processes, as it were, and insert the steps to fill in his intuitive leaps.

Fremont. . . . Without her he felt as if an essential piece of himself were missing. It was not a good feeling.

Michael grunted, swung his feet around abruptly, and stood up too fast, bumping his head on the luggage rack above. "Damnation!" he swore as he sat down hard on the edge of the bunk. He rubbed at his scalp furiously, as if to erase the pain. In this he had some success. Too bad he couldn't rub all the fears for Fremont out of his head as well.

He would find Fremont held under some kind of restraint, he was certain of that much. Whether physical or mental, compelled by some failing on her own part or by malevolence on the part of another, he did not know. All Michael knew was that Fremont was an extremely resourceful woman. She would have managed somehow to get a message to him, or to Wish and Edna Stephenson back at J&K in San Francisco. Or to her father, who had been waiting for them in Boston, at the other end of their ill-fated train ride. But there had been no messages from her anywhere.

Slowly this time, Michael stood up and began to dress in the dark. Like any fine club, the club car stayed open around the clock. He would go there, have a drink and a smoke, and hope the company of other people (who at this hour of the night were quite likely to be as morose and strange as he) would help him gain control of his demons.

As Michael Kossoff tucked in his shirt and fastened up his trousers, those demons planted in his brain a picture of Fremont Jones, dazed and battered, wandering away from overturned train cars in a mindless fog, wandering into a wilderness of forest, wanting only to get away from the fire and the noise and the destruction. . . .

He knotted his tie by feel and shook his head. "No," he said aloud. He had thought that at first, but no longer. He didn't believe she would wander off, not even if she had been the only person conscious after being thrown clear of the wreckage. One passenger was unaccounted for; surely this one was Fremont Jones. Unless someone had made a mistake, and she lay among the dead, after all.

"No," said Michael again. He opened the door of his compartment and stepped out into the narrow passageway. After taking a moment to get the feel of the moving carriage, and to appreciate the fresh, cool air that flowed from an open window or door somewhere close by, he walked slowly, quietly back through the train to the club car. Steel-on-steel, wheels hummed over the tracks, clickety-clacking at every join, a marvel of engineering.

*And a monument to the fortitude of thousands of Chinese laborers,* Michael thought.

He realized he had passed Meiling's compartment without even noticing. Yet how many times on the previous trip had he stood outside Fremont's compartment door, hesitating, longing, deliciously waiting . . . for an invitation that had never come, and now might never come again.

"No!" Michael said.

# 8

THE CLUB CAR was sumptuously furnished, its armchairs upholstered in the same rust-colored velvet that paneled the walls. The tables were of dark walnut, matching the woodwork around the velvet wall panels. A handsome walnut bar occupied the wall at the far end. The bartender, at the moment, was not in evidence.

The air was pungent, but not unpleasantly so, with pipe and cigar smoke. The slap of cards, punctuated by mutterings, came from a gentlemanly game of poker being played at a table in the back, near the bar. Michael sank into an empty chair with a sense of relief. If one could not sleep, surely this was the best place to be —in quiet company, with smoking and drinking the prime order of business.

When the bartender approached his chair, having quietly appeared it seemed out of nowhere, Michael asked for a brandy with a large glass of soda water on the side. While the drinks were being poured, he took from the pocket of his jacket a small book with tissue-thin pages, a novel that had been popular a few years earlier, *The Wings of the Dove* by Henry James, younger brother of the Harvard philosopher William James. As the book was small in size, its print was proportionally tiny, and Michael's eyes were not as young as they used to be. He frowned, moved the book back and forth in an attempt to achieve the optimum distance for good focus, sighed, and wished for stronger light. But that would alter the ambiance, and was not available in any case. So with some regret he returned the book to his pocket. The bartender served his brandy and soda. Michael smiled, and somewhat awkwardly, due to the one-handedness enforced by his injury, dug a bill out of an inner pocket for payment.

The first sip of brandy seared its way satisfactorily down his esophagus. He took another, which ascended nicely into his head. He crossed his legs, and with a small sigh was wishing he could afford to get blind, stinking drunk—when from the corner of his eye he saw movement. In his whole body he sensed danger. He did not move a muscle, but rather reached again for the book, opened it, and pretended to read.

Soon a man came within visual range, so that Michael could observe him with the mere flicker of an eye. No wonder he'd sensed danger! The man who strolled past had once been Michael's nemesis. His name was Hilliard Ramsey.

*My God,* Michael thought, *he's supposed to be dead!*

What to do? Hiding behind *The Wings of the Dove* was not an option—the small book could not protect him for long. Leaving the club car immediately was of course one option. Yet that would be pointless, would it not, seeing as how a train is not that large a place and everyone on it is more or less consigned to remain aboard, at least between stops. They were almost bound to cross paths again.

So Michael continued to read *The Wings of the*

*Dove,* at least ostensibly. He wondered how long it would take Ramsey to recognize him. And what the man would do when he did.

Michael took another sip of brandy.

How long had it been since their last encounter?

Once the memories started pouring back, the time seemed short indeed. Yet it had been six years, almost seven: 1902. The signing of the treaty that formed the Anglo-Japanese Alliance—they had both been covertly involved, on opposite sides of course, Hilliard Ramsey working for the Japanese and Michael Archer (as he'd called himself then) for the Tsar. Michael's job had been to subvert the agreement, which was not in Russia's best interest, and he'd found Ramsey—whose allegiance was only to whoever was paying him at the time, in this case Japan—working against him at every turn.

The role of Russian spy was a family obligation that had fallen on Michael at an early age. He'd been only nineteen, flattered when both his mother and his grandfather had urged him to take over the clandestine duties the grandfather could no longer perform, and for which his father was temperamentally ill-suited. How could a boy with fire in his loins and a sense of adventure in his heart have resisted? And he'd been performing, playing that role ever since. Trapped.

Michael felt only a faint loyalty to the Tsar, and none to Russia as a nation. He was an American through and through; he did not care to be a Russian duke, though being a duchess had meant much to his mother—if truth were told, she would have been glad to reside year-round at the Russian Court. His mother had been, before her death a few years previous, like a lot of Russian nobility—blind to anything but her own pleasure. Oddly enough this Tsar, Nicholas, was probably the best of an increasingly bad lot. Yet with his well-meaning nature went a weak ego and an even weaker will—a dangerous combination, especially for an emperor, allowing him, as it did, to be so easily misled.

For a moment Michael again entertained a thought that had often plagued him during the months leading up to the Anglo-Japanese Treaty, when he'd been gathering information undercover in Japan: If Victoria were still alive, that treaty would never have been signed. Victoria would not have abandoned the kinsman she'd called "Nicky." That shrewd little old lady would have seen the treaty for exactly what it was, a clever ploy on the part of one island nation (Japan) to obtain the support of another (England). But it was a dangerous entanglement, especially for Russia, because Russia needed Korea for access to the Pacific. Japan had coveted Korea for eons. And so in 1902 Michael had foreseen the war that in fact did break out three years later between Russia and Japan.

It was a bad memory, causing him to move restlessly in his chair. Agony, a particular kind of hell, to see war coming and be unable to prevent it.

At least Russia and Japan had ended that one rather quickly without the treaty being invoked, because if England had been obliged to enter a naval conflict in support of Japan—well, the consequences could have been worldwide.

Thank God the United States had had the good sense so far to remain neutral. But Michael very much feared the time might come when all these tangled alliances would have disastrous results.

So what the devil was Ramsey doing here now? Quelling a growing anxiety, Michael turned a page in his book and darted a quick glance toward the bar. Ramsey had taken a seat close by the poker players and appeared to be interested in their game. So much the better for Michael to escape observation a little longer, at least. Of course there was always the possibility that they were both perpetrating the same ruse. Ramsey might already have seen him and might also be hoping, by keeping a three-quarter profile focused on the poker players, that he too could escape notice.

Michael's nostrils flared as he took a deep but silent breath. He uncrossed his legs and put the book away, his movements slow and deliberate. From his other pocket he took out his pipe and silver tamper, and from an inner pocket he extracted a sealed leather tobacco pouch, then proceeded with an air of calm resignation to fill his pipe.

The poker game grew suddenly lively when two players got into an argument and raised their voices. "I never!" one said indignantly, standing up so rapidly that his chair fell over backward but almost sound-lessly, as it fell onto the heavy carpet.

"I saw ya!" shouted the other, likewise jumping to his feet—but the man seated next to him quickly grabbed his elbow and tugged him back down.

*An accusation of cheating?* Michael wondered. He continued to fill his pipe with more than the usual care. In order to light it, he slipped his left arm out of the black broadcloth sling that kept it immobilized. Care-fully holding the pipe by the bowl in his left hand, and keeping that arm clamped close to his chest, he gripped the pipestem between his teeth. He lit the sulphur-tipped match, which flashed and flared up, then applied burning match to waiting tobacco.

That was when Hilliard Ramsey slowly turned his head . . . and Michael's body seemed to make a deci-sion for him independent of his mind. He dropped the match, still lighted, onto the floor and quickly bent down to retrieve it. The action shielded his face from view. Now was the time to leave, to run, if that was what he chose to do.

It wasn't. Instead he shook the match out, deposited it in the ashtray, slipped his arm back into the sling, raised his head, and smiled toward the poker table. Not a smile of pleasure, but a genuine one nonetheless, the rather grim smile that accompanies acceptance of the inevitable. A smile of masculine pride at a battle considered and joined. Michael raised his good arm and beckoned with his fingers: *Come to me, you bastard, come on!*

Hilliard Ramsey stood. He was of average height and average weight, with regular, unremarkable features, which made his exact appearance hard to recall. Because of this he never bothered to go in disguise, but he did have to guard his eyes. Those eyes were hard to forget, if ever they'd looked directly at you: almost colorless, entirely without expression. Looking into the eyes of Hilliard Ramsey was like being impaled on a spear of ice. His smile, which he was smiling now in return, had a reptilian quality. Ramsey came on.

With a quickening pulse Michael watched the man approach step by step. He was beginning to welcome this encounter, to want it, to enjoy in a rather perverse way the heightened course of blood through his veins, the exquisitely enhanced impulse of nerves along the skin.

"As I live and breathe," Ramsey said in Russian, "Mikhail Arkady Kossoff. I hadn't expected you to be quite so easy to find."

Michael stood up. He was taller than Hilliard Ramsey by half a head. Choosing to speak English, Michael replied, "I hadn't expected *you* to be found at all. I was told you were dead, fallen overboard into the Sea of Japan and drowned. Let's see, how long ago was that . . . ?"

Both men were masters of the slow move, seeming languid and unconcerned while beneath their casual surfaces a thousand calculations ran. Ramsey lowered himself into the chair directly opposite until he was sitting on the edge of the seat, thighs spread, weight shifted forward, elbows on his knees. Taking Michael's cue and keeping his voice low, he shifted to English, which he spoke with a British accent: "Six years and not true, as you may see with your own eyes."

"Hmm," Michael commented, stroking the silver streaks in his beard, which ran downward from the corners of his mouth. He pressed a subtle advantage by not sitting down but leaning instead against one of the wide arms of his chair and crossing one foot over the other. The advantage was psychological only, as it required the other man to look up; physically Ramsey already had the advantage due to Michael's injury, which he must surely have noticed by now. And with his weight forward, solidly balanced on both legs, Ramsey could bolt up to attack in a heartbeat. Well aware of all this, Michael played his mind game, saying in a drawl, "Since you thought me easily found, you can't have been looking too long. Where've you been hiding all these years, old boy?"

Ramsey dismissed the question with a well-manicured gesture. "None of your concern. I'd still be there if I hadn't run out of money."

"Living high off the hog, were you?"

"Not exactly. But I heard you were. In fact, Misha, I've heard a number of interesting things about you."

Michael continued to stroke his beard. "Such as . . ."

"That you were leading a dissolute lifestyle in some bohemian artists' colony."

"True enough."

"That you'd publicly taken back your Russian name."

"A matter of record."

Silence. Hilliard Ramsey merely inclined his head.

Michael wondered what he was playing at. Then a new and fascinating thought came to him. He said, probing, "Then perhaps you also heard I've retired from the game. What about you? Maybe you faked your own death. Maybe you also wanted out. How about it, Hill? Am I on the mark?"

Both eyebrows rose in that unremarkable face, and the pale, pale gray eyes, the color of water, sharpened in their intensity. "You know people who have done what you and I do for a living never get to retire."

"Michael Archer did." The man who no longer went by that name shrugged his good shoulder.

"Is that so."

"Absolutely." It was quite true that Michael Archer no longer existed, that his name had been expunged from the U.S. Government payroll. It was Michael Archer who had been the double agent. Michael A. Kossoff was, however, another matter.

"The people who hired me to watch you think differently. They think you're up to something. Have a care, old boy." On these parting words Hilliard Ramsey shot up from the chair and strode without haste from the club car.

"Hmm," Michael said, stroking his beard. He had not moved a muscle, not flinched at the other man's sudden movement, not even so much as uncrossed his ankles. Yet his blood, which had felt the heat of challenge only moments earlier, now felt a paralyzing cold.

---

I felt as if I'd been chosen by the hive to become queen bee, which as we know from scientific study is not an honor but a lifetime sentence to do nothing but reproduce. For a few more weeks I could lie encased in my pupa—or whatever queen bees are encased in before they emerge full-blown to replace the one who has worn herself out and died—but after that I'd better get out there and lay those eggs, produce those children, or else. No matter how I tried to find the absurdity in this, I failed—because there was no one to laugh but me. And I was not amused.

I allowed myself to sink into melancholy.

When I had been in this funk for about two weeks, that is to say, around the beginning of the month of November (in my melancholy I'd lost precise track of the days), Selene came to see me. For the most part up until that time Melancthon Pratt's youngest wife had ignored me, and when she appeared at my bedside looking rather like an angel herself, with her long corn-silk hair and wide light blue eyes, I felt a bit of my old curiosity stir. It was like a tickle, or an itch.

Not only was Selene in my room, beside my bed, but she also spoke to me. "Father thinks you may die. He is convinced it is his fault, that he has failed to heed the angel's direction in some way," she said. "He is a good man, and so I have come to see what I may do."

A rather remarkable statement, coming from a girl of fifteen who had been subjected to the barbaric custom of polygamy, bedded God knew how many times by a man old enough to be her grandfather—well, almost—not to mention that she was a tiny thing and he a very large man. It had to be one of the Wonders of the Western World that he did not simply crush her in The Act. Yet here she was, gravely lovely and sweet, standing up for him, which made my heart go out to her.

"I'm not dying," I said. My seldom-in-two-weeks-used voice sounded like the hinge on a rusty gate. Then suddenly my sluggish mind produced one clear thought, an idea that shone like a ray of hope. I cleared my throat and spoke again: "However, I do need the doc-tor to come because I'm not recovering properly. As anyone can plainly see."

Selene nodded solemnly. Her skin was so fair that at her temples I could see the blue veins beneath its alabas-ter surface. "We know. Your fever broke, you seemed to be getting better, you were more lively, the wives were getting to know you, but then—"

"Something happened," I supplied when she stopped,

obviously at a loss for words. "I need the doctor. If you want to help me, and Father too, then ask him to have the doctor come."

"I will tell him," Selene said. Then she went away.

I lay there thinking about my plight. I knew full well there was nothing physically wrong with me except my broken legs, and they were getting better. No, what had happened was that by a certain light in Pratt's fanatical eye when he told me exactly why the angel had brought us together, I had understood the depth of his obsession, and I had simply lost hope. Physical escape being impossible, I had dropped instead into a gray land of silence and inaction. A land called Melancholia, which existed solely in my mind.

While living in this gray land I had unwittingly stumbled upon something that proved very useful to me: Melancthon Pratt could not bear to be ignored. If I did not talk to him, if I did not respond when he read or lectured in continuance of my "lessons," he went wild with frustration. Yet he would not strike me in order to make me respond. I believed he may have wanted to, because his face would flush a purplish red, and once he even raised his hand to me. But still he did not strike; instead he went away. He did not come again for at least three days, and since that day he had been less and less often in my room.

I thought about his not striking me. Perhaps he'd only refrained from physical violence because he believed I was under the protection of that angel of his; or perhaps because, although no one could deny Melancthon Pratt was a religious fanatic, he was simply not an abuser of women. He liked women. He liked them very much. Why he could not get any children on his women I had not the slightest idea.

One thing I did know for certain. It was only common sense: When a man tries repeatedly and fails to have any children with five different, healthy women, the fault most likely lies not in the women but in himself. Pratt was not impotent, and he must have been physically satisfying the wives, for they vied for their time in the Big House with him. All, that is, but Sarah, who could probably have done without her turns. So if not impotent, then he must be—whatever was the male equivalent of barren? Ah yes, sterile. Such a charming word. No wonder one would not want to admit it, especially someone like Pratt.

Sarah and her sister Tabitha often sat with me during the two weeks of my sojourn in the gray land of Melancholia, and I listened to them talk. Once when they'd gotten up to go, as if it were a waste of their time to sit with a woman who lay immobile, no longer smiling or laughing or speaking, I had whispered and asked them to stay. So they'd stayed that day, and continued to come regularly even though I was about as much fun for them as a knot in a pine board. But I learned a lot from listening to their quiet talk as they sewed. Mainly I learned that the Pratt household—in fact his entire colony of True Saints—was a mass of contradictions.

Imagine, if you will, a society where all grown men are priests; whose members believe that when they die and go to heaven they will all be gods—even the women if I'd heard that part right; where a man may have as many wives as he can support (this was true only for Pratt's so-called True Saints—the main body of Mormons had given up polygamy years ago); where the wives in fact like that situation because they aren't alone, they have each other's help and companionship, and no one of them has to be everything to a demanding man all the time, every single night and day.

After listening to Sarah and Tabitha—not to mention the others—for all this time, I was beginning to be afraid that if I didn't get away soon it would all begin to make a kind of crazy sense to me.

Of all the wives, the one most likely to come to my

aid was Sarah. Norma, oddly enough, was a close second. Norma doted on Melancthon Pratt. She alone was jealous of the other wives, and would not welcome one more candidate for her idol's affection. She was also physically the most intimidating. She would be good in a fight—or so I thought. Not due to sheer strength (that would be Verla), but because she had a large, firm, voluptuous body and she was not afraid to use it. When Norma entered a room, she filled it with her presence. Altogether she'd have been good to have on my side, except for one thing: She could not be trusted with a secret. Norma's need for Pratt's approval was so great, she'd do anything for him, tell everything to him—he had only to ask. Even though she herself wanted nothing more than to have me gone, she would capitulate in a heartbeat to his least importuning.

Verla I'd ruled out as a participant in any escape plot because she had no imagination. She was perfectly content to be first wife to a Great Man. Tabitha was smitten with this same Great Man, though nowhere near as much as Norma. So that left Sarah . . . and the unknown quantity: Selene.

Selene, more child than woman, and yet she was the one in whom the Great Man had confided his concern about me. Or perhaps he had told them all and she had been the only one to come to me and plead on his behalf. Again I felt touched, in spite of myself; touched and something more, though I was not sure what. I had a sense that there was much more to that young woman than met the eye.

Ah, here was another puzzle to occupy my mind: How could I gather information about Selene without calling attention to the fact that my melancholy had been short-lived? I certainly didn't want Pratt to know it had lifted.

*Well, I shall just have to dissemble*, I thought, then

grimaced in dismay. I had never been particularly good at play-acting, unless I was wearing a costume or disguise. Hmmm . . .

I folded the top sheet and quilt down to my waist and scrutinized the nightgown I was wearing. Never in a million years would I have chosen such a garment for myself: It was bulky cotton flannel, gathered to fall shapelessly from the shoulders, buttoned from neck to waist and at the hem of the long sleeves; a garment altogether without redeeming value . . . save warmth. The color, a medium blue, was one I might have chosen —but as for the rest of it, never.

*This is a costume,* I thought, *this is Carrie's costume, and Carrie is a role I play. Fremont Jones may feel her legs getting stronger, but Carrie James is languishing. Carrie needs a doctor in the worst way.* I didn't know exactly what Carrie's symptoms were, but suddenly I realized I would soon find out.

The sound of the door handle rattling had me pulling the covers up to my chin, and then I barely had time to lean my head back against the pillow and arrange my face in what I hoped might appear as lines of suffering.

"What's the matter with you, then?" asked Pratt in a stentorian voice as he strode into the room. I have often observed that big, powerful men will bluster and assume an angry tone when in fact they are emotionally upset, being unable to express their more tender feelings. I hoped this was the case with Pratt. He might not be violent with women, but still his anger had felt dangerous on the one or two occasions I'd seen it.

I coughed and brought my hand up to partially cover my face, as if I could not bear to look at this man who had called himself my savior not so very long ago. I affected a hoarse half-whisper: "I am very ill. I need the doctor. It's entirely possible I may not have long to live."

"Nonsense. The doctor said if you stayed off your legs, once you'd gotten over the inevitable infection, in about six weeks you should be right as rain. They're not bad breaks of the leg bones, more like cracks."

I wondered how the doctor could tell that, since one could scarcely look beneath the skin to see. Feeling about, I supposed, when I had been unconscious— I put that thought away.

Screwing my face into a frown, I clutched my midsection with both hands. "But I have persistent pain, right here. I'm sorry to be such a disappointment to you. . . ." I let my voice trail off plaintively.

Pratt came to my bed, frowning hard too, though his was genuine and mine was faked. "Show me," he commanded, holding out his hand palm down and fingers spread, "place my hand where you are hurting."

"Oh no," I said, cringing with false modesty, "I couldn't do that, you're not a doctor." Even as the words came from my mouth I recalled how minutely Pratt had examined my naked body that first night he'd found me.

Whether or not he himself remembered, at least he did not argue. He didn't capitulate either. "How long have you had this pain?" he asked, withdrawing his hand and looking at it for a moment as if not knowing what to do with the appendage. Then he let it drop by his side.

"Since the first, off and on," I said, feeling almost as if the pain were real and I did have it. "It never really goes away."

Pratt frowned mightily. I could almost feel the weight of his indecision.

"I couldn't very well tell the doctor about it, could I," I persisted, "seeing as how I was either unconscious or delusional with fever when he was here before."

"That is true." The truth of it seemed to make up his

mind, for he bobbed his head up and down in a nod, rubbed his hands together, and said, "Very well. I'll fetch him. As before, it will take two days."

Two days! I had forgotten that little detail, but now I remembered hearing him say it before, eons ago, which in fact had been less than a month. Suddenly I was thinking of all the things I could do in two days, if only my legs would hold up. I wondered if he had horses, but of course he did; no one could survive out here in the wilderness without them. Wondered too if he had a wagon or a carriage or some such conveyance, and if he did, how I might gain access to it.

But I was forgetting my manners. "Thank you, Father, very much," I called after him, inwardly cringing at my own slip of the tongue. He had already reached my bedroom door.

"Humph!" he replied in his all-purpose grump.

———

As soon as Pratt had closed the door behind him, and I'd waited long enough to be sure none of the wives had been waiting outside, I flung back the covers and turned my body so that both feet swung out over the side of the bed. Then slowly, painfully, for I had not allowed anyone to help me sit up in a chair for many days, I bent my knees until my feet touched the floor.

Two whole days! I was thinking, *If only I can do this, if only my legs will take my weight, everything else will fall into place. There will be a cart, or perhaps even a carriage. There will be horses to spare. I'll go at night, no one will see me, no one will stop me. When he comes back with the doctor two days from now, I'll be long gone.*

I shifted, inching my backside farther and farther toward the edge of my mattress. If only I had something to hold on to while I got my balance—but the room's only chair was impossibly far away. My knees were stronger, I was so sure. . . .

At last I could wait no longer. I felt it was better to stand quickly and get it over with, so that was what I did. I stood up, my head swam—and everything went black before my eyes.

# 9

MEILING LI could be just as stubborn as Fremont Jones, Michael was discovering. He had waited until an hour after sunup to knock on her door, and now they sat in her compartment talking. Arguing, more precisely.

He had told her about running into Hilliard Ramsey in the club car, identifying the man only as "an old enemy"; and since then had been trying to persuade her that although he himself was in no real danger, it would be in Meiling's best interest not to be seen in his company for the rest of the train trip.

Meiling cocked her head to one side and studied him with serious dark eyes. "I think you are not telling me enough of the truth," she stated eventually, but not until her silence had let him know that this observation was most carefully considered.

"What more shall I say? It would take all morning to tell you even half of what has happened between Ramsey and me over all the years I've known him."

"How many years would that be?"

Michael had to stop and think. Their first encounter had been in Hawaii, around the time of annexation, and Hill had been working for the Japanese then too, only Michael hadn't known it. He'd thought Hilliard Ramsey was only an Englishman who liked his Pacific adventures—as indeed did Michael. So the year would have been . . . 1898. He told Meiling, "Ten years. Why do you ask, what difference does it make?"

She shrugged, a pretty gesture the way she did it, especially in her rose silk robe, whose neckline revealed the curve where neck met shoulder. So often Meiling was buttoned clean up to her chin.

"I am trying to make my own decision," she said, "and I have a strong sense of more danger than you say. You carry it upon you this morning almost as a scent, like a strange perfume."

Her words made Michael's skin crawl. He said, untruthfully, "I don't know what you mean."

Again, that slight tip of the head to one side, the scrutiny of those fathoms-deep eyes. She said, "On the heads of my ancestors, Michael Kossoff, many of whom you have known, I swear to you this is true—you carry the scent of danger. And further, you *do* know exactly what I mean. It is not protection I want or need from you now, but information. Ten years is a considerable time for an enmity to be nurtured into dangerous hatred."

Michael rubbed his hand through his hair. He felt honestly perplexed. "Yes, but the last time Ramsey and I were involved in, um, something, he was definitely the winner. There was no physical bloodshed; nevertheless, I was badly beaten. It was a diplomatic matter in which influence was sought in various ways. He worked for Japan. You know, Meiling, what was the outcome of the Russo-Japanese War."

"The Japanese got what they wanted, as they so often do. But this man is British, you said."

"He carries a British passport and speaks the Queen's—beg pardon, the King's—English. I mean to say, with an upper-class accent. But the truth about Hilliard Ramsey is that he has no country, and he is at heart a killer. He hasn't the patience for long, involved intrigues, he would sooner go in the cloak of night and darkness and slit a throat or two."

"If he was the winner of your last encounter, then he has no personal enmity toward you?"

"I believe that to be the case, yes." Michael nodded. "He did say he had been hired to watch me, that's all."

"So you prefer that I not be near you because I will be watched also, is that it? Or"—Meiling held up a long-fingered hand to warn Michael that she was not yet ready for her question to be answered—"could it be that you do not in fact believe this Mr. Ramsey will confine himself to merely watching?"

Michael got to his feet, which in the tight space of the small compartment meant that he towered right over Meiling. "It doesn't matter what I believe, Meiling. What matters is that I want you to be safe and to feel safe, which you will not—nor can I feel safe on your behalf—if we're together on this train."

He was physically crowding her, intentionally, because he was annoyed. He wanted her to give up, to give in.

Meiling's eyes flickered up to him and then away, almost in a disinterested fashion. She said, "I'd like you to leave now. Come back in an hour and I'll give you my decision."

Oh, she was good all right, Michael had to give her that. He supposed it was in her training as well as in her blood. Fremont would have given him some hot reply for looming over her like that, but Meiling simply dismissed him like one of the many servants to which her family background had accustomed her.

Michael clamped his mouth shut lest the heat of his

anger leak out like dragon breath. With an effort of will he took two long steps, all that were required to reach the compartment's door. Then he turned back, unable at last to keep still. "Damn it, Meiling, what could you say in an hour that you can't say now? The matter is not that complicated!"

"Oh, but it is," she replied coolly. "When you asked me to come along, I brought with me my own set of special skills, my own ways to help my friend, Fremont Jones. That is why I'm here. Not to find out who has blown up the railroad, or even who may feel malevolence toward you, Michael, although you are a most honorable friend of the House of Li. To find Fremont and bring her home is my only concern. Before I can tell you how we might best do that in the light of this new development, by which I mean the appearance of your dangerous Mr. Ramsey, there is an action I must perform. It will take about an hour."

"Meiling, I can't have you running off in some direction of your own. We have to work together here."

"Precisely," Meiling said.

She stood now, folded her arms into the sleeves of her silk robe, and gave Michael a small bow such as Chinese women give the men who have some control over their lives—a formality meant to placate, he supposed. It worked, a little.

But he was not yet entirely placated. "What do you mean?" he asked insistently. "What is it you're planning to do with this hour?"

"I will seek the wisdom of my grandmother."

"But your grandmother is dead!"

"Not precisely," said Meiling, with a mysterious smile.

---

I was lying on the floor when I awoke from whatever spell had overtaken me. Using my arms I pushed myself up into a sitting position with my legs straight out in front of me; my head was spinning. I supposed I might have stood up too fast. That would sometimes cause a person to lose consciousness, I knew.

Whatever the cause, I hadn't been out of my senses for long.

The passage of time is palpable—I know this from experience. I'd gone for almost two years after the Great Earthquake without a watch; in that disaster I'd lost a pendant watch that had been more to me than just a timepiece, as it had been a gift from my father for my twenty-first birthday. So in a sense the pendant watch was irreplaceable, but it was also true I simply hadn't been able to afford a new one. During all that time without a watch I had learned what our ancestors must have known in the ages before watches and clocks: how to feel time and sense the rate of its passing with one's body. How to ascertain the hour from the movement of shadows across a surface, by the angle of the sunlight falling through any opening, by the slow rotation of stars in the heavens at night—and most of all by some kind of innate built-in mechanism I could not describe. My two watchless years had proven its existence in me.

By now I knew how a minute feels in passing, or five minutes, or ten. And so I judged I had been unconscious for no longer than five minutes, probably less.

With probing fingers I explored my bound-up legs, though I wasn't at all sure I'd be able to tell if I had done any damage. These poor, damaged limbs were tightly wrapped from knee to ankle, with some kind of stiff, board-like brace on either side to keep the whole arrangement immobile. Only the outermost layer of wrapping was ever changed. Thus there arose from my legs a faint, unpleasant odor of unwashed skin. At least, I hoped that was the odor's only source.

I squeezed and poked at my own limbs until I was

satisfied there was no new injury—or at least none that signaled itself by anything other than the constant deep ache with which I had become all too familiar. It appeared, through my risky experimentation, that the sharp pain came only when I tried to force the legs to bear my whole weight. As pain is a sign that something is wrong, I deduced I was not yet able to stand and walk.

*Very clever, Holmes,* I said sarcastically to myself.

After a brief pause in which I allowed myself to feel an altogether different kind of pain, the one that came from missing my Watson—in other words, Michael—I turned my attention to the task of getting back into bed before anyone could discover me out of it.

This proved impossible. The bed might as well have been some mountain in the Alps, and I was no mountain climber. I confess mountain climbing for sport has always seemed completely inexplicable to me. I mean, when you have climbed a mountain what is there to do but stand on the top of it? What sort of thrill is that? It's not as if there is really anything up there except, one supposes, a lot of snow; and then when you are done with standing on top, there is nothing to do but come down again. How very tedious.

Just as tedious as all my efforts to get myself back into that bed. There were mountains, one had heard, in India or some such outlandish place, that were unclimbable. Well, so was this bed.

Getting myself into the chair, however, proved merely difficult, not impossible. That is, once I had crawled over there. I was greatly assisted by a fortunate happenstance: The last person to sit in the chair had left it by the window, and so I had both the chair itself and the windowsill to lean on with my hands and arms, to support my weight while I hauled myself upright. Then I plopped into the chair none too gracefully . . . and none too soon.

I had scarcely tidied my hair and arranged the night-gown neatly around my legs and ankles when—after a brief, one might say peremptory knock at my door—Norma came in with a lunch tray.

"Well," she said a bit huffily, "how did you get out of bed? I didn't think you could do that. Or are you a malingerer?"

"No, of course I'm not malingering. Mr. Pratt was here, he helped me into the chair."

"That's funny. I heard you were so sick he had to go for the doctor. That's a long trip, Carrie. That's asking a lot. But then, you don't have any trouble with asking a lot, do you?"

"I *am* sick. Going for the doctor was his decision." This should have been obvious, especially, I would have thought, to one of his wives: Melancthon Pratt never did anything that *wasn't* his decision.

Norma unfolded the gateleg table that had been brought into the room some days earlier as a place to set my meals, and she brought it over to the chair where I sat. Then she went back for the tray, which she had temporarily placed on the dresser.

I decided to take a risk, to play on what I knew of Norma's personality and see how far I might get. "I don't mean to be offensive. In the real world, I mean the world outside this, this—"

"We call our community New Deseret, home of the True Saints," she said, rather smugly I thought.

"Very well," I agreed. "As I was saying, in the real world outside New Deseret, I am a wealthy woman. I know Mr. Pratt doesn't like me to talk about it, but—"

"That's right. He doesn't." Norma sat on the edge of my bed. "But he's not here, and I'd like to hear what you have to say. I may as well keep you company while you eat. That way I won't have to come back for the tray, I can just take it with me."

The soup was a vegetable broth that smelled deli-

cious. There were yeast rolls that looked light as a
feather, and a fancy little pat of butter from a mold that
had left an acorn shape embossed on top. And a lovely
red apple that I would keep for later.

I thought perhaps if I wove a fascinating enough
story for Norma, she might not notice how much I was
eating. All that climbing of mountains—or rather attempted climbing into bed—had left me starved. So I set
about feeding myself while I made up for Norma a
fancy tale around a core of truth. You never know
whence help may come, after all.

"As I was saying, I have wealth of my own, to dis-
pose of as I will. My first husband was much older than
I am, and he left me a lot of money when he died. I
know Mr. Pratt doesn't care about things so mundane
as money—"

"Whatever gave you that idea?" Norma asked.
"Money is part of life, it is a necessity. We Mormons
are better at getting money than most people. Therefore
the True Saints must be even better at it than your
average Mormon—I mean because, because"—she
floundered—"well, just because. And Father is the head
of the True Saints on earth, so . . . Well, so tell me all.
Everything. If you start to stray into forbidden territory, I'll warn you. Will that be satisfactory?"

"Oh yes, absolutely," I said with enthusiasm, particularly since during her explication of the proper Mormon attitude toward money I'd managed to eat a roll
and several spoonsful of soup. I said a quick little silent
prayer to whatever gods may exist, as I needed all the
help I could get from any quarter, and commenced to
beguile Norma.

"It seems to me," I said, pausing to consume more
soup and to draw out the suspense, "that Father has
quite enough wives. He doesn't really need to add me to
his number."

Norma cocked her head to one side; her eyes, glistening like onyx, betrayed her avid curiosity. She moistened her lips with the tip of her tongue, yet she said nothing. Perhaps she didn't trust what she might say.

I helped her out: "I imagine you would not be sorry to see me gone from here. It must be difficult to be the third wife, something like being the middle child in a family."

Now she bit her bottom lip. Still she didn't speak.

I said, "Though it's clear to me that even considering all the others, you, Norma, have—how shall I say this without being offensive?—something of a preferred position."

Norma dipped her head in acknowledgment of this. Whether it was true or not, I had no idea, but I did know she wanted to be the favorite. Her flaming cheeks attested to the source of her interest in Pratt's attentions, and in spite of myself I wondered. . . . But never mind.

I pushed that thought away as unworthy of me, not to mention of Michael, and said to a second roll as I began carefully to butter it, "If I were no longer to be here, I should think that would only be in your best interest."

Some moments passed, during which I could almost feel Norma struggle within herself. Finally she said, "You can't really want to leave! No one, no *woman* would want that. We five wives of Melancthon Pratt are the envy of the whole community. No"—she tossed her head and crossed her arms over her breasts as if to protect herself—"you are only trying to get me in trouble."

I ignored that. I finished the roll and returned to the soup, which was truly delicious. Then I said softly, "I've seen much more of the world than you have, Norma, and believe me, it's much bigger than New Deseret. I do want to leave. And you may as well admit it: You'd like to see me gone just as much as I would like to get away from here."

I continued to eat without looking at her. I heard her clothes rustle as she fidgeted, and at last, unable to keep still, she got up and began to pace back and forth across the room below the foot of the bed. "What has money to do with this?" she asked, coming to a stop near me.

"Money is always useful," I said, looking her straight in the eyes.

"Father will never let you go," she said desperately, "because you are Chosen. You mean more to him than money."

"Chosen?" I knew what she meant, but wanted to hear Norma's interpretation.

"The angel chose you. The angel who prophesies and interprets, who mediates between Father and the Heavens where Joseph Smith dwells and where we will join him at the Rapture."

I shook my head slowly. "No, I don't think so."

"Blasphemy!" said Norma. Her cheeks flamed, she was hot with desperation. I hadn't miscalculated how badly this woman would like to see me removed from the Pratt household. Yet again she protested: "You are only trying to get me in trouble! If I say the wrong thing, you will report me to Father, and then I will be the one who is cast aside!"

"No, no, no!" I pushed away the gateleg table as best I could and leaned forward with my hands outstretched, wanting to bring Norma to me. If I'd been capable of standing, I would have gone to her and put my arms around her, because I hadn't meant to upset her quite so much. "Norma, please"—I gestured with my fingers—"listen to me. I haven't the slightest desire to get you into trouble. I know it is usual for women to regard each other as rivals, especially where a man is concerned, but really, we women would do better to stick together. We should work in one another's best interests, that way we can accomplish things. Divided among ourselves, we have no chance of making improvements."

"The angel cannot be wrong," she said stubbornly. But she sank down on the floor next to me, in a pretty puddle of skirts.

"No, but even a holy man can be misguided sometimes."

"What do you mean?"

"Norma, this angel has supposedly told Father that I will bear him children, isn't that right?"

She nodded. "That is why he'll never let you go. We must have children in this family, we MUST! We must release the souls of those who otherwise will never get to be with God—it is our bounden duty."

"All right, I won't argue that, it's part of your faith. But you are a practical woman, Norma, so think on this: There are five of you wives, but only one husband. It takes the healthy seed of both husband and wife to make a child. If a man mates with one woman and no child results, the problem could be with either one of them, it is impossible to tell which. But when the same man mates with five different women, and still no child results, the chances that the problem is with the man are greatly increased."

Norma frowned; indeed she positively glowered. "Are you saying Father's seed is unhealthy?"

"No, not exactly," I said hastily. Egad, but I was putting my foot in it. I began to regret having taken this tack but it was too late now to pull out. "What I'm saying is, Father may have no seed."

"But he does!" Norma's shapely chin came up indignantly. "I know he does, for I, I have seen it, and felt it, and therefore it exists, absolutely, for a fact!"

"I must take your word for it," I said dryly, giving up. Melancthon Pratt would remain perfection in his middle wife's eyes. Clearly I would get nowhere going that route. "Nevertheless, I do not want to stay here and become Wife Number Six, the mother of his children. You realize, I presume, that I'm taking a risk by telling you this. I wouldn't tell you if I were trying to get you in trouble. I'm doing it because I want your help, and I'm willing to pay."

"You are not to be sixth wife," Norma said, squirming, hating every word, "you're to be first, elevated over all of us, even Verla, who has been with him since he was very young and first elevated to the priesthood. She will become second, and so on, down the line."

"But that's not fair!" I exclaimed.

She shrugged. "We don't think so either, but the angel has said it. Because you alone are to be the mother, you see."

"Oh, for heaven's sake." Completely disgusted, I stared blindly out the window. Never in my entire life had I been more frustrated, felt more as if I wanted to get up and run screaming into the distance, as far as I could go, and not even caring if I got lost or not.

"Carrie . . ." Norma's hand touched my knee, drawing my attention back to her when the unfamiliar name did not engage me. "What exactly did you have in mind?"

I exhaled a long breath. At last!

Eagerly I explained: "I'd be willing to buy my way to freedom, like a straightforward business transaction. But I don't suppose that would interest Father if everything you say is true, and he sets more store by what he believes the angel has said than by money. So what about this: You and I make an agreement, just between the two of us, that you will help me get away from here just as soon as these infernal bandages come off my legs."

Again that little pink tongue darted out to moisten Norma's lips. "I might be able to do that."

"When I'm well away, I'll get in touch with the bank

in San Francisco where my money is. And I'll set up a bank account for you, in your name, wherever you say."

"Provo!" Norma blurted. Oh, I'd beguiled her, all right, with the oldest substance of all, money.

"Provo it shall be. You'll have your own money, Norma, to spend however you wish. But only if I get away free and clear. Let us shake hands on it."

Norma's hand, when I took it, was rougher to the touch than its paleness would suggest, and cool. She whispered, "You'll never tell, you won't betray me?"

I said, "Of course not. I just want to go home."

"Carrie, there are tears in your eyes."

I wiped them away with the back of my hand. "That's how much I want to go."

———

Michael used his hour for breakfast in the dining car. But the luxury of coffee in individual silver pots, creamy eggs, perfect toast, and grilled bacon with its inimitably delicious smell, all set against a background of snowy linen, was wasted on him that morning. He simply put his head down and ate.

From time to time he cast quick, sideways glances at the other diners. All his considerable will power was required not to look up whenever the door to the dining car opened, but he kept his head down and identified the newcomers by their feet alone. None of the feet belonged to Hill Ramsey; that was all he cared about.

After he'd eaten, with still more time to kill before he could return to Meiling's compartment, he wandered back to the club car for a smoke, tried to read a *Collier's* magazine he found lying on a table, but couldn't concentrate worth a damn and gave it up for a lost cause. The damn clickety-clack of the wheels over the track was beginning to get on his nerves, it was so incessant, so relentless, so, so . . .

Michael drew in a deep breath; his fine nostrils flared and his eyes looked daggers at no one in particular. He was thinking malevolent but unfocused thoughts. His fingers grasped and released, grasped and released, as if working on the throat of the dastardly, subhuman creature who'd blown up the tracks and taken Fremont from him.

Then he realized what he was doing. He wiped his fingers on his trousers although they were dry already, as if he could wipe away the bad thoughts. Then he stood, adjusted his jacket until it sat as perfectly as possible on his one good and one bandaged shoulder, checked the knot in his tie, and looked around to see if he had forgotten anything.

He had. He'd left a thin brown cigarillo burning in the ashtray. He ground it out, nodded at a white-haired man whose glance met his over the open newspaper the man was holding, and sallied forth to once again confront the inscrutable Meiling Li.

# 10

S HE WAS BUTTONED up to her chin again. Michael had to admit he was, if not exactly sorry, then a bit disappointed. He held the opinion that when a man ceases to enjoy looking at women, he must either have grown very old or be in some big trouble.

Meiling looked elegant, if buttoned up, in a dress of black brocaded silk. The top half of the dress was Chinese in style, with narrow black braid around all its edges; but the skirt was full, so that she could move more freely than in the traditionally narrow skirts of Chinese women. The fabric was rich and splendid, but its gleaming black depths made him think of crows, and of mourning.

"Come in, Michael," Meiling said, moving back from her compartment's door.

He did, and slid the door shut behind him.

Now that this moment had come, oddly enough he wanted to postpone hearing what she had to say. Mysticism or any form of mumbo-jumbo made him uncomfortable, all the more so because he'd had enough strange experiences to make him believe at least some of it could be possible. So he delayed.

"Meiling," Michael said, "please forgive me for not having thought to ask if you've had breakfast. Shall we go along to the dining car so that you may eat while we talk?"

She didn't reply but simply sat and gestured for Michael to take the seat opposite.

Outside the small window between them the landscape streamed by, a blur of brown and different shades of green, with occasional patches of white. More mountains, now in Nevada, Michael assumed. Truth to tell, he'd been so distracted he hadn't paid attention to their exact whereabouts.

"Thank you, but I am not hungry," Meiling said a little belatedly. "I paid the steward to fetch me coffee and biscuits earlier, when he came to make up the bed."

Michael sat leaning slightly forward, fingers of one hand splayed upon his knee. Feeling idiotically ill at ease he nodded, said, "That's good, then," and fell to reflecting on Meiling's physical resemblance to the men, rather than the women, in her family.

Perhaps Meiling really had inherited her grandmother's peculiar spell-casting skills, but at least she didn't look like that old Chinese witch. Michael had been very fond of Meiling's grandmother, but he'd been sensibly wary of her too. Now he felt wary of Meiling, which seemed a bit ridiculous, seeing as how he'd known her since she was only a babe in her unfortunate mother's arms.

Meiling smiled, not broadly but rather with the faintest hint of amusement. "I am not—what is that word, crazy? Yes. I am not crazy, Michael. You do not have to be afraid of me."

"What?" His head snapped up and he felt a sudden chill. Uncanny!

"When I said that I would consult with my grandmother, what I meant was, I would consult the sources of wisdom that have been my legacy from her. To do this I need uninterrupted quiet; therefore I must be alone, and so I asked you to leave. It is true that sometimes I do, at such moments, seem to hear her voice speaking to me. But I know that is an illusion."

Michael forced himself to lean back in a more relaxed attitude. He crossed one leg over the other, adjusted the crease of his dark trousers, flecked an invisible speck of dust from his black socks.

The train rumbled around a curve. Meiling swayed with the motion of the car, tipping her head to one side as if to better observe the man across from her.

Michael counted the buttons that punctuated the upholstery of the bench seat behind Meiling's sleek black hair—anything rather than look into her eyes. Suddenly he felt as if she could see right into him, as if nothing he might do could stop her from seeing into his mind and heart. Not even Fremont could do that, at least not when he deliberately closed himself off. No one could. Except now, maybe, Meiling. He didn't like it; it made him feel vulnerable. Yet he kept still.

Finally she spoke: "The signs tell me we must both get off this train as soon as possible. You must decide when and where that should be."

"Nonsense!" His eyebrows rose in surprise. "I can take care of myself. If your mysterious signs foretell so much danger, then *you*, Meiling, can get off the train at the next stop and return to San Francisco. I am certainly not leaving!"

Slowly, with that maddening calm possessed by so many persons of her race, she shook her head back and forth. "We each need the other for our task. We will find Fremont more quickly together. Without each other, we may not find her at all."

Michael considered this statement, which did not sit well with him. For a very long time—certainly his

whole adulthood and probably even before that—he'd
been convinced he did not need anyone or anything, in
either his professional or his personal life. In point of
fact, the one and only time he'd allowed himself to
want someone to the degree of *need*—it had been a
woman of course, Russian, named Katya—disaster had
been the result. Katya had died. Her death had been his
fault. They—the nebulous *they* of the spy's world—
thought he'd confided secrets to her, secrets worth kill-
ing for.

A bitter memory indeed. Michael had not told Katya
anything. He'd deliberately kept her ignorant, thinking
in his youthful inexperience—for he'd been young then
—and amid the vigorous delusions of new love, that he
could keep her safe. Katya had died because he'd loved
her, *needed* her, thought he couldn't live without
her. . . .

"Michael?" Meiling called him back.

He put his good hand to his head and rubbed his
forehead. "Sorry. I . . . I must admit, I'm . . . that
is, I'm . . . confused."

"The immediate question to be answered is, how
soon can we leave this train?"

Michael rubbed harder, as if he could rub away the
beginnings of what promised to be a blinding headache.
"I should not have asked you to help, Meiling. It was
selfish of me."

Then with resolution in his voice he looked straight
into her eyes and said, "I made a selfish mistake for
which I apologize. You must go back. I will continue on
alone, and that's all there is to it." He stood up, intending to leave the compartment.

Meiling put out her hand and snared his sleeve with
slim fingers. "Wait, Michael," she said with sudden,
new urgency in her voice, "forget that. Be quiet instead
and listen. What am I hearing outside the door?"

Of course I worried myself silly that Norma would tell someone of our arrangement. Good common sense, of which I like to believe I have plenty, suggested that she would not tell, because it would hardly be in her own best interest. However, on the basis of good common sense I got perhaps ten minutes' rest for every hour of worrying. The days of Pratt's absence on his doctor-fetching errand crawled by, with me having a devil of a time pretending to be sicker than I was.

In truth, I had taken a sudden turn for the better, and hence was ravenously hungry almost all the time. I would have given much for a chair with wheels, so that I might wheel myself to the kitchen and sneak some food. I had fantasies about such forays all the time. Yet the reality was, I didn't even dare eat everything on the trays the wives so faithfully brought. It was essential that I appear much more ill than I was; essential, but so very, very difficult that I began to fear less for my body's health than for my sanity. All this close confinement was putting odd thoughts and strange longings into my head.

Somewhere I'd read about prisoners who began, in their extremity, to eat dirt . . . and I lay in my bed gripped by a passionate desire to hurl myself, useless legs and all, through my one window, for then I could land in the grass and claw my way to the bare dirt, feel it all soft but slightly gritty in my fingers. I would smell it—it would smell of dust and freedom.

Two days, Pratt had said, one there and one back. On the second day I'd yelled at Sarah: "Leave me alone!" Not because I wanted to be alone, oh no, but because I wanted her company, indeed *any* company, so badly that I could no longer trust myself. Who knew what I might say? Oh, I made a poor prisoner, that was certain.

The one person I could have talked to openly was Norma, yet perversely she was the very one, the *only* one, who did not come to my room. The more time passed without her appearance, the more I worried that I had made a mistake in asking her to help me.

After I had yelled at Sarah, Tabitha, and Verla each in turn, it came as no surprise that it was Selene who then appeared with my supper.

Selene was of such a sweet nature that I could not yell at her. It was very hard for me to be rude to her at all. Impossible, in fact. The merest frown refused to wrinkle my visage at the sight of her luminous youth and beauty.

"May I stay?" she asked in her characteristically gentle way.

I just looked at her, trying to harden my stare and my heart, but without much success. If there was any angel spending time in Melancthon Pratt's proximity, it was this girl with the long, fine, straight blond hair.

"If you will tell me a story," I said, "while I try to eat something. I do not have much appetite, so this should not take long. Pointless, I suppose, for you to go away and then so soon have to come back again."

Selene smiled and said, "Thank you."

She brought the chair that was by the window closer to the bed.

She went on, "I'll tell you a story, but you must promise—*promise!*—to eat everything on your tray!" In mock admonishment she waggled her finger at me. She sounded like a child playing house, being the mommy to her dolls.

*Thank you, Jesus!* I thought, though most likely he was the wrong personage to thank in this Mormon household.

Eat everything on my tray? Heavens to Betsy and Saints be praised! That would not be a problem in the least. The roast chicken was making my mouth water to an embarrassing degree.

"I'll try," I promised demurely, all the while restraining myself from attacking the chicken with my bare hands.

"What would you like a story about?" she asked. "I don't know very many, I'm afraid."

"Tell me more about the Urim and the Thummim," I said, more because the two names continued to intrigue me, and were what sprang to mind, than out of any real interest.

"Well . . ."

In the long pause that ensued, I glanced at Selene and saw to my surprise that her normally pale cheeks had gone quite pink. Perhaps I had asked her a question on a subject about which she was ignorant?

Nothing, I was about to learn, could have been further from the truth. As it is impolite to speak with one's mouth full, I just continued chewing and let her wrestle with whatever was causing her to blush.

Selene lowered her head and gazed into her lap, getting control of herself. Then she looked at me directly, though her cheeks still flamed. "Someone has been telling tales on me, I think."

"No, not at all. Why would you say such a thing?"

"Because I'm very interested in Urim and Thummim, and I have been trying to get books on the subject of things like that."

"Things like what? From what Sarah and Tabitha told me, those stones are unique, there are no others like them—or rather I should say they *were* unique, because certainly they don't exist anymore." *If they ever did,* I added to myself.

"What, exactly, did the sisters tell you?"

"That the Angel Moroni gave the Urim and the Thummim to Joseph Smith in order to help him read the Tablets of Gold, which were in some kind of hiero-

glyphics. He—I mean Smith, not the angel—went in a
dark room or someplace and put the stones in his hat,
and then buried his face in the hat, and somehow a
knowledge of the translation came into his head. Which
he then dictated to someone whose name I forget."

I hoped Selene would soon pick up the story without
further help from me, because that long explanation
had taken me away from my food for entirely too long.
With the chicken was a lovely casserole of escalloped
potatoes, rich with cream sauce and tender onions, that
was calling to me from my plate.

"Joseph Smith was very interested in mysticism," Selene said. She seemed to have settled into her chair and
was more composed now, no longer embarrassed, as if
she'd also settled something in her mind. "But a lot of
people thought he was a crackpot. Did you know
that?"

I raised an eyebrow. My mouth was full but still I
managed syllables that sounded approximately like "Interesting!" which was what I'd intended to say. I struggled to finish the bite because there were questions I
wanted to ask. But strangling myself on partially
chewed food was not necessary since Selene had the bit
between her teeth now, as it were, and she was running
with it. Every word she said demonstrated something
that came as no great surprise to me: The docile girl we
saw every day was only a part of who this young
woman was. The other part was more than a student,
she was a scholar—and that scholar was lecturing me
now.

"Some say that Brigham Young had his doubts about
Joseph Smith. And it's entirely possible that in later
years, after Father Joseph died, Brigham Young may
have suppressed some of Father Joseph's writings. Some
of the early documents may have been lost on purpose.
Do you understand what I'm saying?"

"Oh yes. Of course I do," said I, waving my fork in the air. "That kind of thing happens all the time."

So much for consistency. Here I'd just commented how Urim and Thummim were unique, but never mind. It is perfectly true that founders of religions tend to be, well, one supposes the word is "visionary"; but then visionaries have certain qualities that can be rather embarrassing, so who knows what may end up having to be suppressed later. Religion seems mostly a lot of bunkum to me anyhow, but I was not about to make such a radical statement to anyone in this household.

"Or so one hears," I added for good measure.

Selene gazed off to her right for a moment. She had placed her chair facing me near the foot of the bed, so her back was toward the bureau against the opposite wall. Over to her right was that small sanity-saving rectangle, the window, which was all I'd known of the outside world for far too many weeks. But something about her expression told me she was not looking at the view, whether to her it might be bleak or bright; instead she was lost in thought.

Presently, about the time I finished my potatoes and was returning to the chicken, she roused herself and turned her head toward me again. Once more the color rose in her cheeks. "Mormon women are not supposed to take much interest in these things," she said rather lamely. Her eyes, full of light, hardly reflected lack of interest.

"Why on earth not?" I asked, even as I understood now how the high color had come to be in her cheeks.

"Only the men can be priests. Only the priests concern themselves with the Mysteries of the Faith. But there is so much they don't tell us! Things that happen behind closed doors in the Great Temple in Salt Lake, old documents kept in libraries on the Temple grounds that we women never get to see. . . ."

I made some noise of encouragement while I cut my

remaining chicken into tiny pieces to make it last longer.

Selene blushed more fiercely and ducked her head. "Of course we at New Deseret are above all that, we have no real need for anything of Salt Lake, as we seek to return to Joseph Smith's ways. But I keep on thinking about how Father Smith, even before meeting the Angel Moroni, had studied all the mystical things. He must have, because he was criticized for it! Yet Father— I mean our husband, Mr. Pratt—is really not at all interested in Mormon mysticism. He says he doesn't need to be because he has his own angel who talks directly to him. Surely it cannot be but good to have an awareness of the past, particularly if we are to return to what Father Joseph really taught, and so I thought it might be, er, acceptable for me to study—"

Selene blurted it all out in such a rush that I had to strain to get the words, especially as they were directed not at me but somewhere in the vicinity of her lap. She had stopped short, her sentence incomplete.

However, I did not have to hear the rest of that sentence to catch the workings of her mind. I was fascinated. So fascinated I forgot all those little pieces of chicken I had just so carefully cut up.

What we had here was a very young woman, extremely bright, consumed with the subject she had chosen, which just happened to be on the farthest fringe of the only world she knew. I could not help but wonder what would happen if such a mind were let loose in the classrooms and libraries of Wellesley, my alma mater. Or perhaps even—because of its access to the libraries at Harvard—Radcliffe College.

"I think this is quite wonderful," I said. "Sincerely."

Slowly she raised her head, and as she looked me square in the eye the heightened color drained slowly from her now-solemn face. "I thought perhaps you would understand," she said, "but I wasn't sure. I mean, I didn't know how I would ever be able to tell you—"

Before she could venture into that ever-awkward territory of too much gratitude, I urged, "Now let's please get on with the story of Urim and Thummim. I am so eager to hear it that I am all ears."

"Very well. My version is quite different from the one told to you by Sarah and Tabitha. No one knows which one is true."

*Most likely neither,* I thought, but said nothing. I was once again eating, but slowly, as I hung on Selene's every word. The content of what she said was not so important as the fact that she had ferreted out and assimilated this material, and was eager to do more along the same lines.

"The Urim and the Thummim are part of a tradition that's very ancient, and it's Jewish, so in a way that makes it Christian too. The Hebrews far back in Old Testament times believed that certain jewels had magical properties. King Solomon was a great magician—that was how he got the reputation for being so wise—and he knew how to use the powers in the jewels. He had a breastplate made, called the Breastplate of Solomon—well, of course it would be, wouldn't it?"—a quick flush just along the cheekbones, just as quickly gone—"and he had all these magical jewels sewn into it. Among them were the Urim and the Thummim. This is in the Bible, and in some Jewish teachings called the Kabbala. I'm not sure what the specific qualities of the Urim and the Thummim were supposed to have been, but considering that the Angel Moroni gave them to Joseph Smith to help him read the hier— er, ah—"

Selene interrupted herself, momentarily looking troubled.

"What is it?" I asked.

"I don't like to be so contradictory—I've been told it's an unattractive quality I have. When someone says something that seems to me wrong, often I have corrected them before I even realize the words are out of my mouth. I was just about to say something that might sound that way to you, Carrie."

"I assure you I do not mind in the least. I have often been accused of the same thing myself."

"Really?"

"Yes, really. So go right ahead."

"All right, but really you must remember, I don't mean to be critical."

"I promise I'll remember."

Selene took a deep breath and returned to her discourse. "The writings on the Tablets of Gold were not in hieroglyphics. They were in what is called hieratic writing, which is different. I am not sure exactly *how* it is different, as I have never seen it. But I have seen pictures in books of Egyptian hieroglyphs, and I should like very much to see hieratic writing someday, and to know how it is different."

*Budding scholar indeed*, I thought.

She was continuing: "Because the Urim and Thummim were given to Joseph Smith to help him decipher the hieratic writing, one assumes these magical jewels might have been supposed to aid something like clear vision and increased understanding."

"Sounds reasonable to me," I said, putting my tray to one side with my dessert untouched. It took a great deal of will power to do this, despite my intense interest in Selene's story.

"So the other story of what happened with the jewels, the one I think more likely, is that they were actually made of a material like the clear quartz that is sometimes found in our Western mountains, polished to a high degree. And they could be held above the writing to make it come clearer, like a magnifying glass. Perhaps this magnification was all it took to make the symbols of the hieratics decipherable for Joseph Smith, since he was a student of such mysteries anyway; he may have known this secret language. Or, as some say, since there were two stones, one may have made the writing seem bigger and then the other may have magically turned the symbols into the language of the one in whose hand it was held."

I murmured, "Fascinating!"

"Yes, isn't it. There's one version of the story I just can't believe, though." Selene shook her head, and I found my own head moving back and forth in the same horizontal plane, in sympathy with her.

"And what is that?" I asked.

"Some people say Urim and Thummim were ground and polished into lenses for a special pair of spectacles, and throughout the rest of his life Joseph Smith wore these spectacles whenever he needed special knowledge. I have even heard tell there's a family out West here somewhere, I forget where, maybe Texas, that owns these spectacles and will not let them out of their sight."

"You don't believe that," I stated, not phrasing it as a question. What I was really wondering was how she could believe *any* of it.

"No. Though it would explain what happened to the jewels."

"Ah yes," I said, fascinated again. "But I thought the Angel Moroni reclaimed them and took them back to heaven, or wherever he came from."

"Nobody knows for sure. It's another mystery." Selene smiled and rose from her chair. "And I've been boring you for far too long."

"But look here"—I gestured to my tray beside me—"and you'll see I kept my side of the bargain. Your story was so involving that I quite forgot how poor my appetite has been, and my dinner disappeared." I winked. "As if by magic."

Selene laughed.

Quickly I added, as she reached out to take up the

tray, "I would like to keep my dessert to eat later, if you don't mind. When Mr. Pratt returns I want to be strong enough to make a good impression on the doctor."

It was a lame excuse, but Pratt's youngest wife didn't seem to notice. Instead, with my mention of his name that all-consuming presence came back into the room just as if he had already returned to the house.

"Why do you call him Mr. Pratt?" Selene asked.

"Because his given name, Melancthon, is rather . . . one might say *unwieldy* upon the tongue."

"Why not call him Father, as we all do?"

"Because I'm not yet one of the wives."

"But you don't have to be. The title Father acknowledges his priesthood."

"I am not yet a Mormon either, Selene."

"Oh." She looked profoundly disappointed at being reminded of my differences, but covered it by removing the slice of apple pie that constituted my dessert and placing it on the bedside table, where I could reach it. Then she carefully covered it with my folded napkin.

And I heard myself say, I swear it was entirely without forethought, "There may be a higher authority than Pratt's angel that has brought me here."

# 11

MICHAEL DID NOT LIKE to admit it even to himself, certainly not to Fremont Jones, but his hearing was not particularly acute. Likely it was in the normal range, but for a man accustomed to push himself out onto the edge of everything in life, merely normal was not enough. Fremont's hearing was exceptional: She could pick up sounds long before he heard them.

So, apparently, could Meiling—because at her words of caution he stood stock still but heard nothing. Nothing except the interminable clacking of the train's wheels, which seemed capable of masking many other sounds.

Then, as if to add insult to injury, the train's whistle let off a blast so shrill he grimaced. An animal on the tracks, he supposed, or the train was approaching a blind curve. At any rate, his ears were not giving him the kind of information he needed.

Michael had a sixth sense, a kind of body consciousness that let him know when another body was in close proximity, whether he could see the person or not. This sense, for some reason unknown to him, did not function as well through closed doors. And so although he thought he sensed someone outside the compartment, he was unsure, and this uncertainty led to hesitation.

How long he stood waiting he did not know. Thoughts tumbled through his mind, primarily the thought that he was unarmed and it was probably no longer a good idea to go about the train that way. He felt it begin to round a curve, registered that this would have been the reason for the whistle, and at that moment knew it was time to open the door—knew it was time, but not how or why he knew this.

Quickly Michael shot a piercing, silent message from his eyes to Meiling, held up a brief monitory hand, then jerked open the compartment door.

There was no one there.

But someone *had* been there until just a moment before; Michael was as certain of it as if that person had left behind his shadow or a trail of scent. Michael scanned the doorframe rapidly, then his eyes moved over the corridor floor just to either side of the door, with explosives on his mind. His hearing might not be hyper-acute but his eyes missed nothing. Printed material closer than an arm's length might be getting blurry, but for distance and in the midrange, he could see like a hawk. There were no explosives, not so much as a length of fuse taped to the seam in the wall.

So why, then, did he have such a vivid picture in his mind of someone lurking outside a train compartment's door, swiftly taping slender sticks of dynamite in place, lighting a fuse, and then running like hell?

"Wait here," he commanded Meiling, then took off at a lope toward the front of the car, where in his peripheral vision he'd glimpsed the connecting door slowly swinging closed. He'd gone no more than three steps before he heard confirmation of his assumption—

the door shut with a hollow metallic thump—and he knew that was the way his quarry had gone.

The chase was on. Follow and be followed in your turn: one of the most ancient games in the world, one that humans share with the animals, one that reduces a human all too often to not much more than an animal. Unconsciously, as he loped on, Michael bared his teeth.

———

Of course I'd had an underhanded plan in asking Pratt to go for the doctor. That is, in addition to a true concern that I was not getting over my injuries as fast as I should have. The great irony was that as soon as Pratt had gone from the house I started to feel better. And since I'd taken the risk of asking Norma to help me get away, I had been making daily progress.

It was not all that difficult therefore—one did not need a medical degree or one of those new-fangled psychiatric degrees—to deduce that my major obstacle to a healthy convalescence was the feeling that I was being kept a prisoner by the very folks who seemed so dedicated to making me well.

A conundrum indeed!

When the doctor at last came through my bedroom door in the company of Melancthon Pratt, my heart rose with hope. But even as they began to cross the room, doubt set in. Certainly initial impressions can be deceiving, but was this severe-looking stranger a man who could help me?

Verla came in behind them and somehow managed, in what was for her a miracle of self-assertion, to slip around her husband and arrive at my bedside before him. She stood with her hand holding the headboard in a proprietary manner.

"Husband," Verla said, staking her claim to him with a precision I'd never heard before, "and Doctor.

Carrie's done good. She's eating a mite better. She feels some better too, don't you, Carrie?"

I felt her glance down at me but I couldn't meet her eyes, for I was about to let loose a powerful spate of lies. Verla had been good to me and I didn't want to hurt her feelings or to cast aspersions on her in any way. And so, for the moment, a reprieve as I managed to avoid the issue.

Glancing from Pratt to the doctor and back, I said, "Thank you for bringing the doctor, Mr. Pratt. Your wives have taken their usual excellent care of me while you were absent."

He nodded gruffly but offered no smile or even the attempt at one.

It was late afternoon and I did not doubt that he and the doctor both must be tired. They had to have been riding all day, but the dust of the road was not upon them. So, they must have arrived long enough ago to have cleaned up, perhaps even bathed, yet I'd heard nothing. Not even the sounds of their arrival, which made me all the more curious about the layout of this most unusual household.

"You'd best introduce us, Melancthon," the doctor said. "She'll not remember me. You recall that last time I was here she was unconscious."

"Grmph," Pratt said, a sound that seemed to combine throat-clearing with acknowledgment. "Carrie, this here is Dr. Arnold Striker. Doc, her name's Caroline James. We call her Carrie. She's to join the family soon's she can stand on her own two feet to take the vows."

*In a pig's eye!* I thought, but I smiled and held out my hand to the doctor for a formal handshake. "How do you do, Dr. Striker."

His hand felt hard and cold. If his appearance was any indication, I suspected his personality was likewise. And he was devious too: Instead of gripping my hand in

the hearty shake I was both offering and expecting, he
slid his fingers up my wrist and deftly turned it over so
that he was taking my pulse instead.

This man was young, probably not much older than
I, yet everything about him appeared to belong more to
the previous century than to our new one. With a con-
strictively narrow black suit he wore a white shirt with
one of those stiff, high collars that have been falling out
of the male fashion—at least in San Francisco—for nigh
onto a year. He was excessively thin, so much so that I
wondered if he had enough natural padding to sit a
horse without injury. His face was long, expression
grave, hair sparse on top despite his relative youth. His
eyes, which he kept focused on a pocket watch held in
his left hand while he took my pulse with his right, were
an opaque mid-brown, like muddy water.

The longer I contemplated Dr. Striker, the more my
hopes plummeted. This man was a very poor candidate
for helping me in the way I'd had in mind. He exuded
narrow authoritarianism—I can sense one of those fel-
lows a mile off, and he was much, much closer than
that.

He dropped my wrist.

I looked away, idly rubbing my wrist as if to remove
his touch, and did not bother to repress a disappointed
sigh.

Dr. Striker frowned, and addressed not me but Verla,
as if she were the nurse. Of course she *had* been my
only nurse for many days. "Symptoms?" he inquired.

"I don't rightly know. Happened she was comin'
right along, gettin' stronger ever week, till maybe a couple of weeks ago she took a turn."

"Describe this turn," the doctor ordered.

"Carrie, you tell him," said Verla. A sensible
woman. Yet right this minute I was not prepared to do
it; I had begun to sort through all the lies I'd concocted,

revising my plan based on my hunches about the doctor.

"I, uh"—I looked from one to the other to the other and back again, rapidly, intentionally building up in myself a sense of panic—"I—I can't talk to a doctor in front of all these people."

"*All* these people?" Melancthon Pratt objected in his booming preacher voice. "Good God, woman, there's only the two of us, Verla and me."

I lowered my eyes demurely. "There are some things modesty forbids."

"In that case—" Dr. Striker began, taking the bait; but Pratt interrupted.

He came closer to the bed and leaned over me, as if his overbearing presence alone would produce compliance—and I supposed, in some people, it probably did. But not in me. The more he loomed and boomed, the more stubbornly resistant I became.

Pratt thundered, "Now see here, me and Verla took care of you like you were a baby. You've got nothing to hide from us, Missy, there's not a hair on you we ain't seen!"

I would not look at him. I kept my eyes downcast. "But I was not in my right senses then. I didn't know what was going on. If I had known, I most surely would have objected. Now, I do object. I will talk to Dr. Striker. In fact, I most desperately need his help, but I cannot confide the true nature of my medical problem unless I am alone with him."

Mainly I was buying myself time with this ploy, while I continued to mentally scrabble through the shards of my previously seamless plan. If Striker was going to be as little help to me as I now feared, it didn't really matter whether Verla and Pratt were present or not, because all I'd get from him was a general knowledge of my medical condition.

I sighed again. Oh well. I needed the facts about my

condition rather badly, so all was not entirely lost. And
perhaps, if I proceeded very carefully . . .

"I really think, Melancthon," Dr. Striker said, "that
it would be entirely appropriate for me to be alone with
Miss James, since that is what she has requested. You
know how some women are."

"Well," Verla spoke up, "I don't see how it's proper.
Woman alone in a room with a man, whether he's a
doctor or whatnot, it's just askin' fer trouble. But if it's
what she wants, I'll go if my husband will go too. Otherwise I'm stayin'."

I had to bite my lower lip in order to keep from
saying something that would not be in my own best
interests, just in order to placate her. Verla had been
kind to me, and I didn't like to hurt her. But if there
was any chance at all that I could come out of this with
even a piece of what I wanted, then I had to take that
chance.

"Melancthon?" Striker put a tone of insistence into
saying the name.

Still Pratt did not agree to leave. I could feel tension
passing back and forth over my head, from him to Verla
and back. Some kind of unspoken message was being
sent. This was fascinating. I had never seen her stand up
to him before, hadn't known she had it in her; in fact,
I'd never seen anyone stand up to Melancthon Pratt
until now.

"You can both wait right outside the door," Striker
said, taking yet more initiative, from which I gleaned a
modicum of encouragement. From the corner of my eye
I saw the doctor touch Melancthon Pratt's arm, turning
him gently but firmly away, while with his other hand
he gestured across the bed for Verla to come along too.

They were leaving, thank goodness. In fact, all three
of them went out, the doctor too, and closed the door
behind them.

I'd had not only one plan, but two. Plan the First

was to enlist the doctor's help, to say straightforwardly that I was being kept in the Pratt household against my will and ask that he order me moved to a hospital or some such place of convalescence, and also that he notify some law enforcement agency that Pratt was a kidnapper. I'd thought I might appeal to the doctor's humanity and morality, as I have always assumed that the men—and the very few women—who go into that profession should have plenty of both. *Should* have— but my adult life, especially in recent years, has been a long lesson in how what *should* happen and what *does* happen are all too often entirely different things.

Therefore I had also come up with Plan the Second, though I did not like it nearly as well because it was heavily fraught with things that could go wrong. This second plan grew out of happenstance: In preparation for this trip, for very personal reasons of my own, I had been studying the actions of various poisons and the symptoms they produce. My plan was to recite a series of symptoms that included those of several different poisoning agents in order to convince the doctor I was seriously ill, with symptoms so difficult to diagnose that I needed to be in a hospital. I reasoned that Salt Lake City would have a real hospital, and probably there was one even closer. And I'd thought that, if I presented the poisoning symptoms clearly enough, the doctor might even conclude for himself that the Pratt household was not a good place for me to be.

Either way, with either plan, my goal had been to get the doctor to have me removed from the house and taken to a hospital. I'd reckoned that once I was safely in a hospital, I could get away. Run away. Flee, fly . . .

I sighed again. Plan the First was definitely out. Some strong instinct told me not to even try Plan the Second, not with this man. I was getting the impression that Arnold Striker might not be the world's warmest human being but that he was a good doctor.

He came back into the room. I looked over at him and said, "Thank you."

"I understand your concerns for your modesty. However, the nature of your injuries, as I recall them, leaves me puzzled as to how so much modesty can be required. I shall begin by examining the head wound."

I had almost forgotten that head wound, except when I looked in the mirror or combed my hair. There was a strange gap where the hair was only just beginning to grow back—it looked rather like a crop of new grass, only reddish brown instead of green.

"Any headaches?" the doctor inquired.

"Sometimes. Mostly I am lethargic. I feel dull in general, in my head too, and that is not at all the way I used to be." An accurate description of the way I'd been feeling up until Pratt left the house.

"Um-hm." He poked and patted and worked his fingers through my new crop of hair down to my scalp in a way that might have felt pleasant had his fingers not been so cold.

"What you are describing," he said, "is a certain malaise that is part of the end stage of convalescence. It will pass. I take it you have never had a serious illness?"

"No."

"How old are you, Miss James?"

"Twenty-five."

"And you are a virgin?"

"What has that to do with anything?"

I tried to remember: Had I told the wives I was a widow? Or had I merely said I had wealth in my own right? That is the trouble with lies—one must remember exactly what one has said to whom; it is such a bother. Easier by far to tell the truth, but that is not always possible. Particularly when one is in the detective business.

"Melancthon wants to know."

I narrowed my eyes. I had rather expected Pratt

might have made his own inspection of my private parts during my loss of consciousness, but perhaps he did not know how to tell manually. . . .

I did not wish to complete that thought. I said, "It is none of his business either."

"The man is to be your husband—"

"I rather seriously doubt that."

Suddenly I was seized with an almost irresistible urge not to tell any lies to this doctor. I wanted to tell him the truth and let him do with it what he would. I was sick and tired of this Carrie James masquerade, of trying to continually please, to be careful; in short, I was excessively weary of reining in my whole personality just in order to survive in this wretchedly peculiar household.

"I am not going to marry Melancthon Pratt," I said. "He has never *asked* me to marry him. Instead he has informed me that he will take me in marriage and get children on me because an angel told him so."

"I repeat, Miss James: Are you a virgin? Perhaps that is why you were so concerned for your modesty."

"Are you hard of hearing? That is nobody's business but my own."

Dr. Arnold Striker frowned at me, then made a concession: "Very well. Since you are so adamant we will come back to it. Let us remove the bandages and take a look at your legs, see how the healing is progressing. Are you ready?"

"Yes, and eager to see for myself."

Dr. Striker did seem to be good with his patients, so perhaps his seeming coldness and severity were only a facade. I wondered if he might be basically shy. It was damn hard to tell. Tempting to think, though, that I might trust him. He pulled back the bedcovers gently, I brought the skirt of my thick white flannel nightgown up over my knees, and he began his poking and prodding routine on both my legs. Every now and then he would ask if what he was doing hurt, to which I generally replied in the negative.

Striker told me to bend my knees, if I could, while keeping the soles of my feet flat on the bed. I was able to do this, to my own surprise. He murmured approval and then slowly pushed first one leg down and then the other. This was slightly painful but not too bad.

"All right, let's have a close look." He began to unwrap the bandages and to remove the corset-like stiffening that had held my legs immobile for—how long had it been?

"Dr. Striker, when were you here taking care of me before? How long ago was that, exactly?" I asked.

"A little over a month, make it five weeks, give or take a day or two. I can't tell you for certain without my book of appointments from last month, and I don't have it with me," he said without a pause in the unwrapping.

I considered this. My sense of that time would forever be distorted by my days of un- and semiconsciousness, I supposed. I thought it had been a little less time, but no matter what, it was too, too long.

"And what, exactly," I asked, "did you find wrong with my legs?"

At that question he did pause, and gave me another of his severe looks. "Surely Pratt or one of his wives has told you."

"Yes, but I would like to hear it from the doctor himself." I forced a smile, and a coaxing tone to my voice. "You are the real authority."

I do so love the male ego; it always rises to such bait, so reliable that way.

Striker perked right up and even managed a faint, fleeting smile himself. "A heavy object had fallen across both your legs. My examination—especially when combined with Mr. Pratt's report that from the time of his finding you and removing the object, you appeared unable to move your legs from the knees down—suggested fractures of both your tibia bones. Fortunately for you, there was no break in the skin, so the fractures were simple, not compound. Do you know the difference?"

I thought I might, but he seemed to be enjoying his explanation and so I simply shook my head.

"In a compound fracture the broken bone protrudes through the skin. It is much more serious, harder to set and to heal. A simple fracture will heal itself in time, provided the bones are aligned properly, and yours were scarcely out of alignment to begin with. They went back in place easily, which means they will knit well."

He continued: "At the time, I was more concerned about that head wound. Your loss of consciousness was due more to its severity, the consequent loss of blood, and accompanying shock. I expect you also had to deal with some infection?"

"Yes. I had a high fever and was delirious, but I came out of it."

Striker smiled, which brought just a hint of warmth to his muddy brown eyes. "You're young and strong, I thought that would be the way of it. Though it must be extremely inconvenient to have two broken legs, I do think you will be right as rain quite soon."

"Right as rain," I muttered.

A not-too-pleasant smell was emerging as the doctor unwrapped more layers of bandages from my legs. It increased in pungency as the process got down nearer to my skin. Yet I was fascinated, as if I had never seen my own legs before, and I quite forgot to be concerned about anything else.

"An odd expression, isn't it?" said Striker. "I've never understood it myself."

I looked up, baffled. "Understood what?"

"Right as rain. What does that mean, do you have any idea?"

"I suppose it has something to do with rain making things grow. But that is a rather wild guess on my part; I really have not the slightest idea— Oh! My God!"

The last layer of wrapping had fallen away from my legs—he had been taking it by turns, so that both legs were simultaneously exposed to the air and light for the first time in weeks. And it was quite a shock.

"They look like chicken legs!" I wailed.

"Muscles are a bit atrophied from lack of use, that's all. I'll have Melancthon get you a pair of crutches; some exercise will soon take care of that. Let's see how you do at a little bit of weight-bearing."

Striker directed me to dangle my chicken legs over the side of the bed, to put both my arms on his shoulders, and to let him take my weight as I eased myself to the floor.

Of course as I did that, my nightgown fell and neither of us could see my legs any longer, but perhaps that was unnecessary. The important thing was how my legs felt, not how they looked. Or so I thought—but a moment later I learned he didn't like the long skirt in this situation any better than I did.

"Lean all your weight on me," Striker said, "that's it. Feet flat on the floor. Now, straighten your knees, give me your weight, that's it, that's it . . . damn these long skirts, I can't see a thing. How are you feeling?"

"Wobbly. And excited. I'm actually standing!"

"Yes, but continue to keep your weight on me. You're not ready to stand alone yet, or to walk without support, but I think you're definitely ready for those crutches. I'll be staying here overnight. Tomorrow morning Pratt and I will go into town. You're as tall as many men, so we should be able to find crutches ready-made. I can teach you how to use them myself before I leave. Will that be satisfactory?"

"Oh yes!" Foolishly, I had tears in my eyes.

"Ready to get back in bed?"

My legs were trembling, so I nodded. My mind had been completely captivated by the thought of these crutches, and the freedom of movement they would bring.

Then in my rather perverse way—I swear sometimes I think my mind operates independent of the rest of me —I leapt ahead to the next question. "How long, then, will I have to use the crutches?"

"That's hard to know precisely. Perhaps only two or three weeks; perhaps longer. You'll be able to tell. If there's bone pain, don't put your weight down. Let your arms transfer the weight to the crutches, the same as they did to my shoulders, and just go easy. Don't worry, I'll teach you, you'll do fine."

"I'm sure I will," I murmured. Of course this was not getting me as much closer to freedom as transfer to a hospital would have done, but somehow it seemed more real and therefore even better.

"Now"—Striker rubbed his hands together in a satisfied gesture—"I'd like to call Verla back to bathe your legs. Then we'll give you new bandages and braces, not so heavy this time."

"More good news!" I said fervently, bestowing on the doctor a genuine smile.

I was beginning to feel quite fond of him, but not so fond as to start thinking again of asking for his help. Exactly how, that was the question.

"Doctor," I ventured, "are you a member of the New Deseret community?"

"No, I am not. The Mormons of New Deseret do not have a doctor among them. They need one, though. I'm too far away to serve this community effectively, yet I am the closest physician available."

"And where do you live and have your practice?"

"Little town called Thistle. Other side of Soldier Summit, right on the railroad."

Neither of these names meant a thing to me. I felt

panic when I thought how far I had to go, what an ordeal I had before me in order to escape.

"Now," said Striker, "before I bring in Father Pratt and his wife, I ask you again. Are you a virgin?"

I remained silent for a moment. Finally I said, "Do you really want to see me married to Melancthon Pratt, who already has five wives? A man who is ignoring the laws of this country, the United States of America?"

"In Utah it is not all that uncommon. For us, Washington, D.C., seems so far away as to be another world, irrelevant to ours. The practice of polygamy has been officially outlawed since statehood, that's true, but, well"—Arnold Striker shrugged eloquently—"I myself have three."

"Three?"

"Wives, that is."

*Oh, for heaven's sake,* I thought. It was all I could do to restrain myself from rolling my eyes.

But then I had a brilliant idea, which immediately translated into an equally brilliant lie, and I heard it come out of my mouth: "All right, I'll tell you. I am not a virgin, of course not. And I can't marry Melancthon Pratt, because I'm not a widow. That's only what I tell people when I travel alone, as I was doing when the train I was on got blown up. I further use the widowhood ruse in order to do all manner of other things alone without censure. My husband, however, is very much alive. He lives in Boston, which is why I must return there every so often. I was on my way to Boston via Chicago when the train wreck occurred, as anyone who checks the passenger list will tell you.

"So you see," I concluded, somewhat triumphantly, "I cannot marry Pratt, or anyone!"

"What's wrong with him?"

"With whom?"

"Your husband."

"Oh. I see what you mean. There's nothing much

wrong with him. He just doesn't like to travel and I do. I'm sure by now he must be frantic to know what's happened to me." I leaned forward, pleading with all my heart, putting all the emotional intensity I could muster into my next question.

"Might you be willing, Dr. Striker, to send my husband a telegram for me? Just to let him know I'm all right?"

"I don't know. I might."

"Please."

"I'll think on it."

"It would have to be done without Melancthon's knowledge."

"I said I'll think on it."

"Perhaps—" I did not want to push this too far, but I'd committed myself now, so I went ahead. "Perhaps you might even, in your telegram, tell him exactly where I am and ask him to come for me."

That produced a very big frown. Yet still he said, a third time, "I'll think on it. What is your husband's name and where can I reach him?"

"Jones, not James. Pratt, er, he misunderstood what I said the first time he asked, and I decided just to let them all call me James, because by the time I was conscious again they were all thinking of me as Carrie James. My husband's full name is Leonard Pembroke Jones, and he lives on Beacon Street in Boston."

---

Michael burst through the connecting door and stood upon the metal linkage platform between the two railroad cars, feeling the thrum of the wheels on the silver rails beneath his feet. The car ahead was coach class, rows and rows of high-backed seats on either side of a long aisle. Michael peered through the glass window in the top half of the door, and caught sight of his quarry just as he sat down. He was all too obvious: the one person in the whole car whose chest rose and fell too rapidly, the one who was breathing too hard because he had been running.

A big man. Both tall and broad. Gray hair, very distinguished, yet with a ruggedness about him. He'd taken a seat with his back to Michael. Did he know he had been followed? Probably not.

It was not Hilliard Ramsey.

The man seemed very familiar, but Michael could not come up with a name. Or, for the moment, even the time and the place where he had known the man.

# 12

EILING, PETULANT? If he hadn't seen it with his own eyes, Michael would never have believed it.

"You eat a second breakfast, if one of us must," she said, tossing her long hair back over her shoulder and refusing to meet his eyes. "I have already told you more than once, I am not hungry. You may order coffee for me, that is all."

Michael had insisted Meiling go along to the dining car and take a table, while he detoured by his own compartment before joining her. During that brief stop he'd armed himself with his revolver, but he did not intend to tell her that. He felt it was enough of an explanation to say he believed they had best seek safety in numbers, at least for a while.

He gave their order to the dining steward—cinnamon toast and fresh-squeezed orange juice for himself, a pot of coffee for Meiling—and then leaned back in his chair, doing his best to relax. Continual tension can drive a man mad. At the moment he felt he was not far from it.

Still, he must make an effort, and so, when he had regained his equilibrium he asked, "What is it that has you so uncharacteristically peevish, Meiling? Are you just venting on me your feelings about the train's policy of allowing women in the club car only at the dinner hour?"

She regarded him sidewise out of her almond-shaped obsidian eyes, and somehow her reply came out sounding a bit like a hiss: "It is a senseless custom made up by men for the advantage of other men. It is unfair to allow only the males all the time access to this—what is it called—clubs car, for the reason that it is the only place where one can go on this train when one is simply bored with one's own company. Or with the company of one's traveling companion. Certainly I do not like it. How could I like it? But there is nothing I can do about it. I prefer not to waste my time allowing my feelings to be consumed by matters I can do nothing about."

This speech, certainly the most direct and lengthy one Michael had ever heard from any Chinese woman, got his full attention. Not that he hadn't been learning by bits and pieces how much she had changed; or if not exactly changed, for she'd always had a strong personality, how much she had grown up. But this attitude and way of speaking were both new and powerfully adult.

Somehow, when he hadn't been paying enough attention, the little girl he'd known from birth had become not just a beautiful woman but a force to be reckoned with. Michael felt a prickle of respect, almost a thrill, for the extent of her transformation.

But never mind that. The question was: How the devil was he going to leave the train? Goddammit, he couldn't look after her safety and also do the job he had to do.

Meiling, apparently having said what she had to say, calmly stared out the window at the passing scenery.

The cinnamon toast came, a golden pile of it, sweetly fragrant upon a flowered plate. The steward, immaculate in his stiff white tunic, served Michael's orange juice in a crystal glass nestled in shaved ice within a silver bowl. Meiling's coffee came in a silver pot; her cup and saucer were fine china, flowered like the toast plate but in a different pattern. Everything so elegant, and so . . . wasted. So impossible, under the circumstances, to enjoy.

It was late in the morning; they had arrived at the tail end of the last seating for breakfast and now had the dining car almost to themselves. One other couple sat several tables away on the opposite side of the train; much nearer a man sat all alone at a table for four. Michael watched him, suspicious of everyone now, until he felt reasonably certain the man was fully occupied with eating and reading the newspaper, and had no interest in eavesdropping on their conversation.

"Come, Meiling," he said, "your coffee will get cold."

She gave him another disgusted look. "No, it will not. The metal of the pot will keep it warm for at least an hour. I will talk when you are ready to be sensible, instead of—I cannot think of the right word for what you are being, either in English or Mandarin."

Michael could read her look, and suspected the word she sought was of the sort proper females, young or old, were taught not to utter. It might not even be in her vocabulary.

But it would be in Fremont's. Fremont could swear like a sailor when she wanted to, which was not often. She contended she had learned all these words from Michael, although he suspected she'd picked them up at a shockingly young age from sneaking into some room at night to listen to her father and his cronies. Her mother had died young, leaving Fremont to be her father's hostess—and an often lonely, if unusually privileged, adolescent girl.

Michael roused himself, deliberately shutting a door in his mind against any thoughts of Fremont except those directly related to this case. For that was how he was beginning to think, the direction his analytical mind was increasingly bent upon. Somehow this was all one case, all related: the harassment of the railroad that J&K had been hired to look into, the explosion of the train they'd been on, everything that had happened since. He just didn't know quite how it all fit together, and if Fremont's disappearance was related to all the rest. He continued to think, to hope, she'd been dazed but not seriously hurt, and had wandered away on her own.

But for now, Meiling deserved his attention. His mind might have wandered for a few seconds, but still he'd heard, even been amused by, what she'd said.

Careful to keep any trace of that amusement out of his voice, he inquired, "Shall I help you choose the word you're looking for? I quite take your meaning, you know. You think I am being—how about difficult? Unreasonable? Stubborn?"

"Like the head of a pig," she said, "or the donkey of a horse."

"I think you mean a horse's ass."

"Yes, that is it. A horse's ass."

"And pigheaded."

"That also." Meiling bowed from the waist, a mockery of maidenly deference.

Michael sighed, shaking his head. Women.

He leaned forward and held one hand out, palm up, on the table in a gesture of concession. "Obviously we need to talk this through. It's not the club car that has you out of sorts, it's me. And I have to tell you, Meiling,

I'm a little out of sorts with you too. So we'll talk, and then you'll agree to get off this train."

"No," she said, eyes flashing, "I do not think so. I do not think that would be wise at all, and if you were not being the donkey of a horse you would see it for yourself, Michael Kossoff!"

"Very well. Explain yourself. I'll listen." Michael leaned back and folded his arms over his chest, sling and all.

"I could have been a help to you earlier. I am quick, nimble, and can defend myself. I am skilled in jujitsu, as I'm sure you know. If we had both gone into the corridor together, I might have pursued the man and brought him down while you did whatever it was you were doing outside my door. You wasted time. He got away."

He had to admit she could be right; in such a situation, seconds did count. But he wasn't ready to admit it yet, if ever. Nor did he want to believe Meiling's jujitsu could bring down a man as big and tall as the one he'd been chasing.

He took a different tack: "I wasn't wasting time, Meiling. I was checking around the door for explosives. I was remembering, I suppose, how the train Fremont and I were on was blown up. Not only that, but the very cars in which we had our compartments appeared to have been targeted. I mean, those were the cars that ended up at the bottom of the gorge. That *could* have been coincidence. *Must* have been coincidence. And yet—"

Meiling remained quiet, calm, watchful.

"And yet," Michael said, "I had the oddest feeling it might be about to happen again. . . ."

"Odd feelings are important," Meiling said, leaning forward, instantly interested, animated. "Tell me more about this."

But Michael was reluctant. Surely nothing so irrational could be worth his consideration, or hers. Yet, irrational or not, these feelings and accompanying thoughts persisted—and since this most recent incident, they had indeed increased manyfold.

He took a piece of cinnamon toast, tore it in two, put half in his mouth, and began to chew. It was good, but he only distantly registered its spicy-sweet taste. At last Michael said, "I've had a feeling, ever since the explosion, that Fremont and I were specific targets. But that's ridiculous. Nobody would blow up a whole train just on the uncertain chance that the two of us, out of two or three hundred passengers, could be hurt or killed."

Now Michael too leaned forward. He kept his voice intentionally low: "Besides, the explosive was not on the train, it was affixed to the trestle that supported the tracks over the gorge. This was confirmed by burn marks on what was left of the trestle's wooden timbers. A part of the detonating mechanism was also found. As I'd thought might be the case, it had a timer, which was tripped when the engine passed over it on the track. A certain pre-set interval passed, during which the fuse was burning down, and then . . . boom."

Meiling blinked, even though he'd only whispered the word.

Michael paused, stunned by his memories, his eyes suddenly staring at a place only he could see.

Meiling said, "Yes, boom, and Fremont lies at the bottom of this gorge. Hurt, but alive. And now she is missing. We will find her. Let us not lose sight of this most important fact."

Now in her turn Meiling paused, to let what she had just said sink into Michael's distracted brain. Then she urged, "You are not finished, there is more. Tell me."

"Very well, but eat some of this damn toast. We must at least give the appearance of having breakfast together."

She took a piece of toast and tore it into small pieces, some of which were destined to disappear on her tongue; others ended as decoration around the rim of her saucer. Her attention was rapt, as Michael found himself slowly but surely opening up to her.

He told Meiling things he'd thought he had to keep to himself. For example, his nagging conviction that someone was conducting a vendetta not just against the railroad but also against the J&K Agency—even though this made no sense, because they had not been in business long enough to have made any enemies.

Thinking aloud, he admitted that as individuals, independent of the detective agency, he and Wish Stephenson might have old enemies. Certain shady persons who could want revenge for something he or Wish had done earlier in their respective lives, his in the spy world and Wish's with the San Francisco Police Department.

Not Fremont, though. All of Fremont's enemies were in jail; she had a tidy way of catching them and turning them in. Didn't Meiling agree this was so?

Meiling inclined her head, not quite a nod of agreement, just recognition of what he'd said, and silent encouragement to continue.

Michael sighed; his life was neither so simple nor so tidy, never. He had years of loose ends that he despaired of ever being able to tie up—but that he did not tell Meiling. Instead, having opened certain floodgates, he went on.

He told her about the dream he'd had repeatedly since the blowup, a dream in which he saw Fremont in a small room, a confined space like a prison cell yet not quite that, with chains on her legs.

Telling the dream unmanned him. Michael had to turn his head away, to cover his eyes with his hand until the tears stopped, and then to unobtrusively wipe them away.

Meiling remained silent, giving him time to recover,

for which he was grateful. The pair who had been dining at the far end of the car left their table, chairs scraping on the polished floor, and walked past in the aisle. The lone male diner had long since gone; Michael automatically noted that with the departure of the couple, he and Meiling would be alone in the dining car. Except, of course, for the stewards, who presumably stood unobtrusively nearby.

The female of the departing pair was a large woman; her dress brushed against the tablecloth, threatening to upset the silver coffeepot, but Meiling reached out a stabilizing hand. In the woman's wake trailed a stink of strong perfume. Heavily exotic, a scent meant for nights in some Turkish bazaar, not daytime hours in polite society, it swarmed up Michael's nostrils and produced a jolt, like ammonia to one who has fainted.

Thus jolted back to the business at hand, Michael at last told Meiling the most irrational, yet oddly most important thing of all: the sudden mind-picture, almost a vision, that had come over him when his hand touched the handle of her compartment door an hour earlier. It was this vision that had caused him to hesitate, and then to take the time to examine the walls and floor in a search for explosives.

"What, exactly, did you see in this mind-picture?" Meiling inquired urgently. "Tell me while it is still fresh in your memory."

"I saw a man planting slender sticks of dynamite along the seam where the wall meets the floor outside a train compartment, also taping and laying a length of fuse. I only saw it for an instant, not long enough to recognize the man, but I had the impression he was large—and it is true the man I followed to the next train car was also a large fellow. But there were no explosives outside your door."

Michael rubbed his chin thoughtfully, then ended with a rueful admission: "Now that some time has passed, and I hear myself tell it aloud, I'm inclined to think my so-called vision was probably no more than the product of a heated imagination."

"Do not be so sure. You are very close to Fremont in spirit. It may be that *she* saw this man, but because of her injury she cannot remember it. You can see him— you are seeing him *for* her—because your mind and hers are linked, just as your bodies have so often been linked. In that way you and Fremont are one."

"Meiling—" Michael felt he should protest this reference to his and Fremont's most private business, but he did not quite know how to do it, and so ended by saying nothing more than her name.

Meiling shrugged. "The two of you are together, you are—how do you say it?—a couple. Married or not."

She nailed him with a direct gaze, almost blinding in its honesty and forcefulness. "Do you think I do not know these things? Do you think I don't know what people do even if I have never done it myself? Stop being silly. You continue to think of me as a child; that is your problem, and you are going to have to stop it, do you hear?"

Michael's mouth fell open, but words failed to come out.

And in that moment, Hilliard Ramsey strolled by. He slowed as he passed their table and tipped his brown fedora, which he wore with a dandified suit of light brown fabric criss-crossed with threads of dark green and red.

"Good morning, Miss Li," said Ramsey. "Don't get up, Kossoff. I'm just passing through."

Neither Michael nor Meiling spoke; nor, apparently, had Ramsey expected it, because he didn't stop but simply strolled on.

Suddenly acutely aware of their being alone in the dining car, Michael let the fingers of his good hand stray toward his belt, where he'd stashed the revolver for quick access. But Ramsey kept on moving, his back presenting a rather tempting target.

Only when his old nemesis had left the car by the far exit did Michael silently wonder how the hell Ramsey had known Meiling's name.

———

It is not as easy as it looks, walking on crutches. But I was fiercely determined, all the more so because although Dr. Arnold Striker had given me the crutches and taught me how to use them, the last thing he had said before leaving was that he would not be notifying my husband of my whereabouts, or even of my survival. To say that I was put out by this would be a considerable understatement.

Striker was a good doctor, even a kind one, as long as he played the role of healer; but as a plain human being he turned out to be as rigid and severe as my first impression had suggested. Never before had I been so sorry to have an initial opinion proven right.

He had told me goodbye, and his hand was already on the doorknob, when he turned back. "Oh, Carrie," he'd said—this had happened five days ago now—"I think you'll want to know I won't be sending that telegram to your husband."

I wasn't greatly surprised, but one always hopes until hope has died, and sometimes even beyond that.

"I had a considerable struggle with my conscience over this," he added in a self-righteous tone, "believe me."

"Oh, I believe you," I conceded, "but perhaps you'll enlighten me as to the details of your struggle."

I wondered if it was too late to dissuade him, if I might yet persuade him to change his mind.

Striker folded his hands and faced me straight on, his features set in the gravest of lines. He declared,

"We Mormons believe in the Angels of the Lord, you know."

I nodded, keeping my face as serious as his, and said, "Yes, I know."

There is no accounting for some of the things people believe. I myself am halfway inclined to believe in God from time to time, but to believe in winged creatures of no particular gender? Semidivine beings, usually invisible, except that rather regularly during the Renaissance one assumes they must have come down from heaven to pose for numerous religious paintings? Hah! As for the one most famous around these parts, the Angel Moroni, double hah. And Pratt's angel? I would not waste even a hah on that one.

When Dr. Striker did not continue, I inquired, "So your point is?"

"So while I am not a member of Melancthon Pratt's community, I do respect his beliefs and his right to have them, including his belief in the angel that appears to him from time to time. I am willing to accept that his angel led Father Pratt to you, that this was a miracle, and that all will work to your own good as well as to the good of the whole Pratt family. Therefore I have decided not to notify Mr. Jones."

I nodded again. I was doing my best to be civil. "Mr. *Leonard Pembroke* Jones," I intoned, because my father's name—which Striker believed to be the name of my husband—did have a calming effect on me. My father's name also gave me courage, along with a very great determination to get out of this situation so that I could complete my journey to Boston—a journey I had undertaken not only as a job for the J&K Agency, but also because at the end of it I had expected to see my father again.

Resolutely I pushed to the back of my mind the nagging fear that now I might never make it in time, that when at last I got there I might be too late.

"I recall the name, Carrie," Striker was saying, "but better you should forget. It is of no further consequence now."

I could have struck him for that, be his own name Striker or not, and very likely I might have if I hadn't needed both hands on my crutches in order to keep my balance. My feet could not yet bear my weight for more than a minute, not even two.

So I had simply stood there and listened to him build his argument, brick by verbal brick—and with each one my own determination to get away quickly grew and grew.

"Surely you see," he argued, "that you are better off here with a fine family who all care about you than with a man who cares so little that he allows you to travel around the country alone!"

"That man is legally my husband," I lied, maintaining the ruse. My jaw ached from controlling my tongue, which longed to lash at him while my body could not.

"Sometimes it is necessary to put aside a set of laws, if in doing so you accomplish a greater good. Pratt will marry you in the Temple, Carrie, once you have converted. This good, generous man will save your soul by marrying you. You will join The Elect for all eternity. And you will prosper here on Earth as well."

"I see you did indeed think it all out," I said, biting off the words.

There had been nothing more to say. To my great relief, Dr. Striker also considered the matter closed, and had taken his leave.

In the five days that had since passed, I'd realized I could not find fault with Striker's logic, given that he could operate only out of his own set of peculiar beliefs. If there was any one single thing I both admired and detested about the Mormons, it was this: They were always so very sure of themselves, no matter what the subject or the situation.

I gripped the crutches under my arms firmly, pushed down hard on the crossbar, and went swinging across the floor of my room. Back and forth, back and forth, back and forth. Sweat beaded my brow and my underarms ached, but I was getting stronger.

If my Mormon so-called family were sure of themselves, well, so was I. I was leaving, and soon, with or without Norma's help.

Today, for the first time, I intended to go outside.

# 13

MY HEART was pounding, not from exertion but with excitement, as I carefully let just enough of my weight down to allow myself to grasp and tug the doorlatch. Then I swung myself out of the way on my crutches and let the door fall inward of its own accord, as I'd seen it do many times.

"Open sesame," I said softly, for this seemed to me such a momentous occasion that some incantation was required. Then I took a deep, fortifying breath and peered out. I was only partially prepared for what I saw.

The sisters, Sarah and Tabitha, had told me some weeks earlier—I wasn't sure how many, as I never saw a calendar or a newspaper and had given up trying to keep an accurate count—that the Pratt household consisted of a main house plus a sleeping cabin for each wife, plus this guest cabin I occupied. I had spent many of my idle hours trying to figure out how this arrangement was laid out. Trying without success and with considerable frustration.

Now I understood what my problem had been: The guest cabin, my domain, stood at a considerable remove from the others, whose roofs I could see some distance away. The distance was dismaying, in fact, because everything I would ultimately need for my getaway was over there. *All the way* over there.

"Look on the bright side, Fremont," I muttered aloud. At least I was outside again, under the wide open sky!

The air felt wonderful, fresh and clean, scented with evergreens—pines perhaps, though I am no authority on trees and only know about pines on account of having lived for a number of months in a lighthouse on the other side of a pine forest. Since then—to me I guess—all evergreen trees have smelled like pines.

At any rate, I mentally totted up one point for the good, clean, fragrant air. Cold, but never mind; it was, after all, November. Or were we into December now? I really didn't know, which was distressing.

For a moment I wondered if I could have been more downhearted than I'd realized in those days just before asking Pratt to go for the doctor. It was not like me to have lost track of time like this. But never mind, there was no point brooding. I shrugged and almost lost a crutch. Securing it more firmly under my arm I vowed to ask one of the wives—Sarah or Norma seemed the most likely candidate—for a newspaper at the first opportunity.

That made me feel considerably better. I looked around and saw I could tot up another point in my favor: The ground was fairly level and well kept around my cabin, which was important because the last thing in the world I wanted was to trip and fall. Particularly on this first outing. I intended to get out, about, and back inside before anyone was the wiser.

Aha! Three points: a white-painted bench right up against the outside wall near the doorway with its one step down. A place to sit would be most welcome in case of need, and I was tempted. But first, some long-anticipated active exploration!

It was early afternoon, my choice for an outing because I had observed that the others were, for whatever reason, generally busy at this time. If one of the wives came with my midday meal on a tray and stayed to chat with me while I ate, she would always leave soon after. Their more leisurely visits tended to occur later in the afternoon, and sometimes in the evening, though Selene was more likely to come in the morning before going off to her lessons. She did not go to school, but I had learned that Pratt paid for her to be tutored, which, to be perfectly fair, did show the man could at least recognize the girl's intelligence.

I'd always assumed Selene left the house in the morning and went to the tutor, but now that I saw how far off the house and wives' cabins were—roughly five hundred yards, though I confess I am not much good at guessing distances—I realized I had no real reason to think that. The tutor could just as well have been coming there without my knowing it.

In fact, almost anything could be going on over there without my knowing it.

Melancthon Pratt was so hard to know anything about, such a law unto himself, a bit of an enigma.

I paused in my swinging progress as I realized I had not taken Pratt's unpredictable schedule into consideration. He had not been coming to see me so often lately, either before or after the doctor's visit. While I was glad of that, I didn't delude myself into thinking he had lost interest in me, though that would have been an outcome much desired. No, more likely he was plotting something, rather in the manner of a large creature lying in wait to pounce.

I dismissed Melancthon Pratt from my mind—there was no point trying to consider the unpredictable, I should simply have to handle him on the spot, if he came. I had done well enough I thought, in light of the wives' household habits, in choosing the hour or two after lunch for practice of my outdoor navigating skills.

Mornings I practiced indoors, in my room—practiced with an aim toward getting better and better; then I did an about-face and practiced at dissembling, so as to disguise the progress I'd made. I did not want anyone to know how hard I was working to master this art of walking on crutches with my arms bearing almost all my weight; less still did I want to be caught giving any unexpected demonstrations of my rapidly improving skills.

Looking up to check the angle of the sun and its orientation in the sky, I concluded that it was probably around half past one, and the cabin door I'd just exited faced east. Well, I should have known that because the afternoon sun always came through my one window, which was on the side of the room opposite the door.

One window . . .

That was damn odd. Having advanced a few feet into the yard, I turned and looked back at the cabin. It was rustic, but neatly built—not of boards, as those are very hard to come by in the West, but rather of some sort of rough shingles that had weathered to an attractive shade of gray. Some care and expense had gone into its construction. The door and the one step were painted a pristine white, like the bench.

Why then would a free-standing cabin have only one window?

I continued to puzzle over this as I began, laboriously, to make my very first circuit of the cabin's perimeter—my aim, to be as familiar with my former prison cell from the outside as I was from the inside. It shared no walls with any other structure, there was nothing adjoining, and it was not possible to see into the other buildings below, so why should its builder have been parsimonious with ventilation and views?

Why? For economy's sake?

Perhaps, but probably not. Glass was no longer so expensive as it used to be, not even in the West, where most everything had to be imported, either from the East by train or from the West by boat, around the Horn or across the Pacific Ocean.

This business of the single window was a minor point, but feeling trapped as I did, I had obsessed over it. I'd wondered if perhaps there might not be some kind of connecting corridor on the other side of one of my blank walls, like a cloistered walkway in a monastery. Clearly there was no such thing.

Having completed three-quarters of my circuit around the cabin, I stood for a moment with my back braced against its southeast corner, relieving some of the weight from my arms. From this vantage I had the best view of the Big House, and on closer scrutiny it seemed not quite so far away as I'd first thought, appearing to be situated in a dip of land that screened the lower two-thirds of it from view. That is to say, if the Big House had been a person, from about the ribcage down that person would have been invisible to me.

How very interesting! That same dip of land obscured the wives' cabins entirely, except for their rooflines. I squinted against the sun, wishing I could spare one hand to shade my eyes, but I could not. Truth to tell, my arms were beginning to tremble. Oh, bother. I resolved to ignore all discomfort.

The Big House either had a loft—which is to say, it would be about one and a half stories high—or had high ceilings. The cabins of the wives were by contrast tiny, if one judged from the roofs, which were all that I could see of them. Smaller than my guest cabin, which I had thought quite small but now saw was grand by comparison.

Eventually I would check out everything down there more closely, but not now. I would be forced by my aching arms to go back in soon. Yet I lingered, squinting, searching without success for a barn, stables, or any other outbuilding where horses, wagons, any form of transportation might be located. Surely such equipment must be housed down there somewhere. Certainly none of it was up here with me. Here I was in the guest cabin in isolated splendor. As for splendor, hah; but I was isolated indeed.

Turning now to complete that last leg of my circle around the cabin, I made a mental note to remember to be more profuse in my thanks to the wives when they brought meals and other things to me. How they must have rushed to keep the food from getting cold! And no wonder that no matter how hard I'd strained to hear a step outside my door, I never had. Though the grass here was sparse, it was enough to deaden most sound.

With a sigh and a final look around, I pushed open the door, negotiated the one step up in a final burst of effort, and went back inside. No one had seen me. So far, so good.

———

They played double solitaire and argued about when to get off the train.

Meiling won at her half of the game again and again, until Michael began to suspect she was able somehow to influence the cards with her mysterious grandmother-given powers. Either that or she cheated.

But Michael won their argument by virtue of his superior knowledge of Utah geography. He argued effectively that if they were to have a chance of finding Fremont before the onset of winter froze up their passage through the mountains, they could not leave the train before Salt Lake City.

He would have preferred to stay on until Provo; Salt

Lake was a concession to Meiling, a sop he threw to her soothsaying ability even though her part of the argument had been irrational and had irritated the hell out of him. She said she still sensed danger all around him. He didn't want to hear it. Hell, he'd had danger all around him for most of his life.

Meiling knew that about him; she just wasn't thinking clearly. The grandmother's mumbo-jumbo might have restored her Chinese-ness, but it had messed up her mind.

"Everywhere there are mountains," Meiling commented, looking out the window.

"Um," Michael said. He was looking for a red jack, the jack of hearts—he was sure he'd seen it in there someplace, so why couldn't he turn it up? But no. Oh no.

"Where we're going will be mountainous too," Michael said irritably, "but first we'll have to cross the basin of the Great Salt Lake. I hope you know what you're doing by insisting we leave this train before Provo."

She looked over at him, then down at her cards. "I believe I do." She went through the pack in her hand again, turning up every third card. "Oh," she said, then played a huge number of cards in a flurry.

"Dammit, how do you *do* that?"

"Do what? I am playing the game correctly, am I not?"

"Yes, Meiling. You are not only playing it correctly, you're winning. Every goddam time."

A hint of a smile brushed her lips as she turned her head again toward the window. "I think I've played enough for one afternoon."

"Um-hm," Michael said.

He supposed he had too, and began to gather up the cards to put them away.

"I should like to rest for a while before the dinner

hour," Meiling said, not looking at him. "Perhaps you will go to the clubs car for a smoke. I cannot rest with you hovering over me."

"Meiling, I don't hover."

"Then may I express myself in different words: I cannot rest with you present in the same space that I am occupying. Your energy is not restful, Michael. I am sorry to have to say so, but that is the truth."

He riffled through the cards. He gave each pack a forceful tap upon the playing board, which rested half on his knees and half on Meiling's, then shoved them with more force than was required into the side-by-side sections of their pasteboard box.

"My energy will be a hell of a lot more restful when I've found Fremont. If it bothers you I'm sorry, but there's not much I can do about it."

"That is not true. You could go to the clubs car, as I asked."

"It's club car, Meiling, not clubs. One club, singular, not plural." Michael folded the playing board and tossed it onto the bench seat beside him. The two-pack box of cards he tossed on top of it. The cards had been provided by the railroad, and were decorated with the letters "SP" embossed in gold, in a fussily rococo style.

"And no," Michael continued relentlessly, "I can't go for a smoke. Not without you. I'm not leaving you alone as long as we're on this train. If you don't like it, you can get off at the next stop."

"We have already had that discussion."

"Indeed we have."

She turned on him, her eyes blazing again. "I've told you, the danger is following you, not me! I need to rest, Michael! And so do you."

Michael rose wearily. He was both tired and tense, a bad combination. She was right: He too needed to rest.

Against his better judgment, he held up a hand to her, palm out. "Okay, okay, okay. I give up. I'm going to my compartment. We'll both rest for a couple of hours, then I'll come back here for you and we'll go together to the club car for a sherry, and then on to the dining car for dinner. Is that satisfactory?"

"Yes, thank you." Meiling made her customary small bow of the head, sincerely this time, not as an affectation but rather in the habit of her people.

"You're welcome," said Michael stiffly as he slid open the compartment door. He put his head out and looked right, then left. Up, then down. He saw nothing suspicious.

"A couple of hours, then," he said to Meiling, and closed the door behind him.

———

There is that man again," Meiling said. "He is watching you."

"His name is Hilliard Ramsey, and actually I believe, my dear Meiling, he is watching *you*. You're far prettier than I." A glass of smooth, mellow sherry and a cheroot had restored Michael's spirits. The rest in his own bunk hadn't hurt either; in fact, he'd slept like the dead . . . with his hand on the revolver the whole time.

"He is your friend?"

"No, my dear Meiling. He is my enemy, old and sworn."

"Oh, I see. He is the one you have told me of, who says he is only following you."

"Um-hm."

Michael crossed his legs and made a minor adjustment to the black silk scarf that served him as a sling. This broken collarbone was a damn nuisance—he couldn't do a thing with his left hand. In a public setting like this he was vulnerable.

*Of course,* he thought lazily as he let the alcohol warm his veins and cloud his mind, *Meiling can protect me with her jujitsu.*

"Tell me, Meiling," he said quietly, "what do your mystical powers say about that man, Ramsey? Is he merely following me, or does he mean me harm? Is he in cahoots with the big fellow who was lurking outside your compartment door?"

"You are serious?" She looked from Michael to Ramsey and back again, tilting her head only the slightest bit on her graceful neck as her dark eyes slid from side to side.

Michael thought, *She looks like a Chinese princess tonight.* She had decided to play the role of his woman, his concubine. She hadn't had to tell him this, he'd understood when he saw the way she'd dressed for dinner.

Yet in her masquerade Meiling was not just any woman, not just any concubine, but high-born: Her clothes and jewels announced it. Long earrings of amber and gold dangled from her ears, and amber beads were nestled in her raven's wing hair, which she had arranged in some kind of figure-eight thing on the back of her head. Her tunic, in the traditional style with mandarin collar and side slits, was of rust-brown satin trimmed in black satin piping, and her full trousers were also satin, also black. Sleek gold slippers encased her narrow feet.

Michael understood that the elegance of this outfit was deceptive. The amber beads in her hair were the heads of long, needle-like steel hairpins that could be turned into dangerous weapons in an instant. The side slits in her tunic, and the wide trousers, gave her freedom of movement. And the gold slippers, while pretty to look at, were flat-soled—she could run and kick in them easily. Clever woman.

With a pang, Michael remembered how Fremont had envied the cultural heritage that enabled Meiling to wear trousers. And how, not many years ago although it seemed a long time now, Fremont had worn black trousers herself one night. . . .

Meiling said, "There are too many people in this room for me to be able to single out one man's energy at this distance. But if you were to ask him to join us and introduce him to me, so that I might be physically near him for a time, I might be able to do it."

Michael arched a black eyebrow. The thought amused him. "I'll do it. You know what he'll think, don't you?"

"Of course." Meiling bowed gracefully from the waist, dipping her head lower than she normally would have done. "Surely you did not think I would wear these clothes in the normal way of things."

"No, of course I didn't. Very well, I'll bring him over. You know, Meiling, this could be rather entertaining."

But she wasn't smiling. She said, "Enjoy it while you can."

# 14

FATHER IS ILL," Verla said.

I was astounded. Whatever else I may have thought of the man, Melancthon Pratt seemed such a force of manhood and Mormonism as to be immune from the little diseases that strike the rest of us humans down from time to time.

"I am very sorry to hear it," I said.

"He says he would like to see you," she continued.

"Oh, I don't see how—" I demurred, but did not go on to complete my sentence because of the expression on Verla's face. She was obviously in no mood to be contradicted on anything.

She nodded to the other four wives, who had all accompanied her to my room. They'd filed in and now stood in their semicircle in the space at the foot of my bed, not because I was in the bed, as I had been the previous time they'd all stood in that same exact spot, but because it was the only space in the room large enough to accommodate them all standing in that formation. As Verla looked to each of them for support, they nodded, one by one.

*Like choreography,* I thought. Then I chastised myself for not being in a properly sympathetic mood.

I sat on a chair by the window, my crutches beside me on the floor. "That would be why I haven't seen Mr. Pratt in the last few days." I'd wondered a bit, but on the whole had just counted myself lucky.

"He took a chill," Verla said, "fetchin' that doctor for you."

"Oh." I tried to look contrite. Was I supposed to blame myself for his illness? Verla might have thought so. So I said again, "I'm sorry."

They all looked at me. No one else had said a word, only Verla.

I had been in a sad, pensive mood before they'd arrived, a mood probably induced by the weather. Today for the first time I felt the bleak inevitableness of winter approaching. It had been snowing on the mountains; you could smell winter on the wind. After so many years in San Francisco I had all but forgotten what snow was like.

But recently I'd been remembering: Born and bred in Boston, I had that Yankee blood in my veins, and bad winters were no stranger to me. Oh yes, winter was coming soon—and somehow this felt like a bad one.

That was how my thoughts had been running when the wives came, and so it took me a little time to register that something was very wrong.

"It's not just that Mr. Pratt is ill," I said as that realization dawned on me, "there is more. What is it?"

I looked at Sarah, who shook her head ever so slightly, with a hint of warning in her eyes; at Tabitha, who bit her upper lip and wouldn't look at me but instead focused on some point past my right ear; at Norma, who seemed unnaturally wide-eyed and blank, as if she hadn't the slightest idea what I was talking about; and at Selene, who kept her gaze on the floor and her hands clasped behind her back. Perhaps I was being fanciful, but it struck me that Selene had not wanted to come with the others. I could almost feel the reluctance emanating from her like a palpable force.

"What? Who will tell me?" I insisted, as it appeared Verla would not.

No one volunteered.

"Selene?" I asked.

"She's the youngest, leave her alone," said Verla flatly.

Selene might have been the youngest, but she was also the most intelligent—with the possible exception of Sarah—and Selene was certainly not lacking the ability to speak her mind when she chose. I'd learned that gradually during my weeks in this household. If they were forcing her to be here against her will, then I wanted her to have an opportunity to speak her piece.

"She's young, yes, but she can speak for herself," I said.

Selene raised her head and met my eyes. In that moment she did seem a child, not a woman, certainly not one who could be married to a man like Melancthon Pratt.

"We had a meeting," she said. "All the wives. We do that sometimes, when we cannot agree." Her fair skin flushed so much that she looked feverish, her voice faltered for a moment, but then she continued: "Carrie, we cannot agree about you."

Now it was my turn to bite my lip. Something momentous was about to happen, I could feel it. They were going either to set me free or to stone me to death or something equally dire—I hadn't the slightest idea which.

So I waited, saying nothing. My skin turned prickly all over.

Uneasy silence reigned.

I glanced at Norma: Had she told them I'd asked her to help me escape? Was that what had prompted this disagreement among the wives? Norma's face held no clue; she was keeping to that blank expression.

Apparently out of sympathy for Selene, whose face burned so crimson now that I was truly sorry I had called on her, Sarah broke the silence: "We realize that your being here is through no fault of your own. You can't help that you were seriously hurt and ill and all that—"

Selene interrupted, her voice high and impassioned: "They keep forgetting! The angel sent you—Father said so!"

Her young, clear voice rang out like a bell, struck the bare walls of my room, and left its reverberation hanging in the stunned silence that followed her outcry.

After an appropriate interval, I said slowly, "I don't believe in angels."

And I thought, *Let them stone me if they want to, but there, I have told the truth at last, at least about that.*

Tabitha, the gentlest of them all, cleared her throat. She looked nervously right and left at the wives arrayed on either side of her, and then said, "Angels come from God, and God doesn't care whether we believe or not. Sometimes He chooses us first, and then later we come to believe. For example, St. Paul was not a believer until God blinded him and threw him down off his horse. So I'm sorry, but whether you believe or not is beside the point."

Sarah said, "All that is true, but for the moment let's stay with the matter at hand. We had a disagreement, and so we gathered for a meeting."

"Just a minute," I interrupted. "Wouldn't it save a lot of time if you just told me what it is about me that led you to disagree?"

"You're trouble," Verla said suddenly, and darkly.

Well, that was direct enough! Somehow I knew she wasn't talking about extra work. It wasn't the long trek from the Big House to bring my meals that was bothering her or the other wives.

"I take it Mr. Pratt is not involved in these meetings," I said, just to be sure.

"Only us wives," Sarah confirmed. "He doesn't know it's how we keep peace among ourselves. We wait until a time when he's occupied somewhere else."

"We met while he was gone to fetch the doctor," Tabitha volunteered, "but we couldn't reach agreement. Then, after he got sick, we met again. He's too sick to leave his room, you see, so he couldn't know."

Norma's composure broke. "Oh, it's so awful!" she cried. "What if he dies?"

"Hush, Norma," Verla said harshly, "Father's not that sick, he ain't gonna die. He's got the quinsy, that's all. When the fever goes, it'll pass."

Sarah resumed: "This time we were again divided, but it was four to one. So we decided to go with the majority and tell you our decision. But then, before we could get on with it, Father called Verla in and said he wanted to see you."

"And so," I supplied, as I was beginning to understand what was going on, "like the obedient women you are, you all came along to fetch me to him. You were going to let his asking for me override your own wishes. Isn't that so?"

"Yes," said Verla, and the others echoed her, all the way down the line until it was Selene's turn. Selene said nothing, and then I knew she had been the dissenter. Whatever their decision had been—which they still hadn't told me but I thought I knew—Selene had been the one who stood alone when that final vote was taken.

"Yet," I said, "you can't help resenting me." That conflict was all over their faces; indeed it had permeated the very air of the room from the moment they walked in. I just hadn't been able to identify what it was before now.

Verla said stubbornly, "We obey him. It's our bounden duty."

Sarah folded her hands. "Nevertheless, *you* are not yet his wife, Carrie. If you were to, um, to make a decision all on your own—"

Again Selene cried out passionately: "But it wouldn't *be* all on her own, don't you see? And it's not what he wants, or what *I* want!" Tears rolled down her face.

I could not help myself. My arms opened out to Selene, it seemed of their own accord, and she came running to me, threw herself down on the floor beside me, and put her head in my lap, sobbing.

I stroked her hair while looking solemnly at the rest of them. I didn't know what I had expected, but not this. It had never even occurred to me that the wives would turn me out before I was physically ready and able to go. Oh, I was close to it, but not quite there yet; for every two steps forward, I usually had to go one step back. Sometimes literally.

"It's all right," I said, "I understand. You want me to leave. Selene was the only one who wanted me to stay."

"Norma too," said Tabitha, "the first time." She gave Norma a sideways glance. "I did think that was rather odd, since Norma's usually the one who . . . Oh, never mind."

I smiled. I knew why Norma had voted against their asking me to leave. She wanted the money I'd promised for her help. The deal was now moot, with them all wanting me out. Still, Norma hadn't told our secret, and for that I might give her the money anyway.

"I'm on your side," I said to the four wives, glancing rapidly down the line. I continued to stroke Selene's hair. "I can't think of anything I'd like better than to

leave here. I don't want to be the sixth wife of Melancthon Pratt."

"First!" said Selene, raising her tear-streaked face.
"You were to be made first."

"Shush," I said to her as with my fingertips I wiped
her cheek, "I don't want to be his first wife either. Verla
is first and she always will be."

"That's true enough," Verla said, nodding. "Bein'
the first one has its advantages, and it has its problems.
They balance out. Bein' first is no great thing."

"Speaking of problems," I said, "I don't get around
very well—"

"We'd made up our minds," Verla took over again,
"until Pratt asked for you."

"Forget that. Just tell me what you decided."

"It's best you go soon's possible. Since he's asked for
you, I'm thinkin' it had better be tonight. While he's
too sick to come after you. On account of you can be
sure he'll come after you."

Selene had stopped crying. She seemed resigned. Still
on her knees she turned around and faced the others.
"You realize you're all going to have to lie to Father. It
will break his heart when he finds out Carrie's gone,
especially now, when he's waiting right this minute for
her to come to him. You'll expect me to lie to him too. I
don't know if I can."

"I'll need your help," I said to the wives while at the
same time I gave Selene's bony young shoulder a hard
squeeze. I didn't want her to worry. I did want her to
tell whatever lies she had to tell. I was beginning to
have some ideas concerning Selene, but it would take a
while for them to come to fruition and now was no
time to deal with that. First things first. I added, "I can't
yet walk well enough to go on my own."

This was true, and had been a major cause of my
earlier pensiveness. If the Pratt women chose to drive

me out into the night, or dropped me on the side of the road, I probably wouldn't survive.

Norma spoke up—dear, acquisitive, materialistic Norma. "I'll take you. I'll drive you in the wagon along toward dark. We've decided on the best place for you to go."

———

Michael had things to do under the cover of night.

A train at night is peaceful. The rhythmic click of the wheels over the track, combined with the gentle sway of the railroad cars, acts like a mother's lullaby. The lighting is low, sounds are muted, only the conductors and a few nightowls walk from car to car.

Michael was a nightowl, and so was Hill Ramsey; but Ramsey wasn't bothering Michael anywhere near as much as the man he'd chased away from Meiling's compartment. That big fellow was an unknown quantity, and the evil you don't know is always more dangerous than the evil you do.

Somehow the worst thing was not having seen the large man again. Who was he? Where had he gone? How could he vanish? And above all, why the hell did he seem so familiar?

He could have gotten off the train, but Michael doubted it. Instead he'd be hiding out somewhere, watching and waiting for the right time, the right chance, to do . . . whatever dastardly deed he wanted to do.

"He's the one," Michael muttered aloud, "the one. I can feel it in my bones." That vague feeling of familiarity nagged and nagged at him. He'd walked up and down the train more than once during the day, looking for the culprit but not finding him, which was certainly irritating.

Now Michael sat alone in his own compartment. Meiling, presumably, was asleep in hers. The porter had turned the bench seat opposite into a bed for the night, had made it up with a blanket of soft, high-quality maroon wool and crisp, clean sheets that smelled of bleach and ironing. It would have been pleasant to have not a care in the world, to be able to lie between those sheets and let the train rock and lull him. . . .

But never again, not if he couldn't find Fremont. And if he couldn't find her, this would be his last train trip. He wouldn't get on a train again without her. He swore it to himself, then he promised Fremont in absentia, and just for good measure he made a pledge to his dead mother as well.

Restless as hell, Michael sat on the other side of his narrow compartment with his knees up against the bunk and waited for the right time to move.

He always knew when the time was right. Part of the knowing was instinct, and part was the years of experience. You couldn't go by a clock—which was why he liked to work alone. There was too much of doing things by the clock when you worked with a partner; nobody's fault, it just had to be that way.

The train would be pulling into Salt Lake City tomorrow morning. He had to get into the baggage car tonight. Their tickets—his and Meiling's—were for Chicago, and so their bags bore tags that said Chicago. But of course that was not where they were going; the tickets and baggage tags were meant to mislead.

Michael knew he and Meiling were on a hunt that might take the whole winter. He had intended to set up a headquarters in Provo and work from there, slowly fanning out farther and farther up into the mountains until he found Fremont Jones. Because it could take all winter—especially in the Wasatch, where they were likely to get snowed in—he and Meiling needed the contents of their bags. Not that it would cost too much in dollars to replace the things, but it would cost too much in time. It was imperative their baggage be put off the train at the same time the two of them got off. That would happen a few hours from now at Salt Lake City.

This was a problem. It had to be unobtrusively done. He'd already bribed a porter to put the bags off at Provo, but they were no longer getting off at Provo. Now he had either to find that same porter and pay him more to do it at Salt Lake instead, or to find the bags himself and retag them so that they'd be put off in Salt Lake City. If both those options failed, they'd simply have to abandon the bags.

Meiling had been in favor of abandoning them, even though she'd brought a trunk with enough clothes to dress a whole whorehouse. (Not, of course, that Meiling dressed like a whore—it was quantity, not quality, Michael had in mind.) She carried by hand a carpetbag that contained whatever it was she'd inherited from her grandmother, and she said nothing else was that important. Least of all, clothes.

But Michael had something special in one of his two big leather suitcases, something he wanted to give Fremont when he found her, something he'd had especially made up on a rush order when he was back in San Francisco because he knew it would mean as much to her as it did to him. . . .

He snapped off his light, which had been on low anyhow, and raised the window shade so that he could watch the blackness speed by. Nothing out there, nothing to see, nothing at all, which he found oddly comforting. The Void.

But that was an illusion. In reality there was no Void, but rather a darkness teeming with life unseen, with creatures who came out to feed in the night, to kill or be killed.

The wheels clicked; the carriage swayed; he fell asleep.

Michael dreamed that he was on a train, pursuing and being pursued. He ran through car after car after

car, pulling doors open, rushing into the connector area
between the cars, where he could see the railroad ties
rippling by under his feet and feel the wind of the
train's passing in his face, smell the acrid scent of the
coal smoke. Then onward to the next car, and on and
on, until he realized he'd lost sight of the man he was
pursuing . . . who was a big man with hair made of
burning ice, and no face . . . who was now behind
him, so the tables were turned. Michael was the one
being pursued.

The man with no face was getting too close. He
smelled like hellfire, like burning sulphur, in the Bible
called brimstone. Michael jumped off the train and was
running, flailing his legs through the air, falling—

He woke with a jolt, heart pounding, still half in the
dream and in the middle of that breath-stopping leap.
What had happened? What had awakened him?

First thought: someone outside the door.

Listen, listen, listen hard.

He didn't hear anyone—but then, he might not.

The train gave a lurch. After Michael's heart had
stopped and started again, he knew what had awakened him: They'd gone through one of those railroad
crossings where the train slows down but doesn't stop,
for taking on and putting off mail. It was the change in
the train's rhythm that had gotten him. In the dream
he'd converted that into his leap from the train.

"Ah," he said aloud, satisfied.

He took off his sling. He'd try not to move his arm
or the shoulder, but the sling was too confining for
what he might have to do in the course of this risk he'd
be taking. The worst that could happen to his shoulder
was he might rebreak his collarbone; but the overall
worst if Michael didn't have both hands to fight with
was . . . well, most simply put, he'd probably end up
dead.

He had already removed the dress shirt he'd worn to

dinner and replaced it with a black sweater. His suit was charcoal-gray, almost black. His shoes were black. His hair, except for the silver streaks, was black too and so was his beard—again except for the silver streaks. He would blend with the night. All except for the white skin of his face and hands.

The last thing Michael did before leaving his compartment was to tuck the revolver into his belt. Then he went out into the night world, Southern Pacific Railroad-style.

He neither saw nor heard the similarly black-clad figure that slipped from the shadows at the end of his corridor and followed him.

———

There are reasons why civilized people prefer to live in cities. Such as, when they wish to go somewhere they are not confronted with such outmoded means of transportation as the one facing me now.

"What is this thing?" I asked Norma, eyeing it dubiously.

"It's a buckboard."

"Oh. Regardless of what it's called, I don't think I'm going to be able to get up there." The buckboard was basically a wagon with a tall, high-backed seat and not much wagon bed to speak of behind. This conveyance looked as if it had been in Utah since the days when Brigham Young and the others came across the Mormon Trail from—what was that place called?—Nauvoo.

"Well, Carrie," Norma said impatiently, with one hand on her hip and the other one holding the mule's reigns—for this trip we didn't even rate a horse—"you'll just have to, now, won't you."

"Maybe not."

I swung myself on my crutches around to the back of the buckboard. The problem was, I could not put much weight on my legs and therefore could not climb up into that high seat. In any situation where I couldn't get the crutches under me, my only option was to use my arms and drag the rest of my body along behind.

As I'd hoped, the back panel of the buckboard swung down, giving access to its short flatbed. I said, "I can squeeze in back here."

Norma shrugged. "Suit yourself."

The other wives had already said goodbye to me, leaving me alone with Norma; she had brought the buckboard and mule around to the front of my cabin, which had the advantage, for our purposes, of facing away from the Big House.

I let down the panel, then pushed and pulled and rolled myself into the flat space of the wagon bed. But I'd had to let my crutches drop to do it. I waited to see what Norma would do. Damn, I hated to ask for her help!

There was no alternative, however. "Norma, I'm sorry, but you'll have to hand my crutches up here to me."

"Oh all right," she agreed ungraciously. When she'd handed them over, she slammed the panel shut.

"Thank you." I bit my tongue to keep from saying any more. I would have liked very much to ask why she'd agreed to drive me at all if she felt that way about it, but I didn't dare. I was presuming too much on her apparently sparse charity already.

Sarah had given me a little suitcase that contained my one and only dress which she or Tabitha had mended, plus a few more items of clothing the sisters had made for me out of the goodness of their hearts. I was wearing one of these, a nice, sturdy, plain dress of blue cotton flannel with a small white collar and buttons down the front. To keep me warm, for the nights were now very cold, I had an old cloak, probably of military origin, made of heavy, scratchy navy-blue wool. No hat. Not a single one. No purse. No means of identification, as none had been found with me and none provided since.

I am not at all fond of hats, but as I settled as best I could in the back of the buckboard, using the canvas suitcase as a buffer, I would gladly have taken the ugliest hat in the world if it would keep my ears warm.

Norma did not ask if I was ready. By the time I'd gotten as comfortable as it was possible to get, she had turned the wagon and was clucking to the mule. He was an ugly animal, sure-footed but powerfully slow.

This was going to be a long trip.

The sun was low in the sky as we left behind the little meadow where Melancthon Pratt's household nestled in isolation. Soon Norma had turned the buckboard onto what was a poor excuse for a road. I suppose the mountains were magnificent, if one has a fondness for mountains; I, however, am more enchanted by the ocean and watery views, which seldom—except in California—have mountains attached.

The buckboard did have some kind of spring mechanism that absorbed some of the bumps of the ride; at the same time it squeaked quite a lot. I had to raise my voice in order to speak to Norma. Reluctant though I was to try to engage her in conversation, I felt I must do so because I knew nothing about where we were, and somehow I had to survive. Starting out lost would put me at a major disadvantage.

"Norma," I called out, "what are these mountains called?"

"Wasatch," she replied.

I asked her to spell it, realizing too late that she might not know how. But she did, so that was not the problem it might have been. I breathed a sigh of relief and explained to her my need to know more of the geography, the names of things, where we were in relation to the towns I recalled the railroad line passed through.

She relented enough to tell me that the Pratt family's meadowland was called Hagar's Glen. She named Tabbyune Canyon as we crossed it, and then the patient mule began to pull our buckboard up higher and higher into the mountains. The Wasatch. I repeated the name to myself several times.

I have said I do not particularly like mountains, but really it is more than that. Mountains make me nervous somehow; I do not have the slightest idea why, and it is something I forget when I am not actually *in* some mountain range or other. As the sun went down, producing purple shadows all around, and the already brisk wind increased, my nerves went zinging along my arms and down my spine.

We kept going up and up, higher and higher, and this did not seem right to me. Provo, I remembered, was at the base of the mountains. We had gone through Provo and then the train had begun to climb. I recalled that distinctly. So if Norma was taking me to Provo, shouldn't we be going down?

I moistened my lips. Anxiety makes one's mouth dreadfully dry. "How many miles to Provo?" I called out.

Norma's reply floated back over her shoulder—she hadn't once bothered to turn her head. "I don't know in miles. In days, with this mule, it takes three."

She could hardly be taking me to Provo, then. I was dismayed. I had thought that was where we were going, because she had spoken of Provo as a place to shop, as if it were just down the road.

After a while the road entered a narrow defile, a natural passage through the rocky terrain. It was almost entirely dark now. I began to understand that Norma too must be nervous. She was going to some lengths to get rid of me, and she could not help but have an unpleasant trip back home in the dark after she'd left me off . . . wherever she chose to let me off.

The defile seemed to go on forever. "Where are we now?" I asked.

"Going through the summit. You don't get much of a view this way, it's prettier to go over the top, but this is faster."

"I see." I thanked Norma for the explanation, but she had not finished.

As she continued to speak, a bitter tone crept into Norma's voice: "Father knows all these cuts, long and short. He won't go over a mountain if he can go through it, no matter how narrow the path is or how much it twists and turns. Take the low road—that's what he always says. In fact, Carrie, that's how Father found you."

"What? You mean you don't believe that story about the angel?" At this particular moment, with walls of rock looming dark on either side, Norma's disbelief in angels was not the good news it otherwise might have been.

"Angel or no angel, that's as may be. All I'm saying is—and I'm not the only one says it, mind you, all us wives have talked about this amongst ourselves—if it wasn't for Father's insistence on always taking the low road, he likely wouldn't have been anywhere near the bottom of that canyon when your train wrecked. Which would've been too bad for you, of course, but it would have saved the rest of us a lot of trouble."

"Your point is well taken," I said, biting my lip. Her bitterness stung me to silence.

After what seemed an interminable time, from the left I heard sounds of rushing water. We were at last coming out of that passage through the rock, and all of a sudden there was quite an astonishing drop on the left side of the wagon. I closed my eyes. I know mules are the most sure-footed of creatures, and I know they

learn the ways of their beaten paths so well that this
mule most likely could find its way home alone if need
be.

Not much consolation, that. The Devil must have
put it in my head.

I decided to pray. I no longer cared exactly where I
was, or what names humans had attached to this rock
or that gorge or the other farmstead we passed by. I
only cared that Norma would not put me out on the
side of this mountain to die, that she would take me
instead to some safe, if temporary, haven.

My prayer was brief. After all, there was something
more practical I could do. When she reached a flat place
in the road and paused to light the oil lamps and set
them in place on either side of the buckboard, I seized
my chance.

"Would you rather I put that money in a bank for
you some place closer than Provo?" I asked. "I hadn't
realized Provo was quite so far away."

"Provo would be better. It's the only good place
around here to buy anything," Norma said. She looked
at me silently for a moment, and though it may have
been a trick of the lamplight, I thought I saw her expression soften.

"You would still do that for me?" she asked.

"Yes, of course I will," I assured her. "The circumstances have changed slightly, but you are still doing
what I asked you to do. You're helping me to get away.
A promise is a promise."

Norma clucked up the mule again and we lurched
onward.

After a couple of miles she said, "When do you suppose you can do it? By Christmas?"

"That depends on two things."

"What?"

"Today's date, and where you are taking me."

# 15

IT FELT GOOD to be doing something that would most likely have a positive outcome, even if that outcome was something so simple as getting his and Meiling's baggage off the train at the right stop.

Michael hadn't been able to find the porter he'd paid to put their things off at Provo—the man was probably tucked up behind some curtain somewhere sleeping, just as the whole train seemed to be behind doors or curtains sleeping—and although at first that had been bothersome, now he was glad. Glad because to be taking care of things himself felt far more rewarding.

That is, it would be once he found the damn bags.

He wasn't likely to find the bags unless he first found a lantern—the inside of the baggage car was black as Lucifer's heart, he couldn't see a blasted thing.

Michael stood to one side, still in the connecting area, and looked back the way he'd come. On some trains the baggage cars were attached at the rear, but not on this one. Here the baggage was stowed in the first two cars behind the locomotive and the coal tender. The sound of the great steam engine churned loud in his ears as he peered through the small rectangle of glass in the door of the passenger car through which he'd just come.

He didn't see anyone. Didn't sense any movement. He waited.

From time to time as he made his way cautiously from car to car, he had felt as if he were being followed. But it was probably only his imagination, only tension; every trick he knew to make a follower show himself had failed, and there weren't many people on the planet who could succeed at following Michael Archer Kossoff undetected.

Hill Ramsey, maybe. If Ramsey was back there, Michael wanted to lure him out.

That was why he'd looked into the baggage car, then ducked aside without entering and allowed the door to close by itself as if he'd gone on through. Now he waited patiently amid the roar of the engines and rushing air, counting the seconds as they passed by.

At one hundred and eighty—that is to say, three minutes—Michael was convinced he had not been followed after all. Through his nose he exhaled the breath he'd been holding in a bit of a snort just audible over the noise all around, rubbed his hands together, settled his jacket on his shoulders with a semi-shrug, and was ready to proceed.

He opened the baggage car door again, and this time he went in. He struck a match, a tiny orange flare in the murky black, which settled to a small but steady glow. Then he looked around: no lantern hanging up beside the door, curse it.

Three matches later, he spied a lantern where some lazy railroad employee had left it, on top of a trunk a third of the way into the car. He squeezed down a narrow aisle that had been left to provide room for shifting bags and trunks around, grabbed the lamp, and lit it with another match.

Ah, that was better.

Or was it?

The lamplight cast Michael's shadow up behind him in a monstrous distortion. He moved; this monster moved. It was eerie and distracting. His own shape kept drawing his eye away from the task at hand, which was to find one particular upright steamer trunk and two large leather suitcases—the latter of reasonably handsome quality and appearance, if somewhat scarred from frequent use.

Some time later, Michael realized he would have to move on through this car and into the next. The stacks of suitcases and rows of trunks were arranged, front to back, in the order they were expected to be unloaded. In this car, therefore, all the tags were labeled with the names of towns west of the Mississippi. A few Salt Lakes, a couple of Provos, and then towns with names like Grand Junction, Carbondale, Denver, Lincoln, and plenty of others he'd never heard of. Not a single damn Chicago in this whole damn car.

The train lurched and some of the bags shifted, but nothing fell.

What was that all about? He was instantly hyperalert.

It was probably nothing, some inconsequential hitch, which at any rate was not repeated as the train continued on.

Michael had slipped a bit before regaining his footing. Now he noticed the lantern teetering close to the edge of the stacked suitcases where he'd put it down. Just as he put out a hand to steady it, one particular shadow caught his eye.

Michael made a sound low and deep in his throat, an involuntary growl. That shadow had moved, he was certain of it.

With infinite slowness he crept in the moving shadow's direction, silently as a stalking cat. Yet when he got where it had been, there was nothing there. Nothing but a black gap between two trunks, just large enough for a man to hide.

Challenge, or keep silent?

It was six of one and half a dozen of the other. Michael shrugged as elaborately as he could with only one good shoulder, intending anyone who might be watching him to think he thought he'd been mistaken. And maybe he had.

*Time's wasting,* he thought.

He went back to where he'd left the lantern and moved on up to the front baggage car. As he passed from one car to the next, the train sounded its whistle through the night; he'd become so accustomed to its intermittent, lonely wail that for the most part he didn't consciously hear it anymore.

Not good, not good at all.

Michael shook his head as he entered a second car full of trunks and suitcases and valises and boxes and bags, all shapes and sizes, not arranged in any particular order that he could see, except he felt certain most of them were destined for Chicago.

While scanning rapidly in search of his own bags, which he was sure he would recognize, he wondered how many things he might have missed during the last couple of days simply because he'd become so used to them that he wasn't seeing them. Like the train whistle he didn't hear.

In his business he couldn't afford to do that, not ever.

Michael left off lecturing himself a few moments later, when he found what he'd been looking for. He began shifting things around in order to make a path for himself; he would have to take their three items back to the other car, where the pieces labeled for Salt

Lake City were stored. His suitcases were one thing, but Meiling's trunk was going to be a problem.

Not to mention that some poor person was going to end up waiting on the platform at Salt Lake with no luggage because Michael had stolen his tags, and as of this moment was busily relabeling them with his own name in black grease pencil.

*Click.*

Michael's head snapped up. This close to the locomotive engine it was hard to hear small, discrete sounds, but he'd heard that one: the distinctive click of the railroad car's door latch disengaging. He was ready, he'd been expecting this. The moving shadow had been not just a shadow but a person, and that person had followed him.

He set the lantern on the floor for greatest stability. The last thing he wanted was for it to be knocked over in the fight that was going to be taking place at any moment. The safest thing to do would be to put it out—that way he'd know it couldn't cause a fire. But then he'd have to fight in the dark, and he wouldn't be able to see the face of his assailant. He couldn't have that. He had to know who it was. Who was good enough to have stayed on his tail undetected all this time.

When things started to happen they happened fast and furiously, just a few too many yards away, in the midst of too many shadows cast by that lamp on the floor. Michael could not see clearly.

Initially he didn't understand. He was disoriented and confused. He had expected to be attacked, but he was not attacked; it was something else entirely, something totally unexpected.

A rushing, whirling black thing flew into the railroad car, spinning and turning so quickly he couldn't tell if it was human or animal. There were thumps and crashes, blurs of motion, a guttural swear word he couldn't make out, followed by the unearthly howl of someone in a lot of pain . . . and then silence.

Through all this Michael Kossoff stood untouched.

Shockingly still.

Unmoving but not unmoved.

Then the black figure appeared in the narrow space Michael had cleared; tall, long-limbed, and strange, it came walking toward him. Was there something familiar in that walk?

No, not really, but—

But he had seen another figure dressed in black like this, not exactly but very much like this, a couple of years before. And in Japan, even before that. Ninja. All in black: body, feet, hands, black silk scarf wound round the face and neck, everything covered but the eyes . . . and even those eyes were black. They shone in the lamplight like obsidian.

The figure reached up and loosed the scarf at the back of its head, slowly unwrapped the black silk, and let it fall.

Michael said, "Meiling."

She bowed, unsmiling. "I most humbly beg your pardon. Without your knowledge or permission I have been your shadow tonight. I have done this so that there will be no more foolish questioning of my ability in this regard."

Michael was still too stunned to know what to say, so he did not say anything. Meiling? Meiling had done what so few could?

"I have incapacitated the miscreant. For the moment he is in too much pain to move. But I suggest if you wish to question him, it should be done right away."

————

I knew all too well what money of her own would mean to Norma and I thanked God for having the means to offer that enticement, as without it I very much feared she would have dropped me in the middle of the street. This poor excuse for a town was called Hiram, and it was about as attractive as its name.

Instead of dropping me in the street Norma had done only somewhat better: She left me on a wooden board sidewalk, in the approximate vicinity of a couple of establishments from whose doorways light shone. All the other buildings on the main street were dark, shut down for the night.

I stood there trembling inside, feeling the perilous effect of the same state that had made Norma vulnerable to my wiles: I had no money, none except a treasure given to me by Selene, and I was completely determined not to spend that unless my life depended on it.

I had no money because Melancthon Pratt did not hold with giving money to his wives. Not even to Verla, who as first wife was charged with the overall running of his household. He doled out money as it was needed, to the person who needed it, in the exact quantity required, and he asked for a strict accounting. Therefore the wives had been unable to lend me even so much as the price of one night's lodging in this one-horse town.

If need were dire I could spend Selene's five-dollar gold piece, which she had pressed into my hand when she'd kissed me goodbye. She had won this gold piece by taking first prize in an essay contest upon some esoteric Mormon subject when she was thirteen, and had showed it to me some weeks earlier. I did not want to take it, but there had been no way to make her take it back without calling attention to the fact that she had given it to me, which did not seem a very good idea.

I did not want to spend Selene's gold piece; indeed I was determined to go to great lengths to avoid it. I intended to see her again when all was said and done, with this adventure behind me, when my body had completely healed and I could be reasonably sure my mind was clear.

A child-woman: That was how I thought of Selene. In some touching ways she reminded me of myself at her age, though our circumstances were entirely different. We had become close in my last few days at Pratt's house. I knew she had not wanted me to leave, because I'd provided her with a glimpse of a world that was so much bigger than any she'd ever known, and now she was hungry for it. The more I'd told her, the more she'd wanted to know. My leaving had been like turning out a light, or closing a door.

In a sense I suppose I had corrupted Selene. Perhaps I had done that with all of them. "Trouble," Verla had called me in her flat, direct way. To those wives I'd been like the snake in the Garden of Eden, saying, *Eat of the fruit of the Tree of Knowledge.*

"Oh, for heaven's sake, stop it," I muttered to myself. There was no sense making myself feel guilty. What was more, I couldn't stand there paralyzed on the sidewalk forever.

Yet a large part of my mind was still back there at Pratt's. I wasn't used to being out in the world again. By listening hard I could still hear the creak and rattle of the buckboard on its way out of town, and a part of me wanted to run after Norma and beg her to take me back "home." But that was a very small, sick-in-the-head part of me, and I knew it. Thank God.

Resolving to think no more thoughts of that nature, I squared my shoulders, settled the crutches more firmly beneath my armpits, and turned toward the two establishments from which light flowed. One was a drinking establishment to judge by the sounds and smells emanating from within; the other had a sign over the door proclaiming HIRAM'S FINEST HOTEL.

The saloon was tempting, though of course I

couldn't go in there. I would have liked a drink; brandy would have gone down quite well with me right then. But I behaved myself—greatly aided in this enterprise by the lack of any money except Selene's gold piece, which I certainly could not put to such use as buying myself strong liquor.

Leaving my bag on the sidewalk, for I had no way to carry it, I made my laborious, halting way into Hiram's Finest.

If this was the finest Hiram had to offer, the town was (as Mother used to say) in a peck of trouble. The door hung crookedly on its hinges and so neither opened nor closed properly; the carpet, which had once been a burgundy color, had worn to a rather putrid shade of puce and was threadbare where the traffic had been heaviest; the lighting was dim, and to judge by the unpleasant odor that permeated the lobby, came from kerosene lamps.

The old fellow behind the desk didn't care about any of this, though; he'd tipped his chair onto its back legs so that he could rest his head against the wall, and was asleep. Or drunk.

"Excuse me," I said; then more loudly, "Sir? Excuse me!"

"Whazzat?" He opened one eye, which did not happen to be aimed in my direction. "What's your excuse?"

"Sir!" I said sharply, to get his attention.

"Sir who? Where? Where is he?"

Wham! The old man's chair crashed back down onto all four legs with a jolt that made both his eyes fly open —and probably cleared his sinuses as well.

"I'd like a room," I said, after pausing for the dust to settle, "just for the night."

He looked at me finally, and as some comprehension seemed to register in his eyes I went on: "I had to leave

my small canvas bag out on the sidewalk. As you see,
I'm—er—at something of a physical disadvantage."

"You're messed up, that's for certain." He squinted,
then fumbled inside the sheepskin-lined jacket he wore
until he found a pair of spectacles and put them on. It
was cold outside but warm in the hotel—he must have
had poor circulation to wear that jacket inside. In just
the short time I'd been standing there I'd begun to
sweat beneath the old military cape I wore.

"So what happened to you, then?"

"I was injured in that train wreck, the one that happened about a month and a half ago. Please, if you
could get my bag before something happens to it, I'd be
grateful. Or is there someone you could send?"

He snorted. "Not hardly. No need to fret—what can
happen to it? Nobody in this town's gonna be after
some woman's little bag o' goods this time of night. Got
better things t'do."

"Still, I'd be so grateful. I'd make it worth your
while—"

I'd said the magic words, and off he went. He got
around well enough once he put his mind to it. Old he
might be, but he was much more spry than I.

There was a spindle-back deacon's bench against the
wall, a rather nice piece of furniture actually, if you like
your furniture plain and uncushioned. After all that
time in the buckboard I would have preferred a cushion, but never mind. I sat down and had just propped
my crutches against the wall and was removing my cape
when the man returned with my pitifully small canvas
bag.

"Don't see as how you had much to worry about,"
he said, dropping the bag by my feet.

Then he noticed my feet, which I had foolishly failed
to tuck beneath my long skirts.

"I lost my shoes in the train wreck," I said. I wasn't
going to explain to him that I have long, narrow feet, so

much longer than the feet of any of Pratt's wives that shoes were the one item of clothing they could not share with me. Tabitha had crocheted me some slippers that looked a good deal like those booties they make for babies. Only much larger, of course.

"Train wreck. That weren't no wreck, that were an explosion. Somebody blew the blame thing up. What else you lose?" he asked suspiciously.

"Nothing that can't be replaced," I said evenly, looking the old codger straight in the eye, "as soon as I can get in touch with my bank in San Francisco. If there's a telegraph in town, that can be done tomorrow."

More magic words: "bank in San Francisco."

"We got a telegraph. We even got our own bank. This ain't no ghost town, no siree."

"Then I believe we can do business," I said, as if I had been interviewing him as to the suitableness of his establishment, whereas in fact I'd been praying he would register me without asking payment in advance.

"I reckon. You all on your own, then?"

"Yes." I offered no explanation, and wonder of wonders he accepted that.

I signed my real name in the register: C. Fremont Jones. Oh, what a relief it was to have my name back! No more Carrie James!

I felt like celebrating but my joy was short-lived.

My new friend the desk clerk, who'd told me his name was Tom, stood scratching his grizzled head at the bottom of the stairs. He looked at me, sitting on the bench nearby. He had brought the register to me to sign, rather than asking me to walk over to the desk, for which I was grateful.

Now Tom looked from me to the stairs and back again. "What we gonna do about them stairs?" he asked.

What indeed? My heart fell as I saw his point. I said, "Three's my limit. Oh dear."

"Never you mind. Where there's a will there's a way, and I just thoughta one, if'n you're not too fussy."

"I'm not." At least, I didn't think I was, but this was no time for qualifiers.

Tom raised his voice and bellowed, "Sandra! Getcherself out here!"

# 16

SANDRA HUNTER'S ROOM smelled of male musk and cheap perfume, but it was paradise to me. Freedom! A roof over my head, and my time was my own to do with as I liked. This was wonderful indeed.

Sandra was Hiram's freelance prostitute; in other words, she worked for herself (a woman after my own heart), whereas the other ladies of the evening were employed by a madam in a house devoted to that purpose up the street. Sandra didn't mind at all taking the room I would be paying for upstairs in the hotel and letting me use hers instead; nor, in fact, did her current customer seem to mind helping her move the clothes and toiletries that were her only possessions. The point of all this was that I could not climb a whole flight of stairs, and her room was the only one besides the dining room, kitchen, and pantry that was located on the ground floor. So she swapped with me.

I thanked Tom profusely for coming up with this suggestion, and Sandra and her friend—er, customer—

for their willingness to implement it. Then I closed the
door and was truly, completely alone for the first time
in a very, very long time.

Alone and on my own, definitely my most preferred
state.

That is, if I could not be with Michael.

I sighed. I wasn't ready to think about Michael yet;
indeed I was almost afraid to do so. For so many weeks
I'd kept a door in my mind firmly shut on that subject,
and I wasn't ready to open it yet. I would; I would do it
this very evening; but I needed to ease into it.

First, there were bits of housekeeping to do—those
routine, seemingly inconsequential little things are what
keep one sane—or so I had found since having my
whole life turned upside down. I pulled back the color-
ful quilt, which the obliging Sandra Hunter had
quaintly called a counterpane, to make sure the sheets
were indeed as clean as she'd claimed; they were.

I opened a window to air out the room. As pleasant
a person as Sandra had seemed to be, I did not care
overmuch for her choice of scent, nor did I really like
smelling any male's musk except Michael's.

Oh dear, there he was again. He kept popping into
my mind. I seemed to have left my self-discipline back
at Pratt's.

To work: The inside of the chest of drawers also
smelled like Sandra's perfume, so instead of putting my
few things away immediately, I pulled all the drawers
open and left them that way to air. Meanwhile, I spread
my few possessions upon the counterpane and thought
about when my money would come, how I should go
shopping, and what I should buy first. Shoes, most definitely; for though I could not put my weight full upon
them yet, my legs were getting stronger day by day. And
there was nothing wrong with my feet. Good, sturdy
shoes could only aid my progress.

I hung up my cape on a wall peg, hobbled over to the

open window, and breathed deeply of the cool night air. But what was that?

For just a moment I thought I'd seen movement out there in the dark. Awkwardly, with the crutches digging into my underarms, I bent down so that I could see better. It was black as pitch out there, particularly in contrast to the brightly burning oil lamp on top of the chest of drawers. This room, being next to the pantry, most likely overlooked a service alley. In the daytime I'd be able to see, but right now the effort was hopeless.

Still I stood there, crouched, riveted, as if I were once again an investigator on a case. An enormous ache grew heavy in me, a longing for all I had lost, a painful desire to have again all that had been ripped from me in that explosion. And then, an instant later, I straightened up and laughed until tears came to my eyes. A black kitten had jumped up onto my windowsill and stood there arching its back.

"So," I said when I'd regained my ability to speak, "you are the dark disturber!"

The kitten came into the room and watched with interest while I used the basin and pitcher of water from the washstand to wash my face and hands. Too late I realized there were no clean towels, and so I dried them on my skirt. Then leaving the kitten to guard my domain, I ventured out of the room in search of towels, a newspaper, some notepaper, a pen or pencil, and food. I was very, very hungry.

I soon learned why old Tom hadn't hesitated to register me in spite of my inability to pay in advance: I was the only guest. The cook had gone home early for lack of custom in the dining room. But Tom had no objections to going next door to the saloon to get me a sandwich, particularly when I suggested that he tell them to start a tab for me and to put a drink for himself on it while he was waiting for the sandwich to be made.

Oh, how good it felt to be taking care of myself again!

While Tom was next door, I ventured behind his desk and found the other things I needed, including a discarded newspaper in a wastebasket. Immediately I checked the banner at the top of the front page for the date: Tuesday, November 17, 1908. So now I knew the date of my liberation from Melancthon Pratt. A date to be enshrined in my memory, that was for certain.

I trusted I would stay free, that he would never find me here.

At any rate, surely I would not have to remain long in this place—although it did have one great advantage: Hiram was not a Mormon town. That was why the wives had decided Norma should bring me here—it was not a place Pratt or any of his followers ever had reason to go.

If I'd thought about it, I'd have known Hiram wasn't Mormon even without Norma's telling me when we got to the town limits that this was where they'd decided to drop me off, and why. How would I have known? Mormons are opposed to drinking strong spirits, including coffee, yet here was a saloon doing a lot of rowdy business right on the main street. Also, I would have been extremely surprised had any Mormon town tolerated a house of ill repute right in the center of it, as Sandra Hunter assured me was the case just down Hiram's main street.

Surely the wives would not tell Pratt where I was. The story they'd all agreed upon in the end, Selene included, was that on this particular day I had simply vanished without a trace. Verla was to tell him: She'd gone to my room when he asked for me, only to find I was not there.

The angel giveth, the angel taketh away.

I felt safe.

A foolish feeling perhaps, but understandable in the circumstances.

Freedom can go to a girl's head; it had happened to me before.

———

Meiling was looking a good deal less dangerous when they got off the train in Salt Lake City. She was a bit overdressed, perhaps, as befitted her play-acting the role of Michael's concubine, but nobody would have guessed in a million years what she'd done to that unfortunate man in the baggage car. If the fellow could recover enough to father a child in this decade, Michael would be surprised. Not to mention that she'd dislocated his left elbow.

The lovely erstwhile Ninja was nonetheless dissatisfied. Her efforts had not come to much, because she'd brought down a nobody, an impromptu hireling who when questioned confessed he knew nothing about the man who'd hired him except that he was big, gray-haired, had plenty of money and a seat in the coach class.

She was still apologizing; Michael wished she'd stop. "It is my fault," she said for the third or fourth time, he'd lost count. "If I had not hurt him quite so much, he could have gone back to the one who paid him, and we would know now who this man is who lurks outside doors and means you harm."

"Forget it, Meiling."

"He was not even intending to attack you, he was only going to watch. I should not have harmed him."

"My dear Meiling," Michael said, stopping in his tracks, "I am not going to tell you I wish you hadn't done your best to protect me, because it wouldn't be true. I'm going to thank you again: Thank you. Now stop finding fault with yourself and let that be an end to it."

"You don't understand. I did not act *defensively,* I was the *aggressor.* That is against my philosophy!"

"It's the way of the world, Meiling," he said grimly, moving on. "Eat them before they eat you. That's *my* philosophy. It's much more practical."

"Oh, so now you are a cannibal?"

"A cannibal?" Michael raised his dark eyebrows, glanced over at her—he and Meiling were almost of a height—and caught her swift little smile.

"Oh, I see," he said. "It's a joke."

"I very much hope so, yes."

Michael chuckled. "You did make quite an impression on me, you know."

She inclined her head slightly. "Which was also my intent."

"All right, since you've made such an impression on me, there's something else you can do."

"What?" she asked.

Michael placed his fingers under one of Meiling's elbows and gently guided her into the train station's restaurant, which had big glass windows framed by wide arches. He said, "Sit here while I go to find a livery stable where I can hire us a horse and buggy. You know what Hilliard Ramsey looks like?"

Meiling nodded: Yes.

"Watch for him, see if he passes by. I want to know if he gets off the train at this stop. I don't think he saw us leave, and he could not possibly have known ahead of time, but Ramsey's good. As much as I'd like to think we've thrown him off our trail, we probably haven't."

"Very well."

"Oh, and while you're watching, you might as well keep your eyes peeled for this big man with the gray hair."

Meiling nodded and said emphatically, "If I see the big one, I will follow him."

"No, don't do that!"

"Yes. We will want to know where he goes, what is his name, all of these things."

"Meiling, in that dress you're about as unobtrusive as, as—"

"Never mind. I will be careful. I do not like to dress like this anyway; if this man sees me, I will change my appearance at the first opportunity. If you come back here and I am not here, do not worry, Michael, for that will be where I have gone. Stay here and wait for me."

He rolled his eyes but gave up and settled her in the restaurant, in a window seat with a fine view of the railroad promenade. He kissed her cheek, both because he was fond of her and because he was playing the role of jealous lover—a man who would not allow anyone else within whispering distance of his woman, one for whom a woman such as Meiling was private property. Then off he went in search of a livery stable.

Out on the street Michael picked up a newspaper and glanced at the date in passing: November 17, 1908. Tuesday.

———

I was not a banker's daughter for nothing.

I proved it the next day, Wednesday morning. When the County National Bank of Hiram opened at nine o'clock, I was there. By nine-thirty a telegram was on its way to the Crocker Bank in San Francisco, my bank. The story I'd told the bank manager—a careful mixture of truth and fiction that I'd written out the night before and memorized—had been sufficiently credible that I left with a cash advance of one hundred dollars in my possession.

I returned to my room at the hotel to write out more telegrams. Shortly I would carry them up the street to the telegraph office and have them sent, now that I had the means to pay. (The bank, of course, had sent their own telegram—just as I'd expected them to.)

The kitten had taken up residence, it seemed, as he or she was there waiting when I returned. I had no objection, although I knew nothing whatever about animals because we did not have pets in the house when I was growing up. I had left the window open a bit for ventilation, and that was enough of an invitation for this little cat.

The cat was playful. He pounced repeatedly on the moving end of my pencil as I wrote out my telegrams, until I became exasperated, scooped him up, and placed him in my lap, where he turned around a few times as if making a nest, then lay down and began to purr. Thus with a warm, furry, vibrating ball in my lap I wrote:

TO MICHAEL KOSSOFF
J&K AGENCY
DIVISADERO STREET
SAN FRANCISCO CALIFORNIA

DEAR MICHAEL
SURVIVED TRAIN WRECK STOP HAVE BEEN UNABLE TO
WRITE UNTIL NOW STOP AM IN HIRAM UTAH STAYING AT
HIRAM HOTEL STOP HAVE TWO BROKEN LEGS NOW
HEALING STOP CAN YOU COME FOR ME STOP
LOVE FREMONT JONES

I should have liked to be able to say more, such as how to get to Hiram, Utah, but I could not because I did not know exactly where it was. I'd have to trust that Michael would find out. That is, if this telegram reached him at all.

I wrote the second one:

TO ALOYSIUS AND/OR EDNA STEPHENSON
J&K AGENCY

DIVISADERO STREET
SAN FRANCISCO CALIFORNIA

DEAR WISH AND EDNA
HAVE SENT MESSAGE TO MICHAEL STOP IF HE IS NOT
THERE PLEASE ADVISE HIS WHEREABOUTS STOP HAVE
SURVIVED TRAIN WRECK STOP NEED HELP TO GET HOME
STOP WRITE OR WIRE TO ME AT HIRAM HOTEL IN HIRAM
UTAH STOP
LOVE FREMONT JONES

I read it over. Absently I stroked the purring cat, drawing considerable comfort from the soft fur, the simple, undemanding presence of another living creature. I supposed that was the attraction of having a pet; I'd really never thought about it before.

Then I composed my final telegram:

TO LEONARD PEMBROKE JONES
BEACON STREET
BOSTON MASSACHUSETTS

DEAR FATHER
AM WELL THOUGH HAVE TWO BROKEN LEGS NOW
HEALING STOP HAVE BEEN UNABLE TO COMMUNICATE
UNTIL NOW STOP DO NOT WORRY STOP WILL RETURN TO
SF SOONEST STOP COMING TO BOSTON WHEN LEGS
ALLOW STOP
YOUR LOVING DAUGHTER CAROLINE FREMONT JONES

There. I felt a tremendous sense of relief to have written those telegrams, and would feel even better, I was sure, when they were sent.

Although I was quite tired, for I had not had so much exercise in many weeks, I put the cat down, donned the military cloak, put money and the folded papers into its inner pocket, and made my awkward way down the wooden sidewalk to the telegraph office.

The telegrapher wore his name on a badge attached to his shirt: WAYNE.

"Hello, Wayne," I said with a smile. I was glad to be able to call him by name, since he was about to play such a significant part in my life: This smiling, innocent-faced young man was going to put me back in touch with the people nearest and dearest to me.

"Hello, ma'am, Miss Jones," he said, nodding his head in an extra greeting.

"You know my name?"

"Oh yes, ma'am, you're the one survived that turr'ble train blowup. Reckon you're the one they said was 'unaccounted for.' Meaning they couldn't find your body. Counted over and over, they did, always came out one missing. That was you."

All of a sudden I felt chilled to the bone. I had known, of course, that some people had probably died. Certainly I'd come close enough to it myself. But it was not something I ever allowed myself to think about.

Wayne was continuing to talk: "Ever'body here in Hiram's glad to have you here with us, an' real proud too. Glad you got your memory back and all. So what can I do for you this morning? You got some telegrams to send?"

I handed over my telegrams. Made small talk. Paid what I owed the man, and thanked him when he assured me he would bring the replies to me personally at the hotel just as soon as they came through.

Then I went back and lay down on my bed with one arm thrown across my eyes.

The little cat came and licked my cheeks where the tears leaked out. Finally I had let the horrible thought come and stay in my mind: What if Michael was among the dead?

# 17

TAKES ONE pretty hard day, two easy ones, to Provo by horse from here," the stabler said. "You got a wagon 'r a buggy with two people and a heavy load, most likely you should be thinking two. So what you got in mind, mister?"

"I have in mind," Michael said, trying to forestall a major attack of ill temper, "renting your largest and most comfortable rig. I shall require it for at least a month, maybe two."

The stabler gave a long low whistle, shaking his head. "Don't know as I can do that. I mean, there's others as might like to use it from time to time. That's a long while to do without the best I've got. Know what I mean?"

Michael knew. He was in no mood to bargain. "I'm short on time, I need to get going, so I'll tell you what. You name your price and I'll pay it. Not only that, I'll return your rig in the same shape as when I got it from you, or better, or else I'll pay to buy you a new one. Now what do you say?"

"Can't say fairer 'n that, I reckon."

*Thank God.* Michael had begun to think this was going to be one of those situations in which one obstacle is overcome, only to have another take its place, and on and on and on in that fashion unto infinity.

"Getting morbid," he muttered, following the man deep into the stables where the better rigs were kept.

"Say what?" the stabler asked over his shoulder.

"Nothing."

The stables smelled of hay and horses and freshly polished leather. Michael found this old-fashioned, masculine combination of odors bracing. Encouraging, somehow. Though, truth to tell, he would have preferred an automobile.

No such luck. The roads out here weren't good enough. Maybe someday . . .

"This here's a surrey," the stabler said, "best I've got."

Michael shook his head. The carriage was handsome and well sprung, but it was too fragile for what he'd likely be putting it through.

"I'll need something heavier," he insisted. "I said I wanted your largest and most comfortable rig, not the fanciest."

In the end he had to settle for a covered farm wagon; what the conveyance lacked in elegance was made up for by the horse, an exceptional animal of large size that gave an impression of strength, along with a sympathetic eye. The horse's name, the stabler told him, was Chess—not for the game but from "chestnut" for his reddish brown hair.

*Much like Fremont's,* Michael thought, though hers was a bit darker. Maybe having a horse with reddish brown hair was a good omen. He hoped so. He could use a good omen right about now.

Anxious to be on his way, wondering if he'd find Meiling in the coffee shop—though he supposed the

Mormons would call it something else, because wasn't it true that Mormons didn't drink caffeine?—Michael scarcely paid attention while the stabler went over the somewhat detailed procedure of getting the horse into harness, then the harness hooked up to the wagon. All he wanted was to be off.

Meiling was not where he'd left her. He'd been afraid of that, and didn't know whether to hope she was off on a wild-goose chase or hot on the trail of the elusive big man. He decided to worry about her later. Right now there were other things he could be doing.

Michael took the wagon around to the baggage end of the passenger platform, where he'd left Meiling's trunk and his two leather suitcases. He got them loaded into the back of the wagon with the help, well compensated by a generous tip, of one of the redcaps who were standing around waiting for the next train to come in.

So far, so good. But when he returned to the café, whatever it was called, there was still no Meiling.

"Wait for me if I'm not here," she'd said, but Michael was no better at waiting than Fremont would have been in similar circumstances.

Fremont never liked to wait for anything or anyone. It was one of her worst faults, and would sometimes cause her to do things precipitously.

"I have to stop thinking about her," Michael muttered to himself; but even as he said it, he decided to do the very thing she would have done: drive around and look for Meiling.

The worst that could happen would be that he didn't find her, but even so he would have had a fine view of Salt Lake, which was a beautiful city of wide, clean streets with that huge, slightly mysterious Temple of the Mormons in the middle of it all.

There was just one flaw in this logic, Michael thought as he struggled to keep the horse going where he wanted him to go (Michael was a bit out of practice on the reins): Anybody worth following wouldn't likely stick to wide, clean main streets.

So much for sight-seeing and finding Meiling at the same time.

He went back to the train station after all, tied the horse and wagon to a hitching post in an area that also had slots for automobiles, and was on his way back to the café when something caught his eye. Off to his left: the freightyard. A glint of sun off metal. Down a dark sort of alleyway, not a street but merely a passage left between tall stacks of various goods awaiting pickup. These Mormons were apparently a prosperous lot, with plenty of commerce going on.

On a hunch, Michael entered the passage. He didn't take the time to examine the boxes piled up on either side; the boxes weren't what was important. Not *what,* but *who*—who was in here—that was important. And *why* was he here. And was *she* in here too; if Michael was getting to know this new Meiling at all (or had she always been this way?), the answer to the last was probably yes.

The early morning air was so cold he could see his breath. The sunlight had a wintry quality, as if its beams were too thin to penetrate the freightyard's somehow denser atmosphere. This was a good place for someone to hide—the deeper in Michael went, the more he realized that.

It was also a good place to get lost, because after a while it all looked the same: dark, gloomy, crowded, confusing. Michael began to feel as if he'd been in this place before, yet he knew he had not. Only in maybe a hundred similar places . . . much too similar.

The hollow sound of footsteps, not his own. He stopped and stood quietly, listening hard, inwardly cursing his relatively poor hearing. Where? Maybe a couple of rows over that way . . .

The rustle of a skirt: Meiling. He was sure he'd heard

it. Maybe his ears were getting better after all. Practice, practice, never give up. . . .

Michael had been walking backward, not quickly, inches at a time, but not looking behind himself either. Too late he realized his mistake.

Suddenly there he was—he'd backed into an open space that, when he spun around, proved to be rectangular, maybe twenty feet long, twelve feet wide. He was vulnerable, an easy target. His hand went to his gun, the revolver in his waistband.

But he didn't yet have it securely in hand, when a shot rang out over his head. Followed by a second shot, the bullet passing so close by Michael's ear that he felt its faint, deathly chilling breeze.

Then a voice from somewhere behind him, a low rasp just above a whisper, in the accent of an English public school: "God's teeth, Kossoff, get down! I'm trying to save your arse here!"

———

TO FREMONT JONES
HIRAM HOTEL
HIRAM UTAH

DEAR FREMONT
MICHAEL GONE LOOKING FOR YOU STOP WE WILL TRY
CONTACT HIM STOP STAY WHERE YOU ARE TILL FURTHER
NOTICE STOP SO GLAD YOU ARE ALL RIGHT STOP
MOTHER SENDS LOVE STOP ME TOO STOP
YOURS WISH

———

I read this blessed telegram over at least ten times. Then, in a silly sentimental fit, I clasped it to my bosom.

"Michael gone looking for you." That was what it said. He was alive. He couldn't have gone looking for me if he weren't alive. And he was well, for that same reason.

My Michael was alive and well!

In an excess of elation I hugged the black kitten, thereby discovering that little cats do not take very well to hugging. This little cat, in fact, did not take very well to anything that was not its idea in the first place. I found this a fascinating trait.

As I left my room to go shopping for some real shoes, I made a mental note to ask Sandra if her cat was supposed to be allowed inside, and what she fed it, and how often. And what was the sweet creature's name.

"I'll be back," I said absurdly from the doorway. Yet it was nice and felt good to have someone to tell.

———

So Hilliard Ramsey was trying to save Michael's ass? That was a switch.

Ramsey had grabbed him and pulled him back between a couple of large packing crates that made good cover.

"Who're you shooting at?" Michael whispered. "Be careful, Meiling is out there."

"I know, believe me. I mean, I know about the lovely Meiling. She and I have both been following this bloke who's been on your tail for days now."

"Hmm," Michael said.

"Who is he? What's he after you for?"

"I don't know. Why are you following him, and me?" Michael shot back, glaring.

"I'm being paid by some people who are more your sort than mine," said Ramsey. "I can't tell you more than that."

Another shot whizzed over their heads.

"But I'm not sure they're paying me enough for all this," he added.

Michael ducked. "My sort, meaning what?"

"Russians, old boy. Disgustingly rich, of course."

"Hmm," Michael said again. It was as he'd surmised, but there was no more time to think about it now. The shooter might have heard their whispers. They must move.

But move where? The shots were coming at them from the other side of that rectangle of empty space. It was like a no-man's-land.

Michael still hadn't aimed his gun. He was afraid he'd hit Meiling, because as far as he could tell, Ramsey couldn't be shooting at anything but shadows.

Another shot rang out, and this time he and Ramsey both returned fire, aiming blind in the direction from which the shot had come. Michael flinched as he realized what he'd done; his response had been automatic —some spot in his brain had calculated the information and fired the gun before his will had a chance to engage and stop it.

*This,* Michael thought, *is how a lot of tragedies occur. That's the problem with firearms, they work too damn well.*

In such a confined space all this concussion was damned hard on the eardrums. No wonder his hearing was not what it used to be—too many nights and days like this one, too much noise assaulting delicate membranes; it was bound to wear them out after a while.

From across the no-man's-land there was a commotion, not shots but a scuffle that sent boxes and crates tumbling down, their crashes covering more human grunts punctuated by a sudden, sharp, unearthly cry.

Meiling!

"Don't shoot, Ramsey, don't shoot!" Michael yelled as he leapt from their hiding place and raced across the empty space, quickly reaching the other side, where he frantically kicked and elbowed all obstacles out of the way. He was using his bad shoulder, probably reinjur-

ing the broken collarbone, but he felt no pain and
wouldn't have cared if he had.

Meiling was out cold, half-hidden under the crate
that had apparently felled her. Quickly Michael shifted
it up and out of the way. She clutched a prize in her
hand: a Colt revolver, old Army issue, a handsome gun.
A hero's gun. Stolen, Michael would have bet. This bastard who was following him was no hero. But he was
clever enough, and tenacious . . . and gone.

"Shit!" Michael said, a word he seldom used, but he
was angry and frustrated and sick at heart. After
quickly ascertaining that no bones were broken, he
picked the unconscious Meiling up in his arms. Her hair
was down and trailed over Michael's shoulder as he
carried her back the way he'd come. He surmised she'd
used one of her long steel hairpins on that bastard,
whoever he was.

"I should've gone after him," Michael muttered. But
there was no point, really. He wasn't going to catch the
big man now. Maybe, if Meiling had managed to
skewer him with her hairpin, there might be a trail of
blood he could follow. Maybe, with the help of the
local police *and* a blood trail, they might actually catch
this guy. But all that would take time.

And every precious minute he spent that way would
feel to Michael like a minute he could have spent finding Fremont. The big man—that whole side of his life,
which he was pretty sure now was connected to the
railroad explosion and other incidents—was going to
have to take a back seat, at least for the moment.

Hilliard Ramsey had disappeared too, Michael saw
when he reached their makeshift blind. He was not surprised.

# 18

_____

WHEN TWO DAYS had gone by without my father's replying to my telegram, I sent a similarly worded one to him at his bank. To this one I received an almost immediate answer:

TO CAROLINE FREMONT JONES
HIRAM HOTEL
HIRAM UTAH

MY DEAR MISS JONES STOP YOUR FATHER NOW RETIRED
STOP HAS BEEN ILL STOP DID YOU SEND TO HIM AT
HOME STOP AM CONCERNED STOP GLAD YOU ARE WELL
STOP PLEASE ADVISE STOP
GLADYS HORNSBEY FORMER SEC TO LF JONES

I remembered Miss Hornsbey, a sturdy, dependable, plainly dressed, and plainspoken woman who had been my father's secretary approximately forever. I had always liked her. I wondered what she thought of Augusta, to whom I still could not refer as Father's wife without getting a bad taste in my mouth.

Well, one thing was clear: Augusta must have intercepted my telegram to Father, or else he would have replied. Only his absence, perhaps on a business trip, I had thought, could have accounted for the lack of a response—assuming, that is, he had received my communication, which apparently he had not. Because *she* hadn't let him.

Immediately I was consumed by an immense rush of anger. Really, how dare the woman keep from my father something so important as the information that I was not dead!

Of course she would doubtless have preferred that I *were* dead. My moving all the way across the country hadn't been enough for her, oh no, she wanted me out of his life entirely. Wanted my poor father all to herself. Selfish, stifling, horrid woman! What had he ever seen in her?

I did know the answer to that: Augusta Simmons, when my father married her, was a voluptuous widow who'd acted as if she worshipped the ground Leonard Pembroke Jones walked on. And perhaps she had. But I doubted it. Unhappily for him, if one could make an accurate inference from his appearance and some things he'd said on his visit to San Francisco the spring just past, Augusta had begun to show her true colors once they were well and safely married. Poor man.

During their courtship Father had been too besotted with Augusta to notice that the woman was a social climber. I must admit, as these social things do not interest me in the least and I would far rather ignore them, people who clamber after social status leave me particularly cold.

Knowing that, I'd tried to make allowances for my extreme reaction to her. And knowing Father, who had always been a soft touch for lost causes and underdogs, the fact that Augusta had come from a less socially prominent family than either the Pembrokes or the Newport Joneses (Father's branch), or even the Fremonts (from Charleston, my mother's maiden name), had probably seemed to him a point in her favor.

At any rate, after knowing her for only six months, he'd married her, and I'd used their honeymoon as the occasion for my flight from Boston to California; from a proper young womanhood punctuated by the inevitable marriage, to the unconventional role of working woman, owner of her own business, and (some would say) living with her partner in sin.

So who was I to criticize Augusta?

I was my father's daughter, that's who. Quick to anger and equally quick to forgive, that was I—and indeed I would have forgiven Augusta most anything if she had been making Father happy. But she was not. The Leonard Pembroke Jones who'd come to see me in the spring had been almost a stranger—a sick shadow of the man he'd been.

*Oh, God,* I thought. And then I went a step further, I prayed: *God, please let me get to Boston in time to see my father again. Don't let him die before I can arrive!*

One thing became quickly clear once I began to think in those terms: Miss Hornsbey could help. So I replied to her telegram:

TO MISS GLADYS HORNSBEY
GREAT CENTENNIAL BANK
BOSTON MASSACHUSETTS

DEAR MISS HORNSBEY STOP HAVE SENT WIRE TO BEACON
STREET STOP NO REPLY FROM FATHER STOP WISH TO LET
HIM KNOW I AM WELL STOP BELIEVE SOME INTERFERENCE
FROM AUGUSTA STOP CAN YOU REACH FATHER BY

TELEPHONE STOP REPLY TO ME HERE STOP WILL
REIMBURSE YR EXPENSES STOP
MANY THANKS STOP
CAROLINE FREMONT JONES

Off I went to the telegraph office again. Wayne and I were becoming fast friends.

When I returned to the hotel Sandra Hunter was in the lobby, leaning on the desk and talking to a woman I'd never seen before. This woman was dark-skinned and black-haired, rather heavy, with a pleasant square-shaped face.

"Hey, Fremont," Sandra said, circling her lanky arm in the air, "come on over and meet Bright Feather. She's Mrs. Tom—takes turns with him here. Feather's a whole lot nicer than her husband, if you ask me."

I suppose this might sound preposterous to anyone thinking of the United States west of the Mississippi as the "Wild West," but Bright Feather was not only the first Indian I had ever met, she was the first I'd ever seen up close. We Americans have done such a thorough job of eradicating most of them, and containing the rest, that as long as one keeps to the urban centers of the West, one might go a whole lifetime without meeting even one example of those who once ruled the North American continent.

"How do you do, Bright Feather," I said. "What a lovely name!"

"Hey," she said informally. "Tom told me what happened to you, how you were in that train wreck, and said you'd lost your memory for a while and all. So now you're here till your friends come for you, that right?"

She didn't sound at all like one thinks an Indian would sound. She didn't say "how" or speak in broken sentences or any of that; her manner of speaking was the same as anyone else's.

I replied, "I think so. I haven't been able to get in touch with them yet. It's really rather ironic—they're out looking for me, that's why I haven't been able to reach them."

"Haw!" Sandra hooted, slapping the desk with the flat of her hand. "I bet what they need's an Indian guide, Feather. Think you could rustle 'em up one?"

"Oh sure, let me just make a note of that," Bright Feather said with a perfectly straight face. Suiting her actions to her words, she really did make a note of it. Then she looked me straight in the eye and said, "I never can remember anything if I don't write it down. And I get lost without a map."

Sandra doubled over laughing, and I joined in because laughter is infectious. Even if I wasn't exactly certain what we were laughing about. I suppose Bright Feather was making fun of herself, in a subtle way—but one must be careful with such suppositions.

Eventually Sandra straightened up, wiping her eyes with the back of her hand. "That Feather," she said, shaking her head, "she's a real card."

Bright Feather winked at me. I winked back, smiling still. It felt good—I hadn't been doing nearly enough smiling lately.

Sandra either had not yet dressed for work or was taking a day off. She was one of those women who appear to be plain until they put on a little makeup—or in Sandra's more usual case, a lot of makeup—because their looks are all in their bone structure. Her lips were thin and her eyes were pale, but these features are easily enhanced. With good clothes and a decent hairdresser, she'd have been a striking woman. Her hair was a vague shade of blond, and unfortunately thin. I wondered if she'd had some kind of illness, a fever perhaps, that had caused it to fall out; or perhaps it was her obvious habit of back-combing it, which I was sure she did in order to make it appear fuller. But this back-combing was not having the desired effect; instead, if my eyes did not deceive me, the fine hair was breaking under the strain and thus compounding the problem even further.

"I have never met an Indian before," I confessed.

"Feather ain't typical," Sandra said.

"I am not surprised to hear that."

"She's been to college and all."

"Really?" I inquired. "How interesting. I went to college too, in the East. Where did you go?"

"Convent school, run by nuns in Chicago. Before that, they taught us heathen savages at a mission school on the Reservation. I was gonna be a Sister but I changed my mind." Feather shrugged. "They felt cheated. Here they'd invested all this money in an Indian's education—and a woman too, to make it even worse—and then I up and left."

"Good for you, for following your own mind," I said.

"Haw!" said Sandra.

Bright Feather kept a serious expression. "I decided I wanted to study the old ways, which was how I took back my Indian name. My Christian name was Barbara Marie."

"That's a pretty enough name, but I prefer Bright Feather," I said honestly. "But now, ladies, if you'll excuse me, my arms are tired and I think I'd better get off these crutches."

"Why's your arms tired," Sandra asked, "when it's your legs that's broke?"

To my surprise, Bright Feather replied for me, and she did so accurately: "It's because she's not supposed to put her weight down all the way on her feet. So she leans hard on the crutches. I can maybe help you some, Fremont. I'm good at healing. That's the main thing that brought me back to my people. I want to be a healer. Medicine Woman."

"How fascinating!" I exclaimed sincerely, though I did wonder how she could be with her people and also married to old Tom, who wasn't an Indian but a white man. A story, I supposed, for another day. "Of course I'd appreciate your help. I'll try most anything to get these legs to mend faster."

"She'll do it too," Sandra called after me. "She's a good 'un, damn straight. Oh, and Fremont—"

I turned back to hear Sandra's parting remark, my hand on the doorknob.

"—thanks for trading rooms. I like it upstairs for a change. See how the rich people live. Haw!" Sandra slapped the desk again.

I smiled, ignoring that embarrassing word "rich," and then I remembered something. "Oh, Sandra, about your little cat—"

"Cat? I don't have no cat."

"That black kitten with the green eyes isn't yours? Whose is he, then?"

Bright Feather looked over her shoulder at me. Her brown eyes twinkled. "Is it pure black?"

"Yes. Sleek as slate, black as coal. Not a speck of white on him anywhere."

"It's good luck when any cat, but especially a pure black one, chooses you for its human companion," Bright Feather said. "So if I was you, I'd hang on to it. That's the mystical answer, the Indian answer: Cat's chosen you, makes him yours.

"But white people's answer is: That cat's a stray. Been hanging around here for the past week or so. Doesn't belong to anybody."

"Oh yes he does," I said, opening the door to my room, "I prefer the Indian explanation. The little cat belongs now to Fremont Jones."

*Or perhaps,* I thought as I went in and closed the door behind me, *I belong to that little cat.* The cunning creature was curled up asleep precisely in the center of the bed, and it was quite amazing how my heart was gladdened by such a simple thing.

———

Leaving the train at Salt Lake City put Michael and Meiling into Provo a day and a half later than they'd expected to arrive. Wish Stephenson's telegram was waiting for Michael when he signed the register at the Mountain View Hotel, where, thanks be to the gods, they'd kept open the reservation he had made before leaving Utah for San Francisco over a month ago.

"Who sends the telegram?" Meiling asked.

She had recovered from the effects of being knocked unconscious by a falling crate, but she was still angry with herself for having captured only the gun, not the whole man along with it. Anger made her surly, imparting a dark cast to her features. Strangely, she seemed less inscrutable this way, more . . . approachable.

And so, though he was wary and careful around her, Michael found an angry Meiling rather attractive. She was definitely a more exciting companion than the quiet, reserved person he had usually known by the name of Meiling Li.

"Wish Stephenson," Michael said in answer to her question. "I expect it's just J&K business, nothing important. Let's go on to our rooms. If the telegram says anything that pertains to us both, I'll let you know. Otherwise, shall we simply meet for dinner in"—he consulted his pocket watch—"two hours?"

"That is agreeable," Meiling said.

They parted, and then only minutes later Michael was pounding on the door of Meiling's room, which was next to his.

He paid no attention whatever to the state of her *deshabille* when she opened the door, but burst right in, waving the telegram in the air. "Listen to this, Meiling, the telegram is about Fremont!" He read it out word for word.

TO MICHAEL ARCHER KOSSOF
MOUNTAIN VIEW HOTEL
PROVO UTAH

DEAR MICHAEL
AM IN RECEIPT OF WIRE FROM FREMONT JONES STOP SHE
WAS INJURED IN TRAIN WRECK BUT IS SAFE STOP NOW
LIVING IN HIRAM UTAH AT HIRAM HOTEL STOP NEEDS
ASSISTANCE TO COME HOME STOP GOOD LUCK STOP KEEP
US INFORMED STOP MOTHER SENDS HER BEST STOP
WISH STEPHENSON

Michael and Meiling both cried out at the same time: "She's safe!" They threw their arms around each other and hugged, until a slightly embarrassed Michael suddenly became aware that he was holding a nearly naked woman crushed against him.

He stepped back. Meiling averted her eyes and drew the rose silk robe more closely around her. But both were too happy to be embarrassed for long.

"We will go to her immediately, of course," Meiling said.

"This is the most marvelous luck," said Michael. He couldn't stay still, and paced the floor with such great steps he almost bounded.

"Not luck," said Meiling. "Fate. Being sensitive to the forces at work. She pays attention. You pay attention, and so do I. The time is right, the energy is right. And so, we come together."

"Whatever you say, Meiling. Get dressed, come downstairs, we must celebrate. Not in two hours, right now!"

He raced for the door, but halfway there, in mid-leap as it were, turned back to her. "Oh say, give me a few

minutes. I have to go out and find a map first. There's
no town named Hiram on the one I've already got."

Meiling's smile faded. "Michael," she said gently, "if
you do not mind so very much, kindly find your map
and have your drink alone. I must withdraw, and consult my grandmother over this new development."

"Oh, Meiling—"

She said firmly, "It is wonderful that we know now
where Fremont is, and so will not waste precious time
in empty searching. But there is still much wrong. There
is danger . . . to us all."

# 19

TO FREMONT JONES
HIRAM HOTEL
HIRAM UTAH

DEAREST FREMONT
MEILING AND I ARE COMING TO YOU STOP UNSURE HOW
LONG FROM HERE TO THERE STOP WILL COME AS FAST
AS POSSIBLE STOP
I LOVE YOU STOP MICHAEL

———

"Damn!" Michael swore. He'd charged at the door
of Provo's Western Union without noticing it was
closed. Now he stepped back and read the sign: HOURS
OF OPERATION, SEVEN A.M. TO FOUR P.M.

He didn't bother to check his watch—he knew it was
after five. So, his telegram would just have to wait until
morning. But by God, he hated that!

What did these people do if they had an emergency
in the middle of the night? There are some things that

just can't wait until morning. . . . Still, there wasn't a thing he could do about it.

After standing on the sidewalk like a fool, tapping his foot and looking up and down the street although he knew damn well Provo wouldn't have more than one telegraph office, he finally folded the paper with Fremont's telegram in half lengthwise and slipped it into his inside jacket pocket, the long one, where it wouldn't wrinkle.

*That's the trouble with small towns,* he thought as he crossed the street, heading for a store with a sign that said PROVO HARDWARE AND DRY GOODS. *In small towns, everybody believes nothing's really that important, just about anything can wait. And then, if they think you're some city slicker, they'll set about proving it to you; they'll go so slow on just about anything you're trying to accomplish that the agony of waiting's enough to make your teeth itch.*

"I need a map," Michael announced to the man in shirt sleeves behind the dry goods counter.

"You going somewheres? Or coming from somewheres. Haven't seen you in here before, have I?"

*Right, here we go,* Michael thought.

He took a deep breath, as unobtrusively as possible, and readied himself for the small talk that was likely to be necessary before any map was produced from behind the counter, or in the corner, or up on a shelf—wherever such things were kept in this particular store. He was right—it did take a long time—and to his dismay, when he got back to his hotel room with it, the map didn't do him a bit of good.

Hiram wasn't on it.

He was explaining all this to Meiling at dinner an hour later, his former elation now tainted with peevishness and fraying around the edges with worry.

Meiling had lost her rather exciting angry edge, and had returned to being inscrutable. The grandmother influence, Michael supposed. She didn't look at him, but down at a piece of fish on her dinner plate. She was slowly separating it into thin flakes. Occasionally she ate one.

"That is odd, yes," she agreed.

"Irritating as hell."

"Perhaps another map?" Meiling did not have the same reluctance about the mashed potatoes and greens that she had about the fish—her vegetables disappeared rather rapidly once she began on them.

"I don't know. This one's the standard; it's the one everybody uses." Her eating habits were getting to him. He'd seen her do senseless things like this before, and there was never any pattern. Michael couldn't stand things he couldn't figure out, even if those things were only another person's peculiarities and of no real consequence to him.

So he said, not bothering to hide his exasperation, "Meiling, if you don't like fish, why did you order it?"

Now she looked up. "I do like it. But I prefer it in very thin slices and in small quantity. This came in a great slab, which I am making thin and small."

Oh yes. Well, put that way, it made perfect sense. "I see," Michael said. Somewhat sheepishly, he resumed eating his sirloin steak. The food was good, but not as good as the elegant meals they'd had on the train.

"Someone will know where this town is," Meiling remarked calmly. "All we have to do is ask, and keep asking until we find someone who knows."

Michael chewed thoughtfully. That approach seemed a lot like asking for directions; he hated to ask for directions. So he simply said "Hm," which was his all-purpose noncommittal reply. As Fremont knew all too well, and maybe Meiling too, it meant "maybe yes and maybe no."

They finished the meal in silence.

Instead of dessert, Michael asked for coffee for two.

He was told by a frowning waiter that there would be a delay—they would have to brew it.

"Then by all means, brew it!" Michael said, frowning in return.

"This is good," Meiling said rather unexpectedly.

"What?" Michael looked out the window where, if it had not grown rapidly so dark, they could have seen a view of the Wasatch mountains rising up from Provo. If she didn't mean the view, what then?

"A time to talk while we wait for the coffee. You've had a good meal, you are calmer now, no?"

"Yes, I suppose I am." Michael leaned back in his chair, adjusted his blasted sling, and tried to get comfortable.

"There is something I would like to know."

"If I can enlighten you, I will gladly do it. You have only to ask." Michael playfully inclined his head, a little imitation of her characteristic bow.

"You seem to believe the two men who are following us, that is, the large one from whom I took the gun and the other one, are doing so for reasons that are unrelated to our search for Fremont Jones. Am I right?"

Uh-oh. Uncomfortable subject. One he'd been trying not to think about.

"Partially," Michael said.

Now Meiling did her little bow. "You will please explain more fully."

"Oh all right. But I warn you, there's no point to it, because we're going after Fremont no matter what they do. I don't care about those two; if I have to, if there's no other way, I'd just as soon put a bullet right between their eyes, either one or both of them."

"There is no need to be so vehement; I do not seek to distract you from finding Fremont. It is what I want most, also. However, I think you will find, Michael Archer Kossoff, that one or both of these men is going to create problems for us very soon."

"Your grandmother told you that, I suppose."

"In a manner of speaking, yes."

He sighed. "Hilliard Ramsey and I, as I've already told you, go a long way back."

"What you have not said is why you believe he is following you now."

Michael stared hard at Meiling. She met his eyes with an unfaltering gaze of her own. Then slowly, deliberately, carefully, he considered the other diners; he was assessing degrees of risk.

Finally he spoke. "This you must tell no one, ever. Not even Fremont. If she is to be told, then I will do it, and I will decide what may be said to her. Do you understand?"

"Yes." Her eyes told him that she told the truth.

"In Russia, the Tsar is in trouble. I have served the Tsar for many years, as my father served his Tsar before me, and my grandfather, and so on since there have been Kossoffs in America."

"My family too has always known this, Michael," Meiling said, "and I have known it."

"What you do not know is that now, even the members of the Russian court are divided. The country of my ancestors is in very serious trouble, Meiling. I have been asked to take one side. To do a terrible thing, so that a good thing may result. I have not yet decided if I will do this thing or not, but those who have asked me are offering a powerful incentive: If I do it and succeed, I will be free. The Tsar will be so grateful that he will grant me whatever I ask, and I will ask for my freedom, never to have to act as a Russian spy again."

Meiling nodded, to show that she understood.

"I am all but certain Ramsey works for the other side. I expect they are paying him to watch me in case I make a move."

"This is serious. But in fact it can have nothing to do with Fremont Jones," Meiling observed.

"That is correct."

"And the other man? The big one, whom I most dishonorably allowed to escape?"

She would never get over it, Michael realized, unless she was the one who, in the end, brought him down. He could understand how she felt because he'd been there himself. Meiling's heart was like a man's, like his own.

"The other man, I think, is not nearly as intelligent as Hilliard Ramsey, but he's dangerous because he's desperate. What causes his desperation, I do not know, but I think it's something to do with the Southern Pacific Railroad. I think he is the one who was behind the harassment that Fremont and I—that is to say, the J&K Agency—were hired to investigate. Somehow, our presence seems to have coincided with a more serious level of disruption, culminating in that explosion. Whether that was intentional, or coincidental, I also do not know. But the more he pursues me, the more I think the man may have a grudge against me, aside from any he may have against the railroad."

"And against Fremont?" Meiling inquired, a line of concern appearing in the center of her forehead.

"Possibly. Not likely, though, because all of her enemies have ended up in jail."

"Not all," said Meiling.

Michael raised his black eyebrows in silent query.

"The one called Braxton Furnival got away. He disappeared from his house in the Del Monte Forest, leaving others—men he had hired—to pay for his crimes. She has told me about him, but she has never given me a physical description of the man. The one I have seen and described to you, could he be this Braxton Furnival?"

Michael felt his heart skip a beat, and all the color drain out of his face, as the realization spread through him and sank in.

"My God, Meiling, that's it! That's who it is!"

She inclined her head, not in one of her little bows but in grave acknowledgment. "I thought so. This man has had months to nurse his hatred of our Fremont Jones. I feel hate pouring out of him like a dark force. And I feel him on our heels, Michael—close behind."

---

Michael had sent me a telegram from Provo saying that he and Meiling would come as soon as possible. Everyone said it should take only two days to ride to Hiram from Provo, and vice versa. Yet two days came and went without any sign of Michael and Meiling.

I tried not to be very disappointed, but I must not have succeeded very well, for on the evening of the second day old Tom asked me what was wrong, why was I dragging my tail feathers. A charming metaphor.

"I was expecting someone from Provo," I said, "but perhaps they have gotten lost. Is the way very difficult? Surely they cannot have run into such obstacles as hostile Indians, robbers on the road, things like that? One assumes all that disappeared with the end of the previous century."

Old Tom chuckled. "These folks, these friends of your'n, they ever been to Hiram before?"

I shook my head silently.

" 'Cause," said Tom, eyes twinkling, clearly enjoying himself, "Hiram ain't on the map."

"But the town exists! It has—what does the sign outside the town limits say?—three hundred people."

"Three hunnert 'n' two. Miz Phillips had twins back in the summertime. Anyways, it's on *some* maps, like for the post office and the telegraph office and so on, all them folks that have to do business here, but the maps as get printed up and sold in stores, Hiram ain't on 'em."

"Why not?" I was feeling slightly sick to my stomach.

"On account of this is a Mormon state, and we're right smack dab in the middle of the most conservative Mormon country you can possibly imagine. Lots of little communities around here think they're holier than holy, they done out-Mormoned the Temple in Salt Lake—"

"That's all right," I interrupted hastily, "you don't have to say any more. I know exactly the type of people you're talking about." And I didn't want to be reminded either.

"Uh-huh." He eyed me as if he were wondering where I'd spent those months when presumably I'd had amnesia; but he hadn't asked before and he didn't now, for which I was grateful. "Anyways, when Utah got statehood, they just conveniently didn't put Hiram, and probably some other little towns with anti-Mormon ideas, on the official maps. We don't care none. Exceptin' when it inconveniences a body such as yerself, of course."

"Oh dear."

"Don't worry. Your friends'll find you. Folks always do. It just takes a while."

"But how?"

"They'll get out on the road and start askin' questions, goin' from town to town. Eventually somebody'll point 'em right here. You got plenty to do in the meantime, you ask me."

"Such as?" I inquired.

"Such as lettin' my Feather heal those legs of your'n. Such as gettin' some more flesh on those bones and roses in those cheeks."

I smiled. Tom and Feather were kind, and he was right. Feather had a real gift for healing, and as far as I could tell she was helping me. Not causing any harm. I was content here; Michael and Meiling were on their way; eventually they would find Hiram, and me; and I had a new book to read from the circulation rental library.

I had nothing to worry about, nothing at all.

# 20

---

MICHAEL REFLECTED that his recent physical exertions, of one sort and another, had certainly aggravated his injury. The pain now ran all the way down into his arm, but he welcomed it as an aid to staying awake. Truth to tell, what with the pain and temperatures colder than he was accustomed to after so many years of living in San Francisco, he was damn uncomfortable. As cold as it had been all day, when the sun went down the temperature had plummeted with it. Now he could see his own exhalations like smoke in the dark night air.

Smoke: He might as well light a pipe, it would help to keep him awake. With his good hand, grimacing unconsciously when even these simple movements pained him, Michael rooted through his pockets. Maybe he should switch to cigarettes—they were unpopular with gentlemen, but a hell of a lot more convenient.

The day had been overcast, with a thin layer of high pale gray clouds; now the night was both moonless and starless, black as pitch outside the small area of illumination cast by two kerosene lanterns that hung by wire handles from either side of the driver's bench at the front of the wagon. It was this near-total darkness that had finally forced him to stop for the night, but only because the road was so poor it didn't deserve the dignity of being called a road. It was more of a track, impossible to follow when beyond the lamplight all was so dark that he could barely make out the ears on the horses' heads.

He hadn't wanted to stop; Meiling had nagged him until finally he had to admit she was right—if they lost the track, they'd be delayed yet further. The last information they'd had from a traveler going in the opposite direction was encouraging—the man had spent the night before in a town he thought was called Hiram. They had only to continue the way they were going, they were bound to come to it, the man said.

So Michael had hoped he could reach Hiram before nightfall, but that hope had been in vain, even though he'd pushed the horses to their limit—and pushed Meiling's patience beyond its limit. She had been quiet for some time now, lying bundled up in the back of the wagon while Michael sat on the ground with a blanket beneath him and his back against the wagon wheel. He hoped she was asleep. All the damn day long she'd pestered him with her premonitions; God knew, he could use a few hours of silence.

The horses, which he'd reluctantly released from the wagon's traces and tethered behind it, snorted softly; the leather of their halters and reins creaked as the animals shuffled, probably seeking closer contact with one another for the sake of warmth. Michael pulled at his pipe, drew some comfort from smoking. Precious little, but any comfort was welcome. The pipe between his teeth, he took his revolver out of his pocket and put it in his lap at the ready, a concession to Meiling and her fears. Then he curled his one good hand once more around the bowl of the pipe, appreciating that small warmth against his palm.

She had wanted to stop much sooner. Stop, hell— she'd wanted to set up an ambush in broad daylight for "the big man," as she called him. The one who might or might not be, but probably was, Braxton Furnival. Meiling was convinced he was close on their heels, and dangerous.

Now it was Michael's turn to snort. He'd known Braxton Furnival fairly well over a period of about a year, during a time when they'd both lived down around Monterey—and while Furnival had certainly proved himself dishonest during that time, Michael couldn't believe the man would ever be truly danger- ous. He was a consummate coward and a bumbler to boot, the type who hired others to do his dirty work and even then managed to go wrong in the planning of it.

Michael frowned, pulling on his pipe. He'd just re- membered that Fremont had known Furnival too dur- ing that same time period, and her opinion of him had been much harsher than Michael's. If Fremont was right, then Braxton Furnival had committed murder. That murder had never been pinned on anyone; the po- lice had long since abandoned the case; Furnival had disappeared. Furnival a murderer? Michael doubted it.

Nursing the pipe along, unaware that his head was dropping lower and lower on his chest, Michael talked himself out of the few fears Meiling had managed to stir in him. He didn't believe desperation had made Braxton Furnival as dangerous as Meiling insisted. Be- sides, the man was unarmed because she'd taken his gun. No gun, no hireling to help him . . .

Michael removed the pipe from his mouth as he let out a long, heavy sigh. His chin rested on his breast- bone, and stayed there. His eyelids flickered, and closed. . . .

Something cold and hard bored into his temple as a harsh whisper cut through the stupor of exhausted sleep: "Don't move, Kossoff!"

Michael's eyes snapped open; simultaneously his fingers let go of the pipe they'd cradled in his lap and fumbled instead for the gun. It wasn't there. He knew he'd put it there, but the gun was gone! His eyes opened wider.

Again the harsh whisper: "If that Chinese demon woman is still with you, call her out here. Say you need her, nothing else; if you try to warn her in any way I'll shoot you dead!"

Slowly, deliberately, Michael turned his head until the gun—which perhaps was his own, he could not yet tell—was no longer at his temple but instead grazed his eyebrows like a cold, slow kiss and came to rest dead center between his eyes. As he had hoped, his captor reflexively took a few steps back. Now Michael could see his face.

So, Meiling had been right all along. Right on more than one count. In the dim, wavering lamplight, Braxton Furnival was not just big but a threatening tower of a man. No longer the dapper dresser Michael remembered from Carmel and the Del Monte Forest: His tattered clothes and beard-stubbled face showed no vestige of the respectability the old Furnival had been accustomed to hide behind.

"Get that woman out here!" he insisted, still in a whisper, so harsh that this time his voice cracked.

But Meiling had already heard or sensed something amiss; through his back against the wheel Michael could feel the small vibrations of her movement inside the wagon. And suddenly Michael's mind was hyper-alert, thoughts and instincts and words coming together like clockwork.

"Meiling!" he roared in defiance of Furnival's warning. "Run, get away, go NOW!"

As he yelled the wagon lurched, and in that same moment Michael lashed out with both feet. Furnival toppled. They fell on each other like snarling wolves.

———

I named my kitten Hiram, which the people in the hotel found amusing, but I knew in years to come the cat's name would remind me of this very special time in my life. I was as happy here as I could possibly be under the circumstances, and grateful for it. This memory would be a good one.

Of course some things could be better, such as: I would have felt much relieved if I'd heard from Father, but I had not, which was of considerable concern to me. Waiting for Michael and Meiling to appear was also rather tedious—four days had passed since my receipt of their telegram. I was confident they would come soon, especially as everyone said it shouldn't take much longer for even the least experienced travelers to find us. Nevertheless, it was a vastly annoying practice of the Mormons to leave whole towns off the map of Utah just because the inhabitants didn't follow Mormonism. Whatever had happened here to the separation of church and state?

For a welcome distraction I had the care and feeding of my little feline, who had been declared by Feather to be a male of its species. Care was easy: In grooming, Hiram required no assistance, as he was naturally fastidious, with much licking of paws and fur and polishing of ears. Also in other essential habits of hygiene the cat took care of himself, coming in and going out the window as needed. Where he did his business was apparently nobody's business but his own.

Feeding, however, was a matter in which Hiram proceeded to educate me. Fascinating! I quickly learned that if I did not want my cat to bring disreputable dead creatures through the window and deposit them at my feet like some sort of macabre gift, I had best provide him with food that was to his liking. Otherwise he'd bring one of these gifts which, after having allowed me time for a proper inspection, he would take back and bat around a few times with his paws in a kind of feral pleasure. Then he would settle down to eat it, which was rather disgusting, although better than starving I am sure. What Hiram liked to eat was meat and fish. Period. If I gave him anything else, we were back to the macabre. To drink he liked water, which I kept always in a small bowl on the floor by the dressing table. His food I saved for him from my own meals. Once I tried to beg cream from the kitchen for a special kitty treat, but the cook would not give it to me.

"You shall have all the cream you like when we get back to San Francisco," I said to Hiram, who lay languidly asleep in my lap, not curled up but sprawled in abandon. A cat makes a gentle weight.

Of course there was no question of my leaving him behind—Hiram was a part of my life now. If Michael didn't like cats, well . . . Michael would just have to reconsider.

The sun had gone down some time before, and the night was so cold that I had closed the window. If Hiram wanted to go out, he had ways of letting me know; in the daytime a meow, at night a cool paw on my nose, in the dark. It was quiet too, in part because it was a weeknight, and in part because Hiram—the town, not the cat—although God-less as far as the Mormons were concerned, was a law-abiding place. During the week most folks went to sleep at sundown, even in winter, when the nights were long.

I generally stayed up for a few hours, though. I hadn't lost my city habits, even if I'd become so accustomed to reading by lantern light that I no longer paid attention to a certain amount of flickering. They used lamps or lanterns exclusively in this place.

The book I'd been reading no longer held my interest, and so I put it aside and wrote a few notes to myself. It was time I began a list of things to do upon my return to San Francisco. Surely it would not be defying Fate to do so at this point? Surely I was merely being prudent?

Number one on my list: Find an intermediary to deal with Pratt matters so that I could do certain things without revealing my whereabouts. Not that I really thought there was any danger of Melancthon Pratt coming after me, but better to be safe than sorry. An officer of my bank would be an ideal intermediary. First, I would instruct him to open an account in Provo in Norma Pratt's name and place on deposit the money I had promised her. Then I wanted to find a way to get a letter to Selene. I wanted her to know she could write to me if she wished, and I would reply, provided we could be sure that Father would not intercept either her letters or mine.

I frowned, wondering how this might be accomplished. The first letter should go in a package or pouch, as in it I would want to enclose the five-dollar gold piece Selene had insisted on giving me. I had not spent it; I thought perhaps I might even have chosen to die rather than spend it, her kindness had meant that much to me. Perhaps I might keep this gold piece as a memento, replacing it with another of even larger denomination?

But no . . . because Selene had won this gold piece in a contest. She had kept it not for its monetary value but because it was her prize.

"She shall have back her prize," I muttered, making note of it, although I was hardly likely to forget. Then I wrote: *Selene—college?* That was my dream, that I might somehow be allowed to send this bright and talented young woman to college, where she would see and learn about a wider world than she had available in the whole state of Utah. Would she want that as much as I wanted it for her?

I leaned back against the bed pillows and mused upon this question, to which I had no answer. In all likelihood I never would, because for the life of me I couldn't think of a way to contact Selene without Melancthon Pratt's knowledge. Eventually the musing over this problem meandered into a reverie, in which at last I allowed all sorts of feelings about and memories of the Pratt wives to wash over me; and from that I drifted into a restless, fitful sleep.

I did not sleep well, not even after I had roused myself to don my nightgown, get under the covers, and blow out the lamp. Countless times I opened my eyes to darkness and lay wishing for morning to come. Thoughts of Michael plagued me, to the point where I was so unable to get him out of my mind that when I did sleep, I dreamed of him. Not pleasant dreams either —I dreamed that he was in some kind of trouble, some sort of danger.

Finally, coming out of one of these bad dreams I opened my eyes to the gray light that precedes sunrise. Such a foreboding was upon me that I felt physically ill, weak, and nauseous.

I had just gathered together the energy to say aloud, "Nonsense!" when I heard a commotion outside my room. My heart rose into my throat as I recognized the source of the noise: Someone was knocking, hard, on the hotel's front door, which had been closed and locked for the night.

I was in a flannel nightgown and had no robe. Yet I did not hesitate, nor was there any question of taking time to get dressed. I grabbed my crutches, flung open my own door, and crossed the hotel lobby as fast as I could possibly move.

# 21

THE DOOR of the Hiram Hotel had a pane of glass in it, with a shade that was lowered when the hotel was locked for the night. In spite of—or perhaps because of—the fierce pounding going on, I delayed long enough to raise the shade so that I might see who was on the other side before opening the door.

It was Meiling.

I could not undo the lock fast enough.

Sandra Hunter had been awakened by the noise—as I flung open the door I heard her say something from the stairway, but I did not, could not, reply. I couldn't do anything, not speak or move or even think. I could only fill my eyes with the sight of my dear old friend, who flew through the doorway and threw her arms around me in an effusive fashion that was most uncharacteristic, not only of all Chinese women but also of the Meiling I knew so well. My crutches got in the way, but somehow we managed a tangle of hugging and greeting, until finally I laughed to see tears spilling from Meiling's eyes and to feel my own cheeks wet.

I had never before experienced this quality peculiar to us humans, that we sometimes cry when we are happiest of all.

Gradually I became aware that Sandra was standing nearby. I disentangled myself, clamped a crutch under an armpit, and wiped my wet face with the hand thus freed as Meiling also stepped back.

Nodding toward Sandra I said, "Sandra Hunter, meet Meiling Li. And vice versa."

Meiling found her dignity, made her small bow, and said, "I am pleased to meet new friend of my old friend Fremont Jones."

With that initial rush of happiness now subsiding, another emotion came swiftly to take its place. The new and far less welcome feeling, a sick and empty dread, established a residence in the pit of my stomach.

I swallowed hard and asked the key question: "Meiling, where is Michael?"

———

Sandra, Bright Feather, Meiling, and I were gathered around the warmth of the small woodstove in the corner of my room. Meiling had first held us spellbound with her tale: How at Michael's warning she had untied one of the horses from the back of the wagon and then ridden it bareback, clinging to that frightened horse for she did not know how many miles as they galloped in total darkness. At last she'd gained control of the animal, and had then hidden in a copse of trees for the rest of the night. As soon as the sky grew light enough to see she set out again, and fortunately it was not long before she found the track that was the road to Hiram.

Meiling had done what she was sure Michael would have wanted: She'd found and warned me. Now what next? According to Feather, we were having a council of war.

There was some disagreement as to the battle plan. Meiling did not want to involve anyone other than the two of us, herself and me. The objective was, of course, to free Michael and at the same time to capture "the big man," as Meiling called him. Her attempt to get her Mandarin-speaking tongue around the name Braxton Furnival would have been amusing in other circumstances.

I let the other three carry on their debate without me for a few moments while I thought about Braxton. Was it really he who had blown up the train, and done all the other things Meiling said Michael believed he'd done? The physical description she gave did sound like Braxton. She said Michael thought he was behind the harassment that the two railroad lines, the Southern Pacific, and Union Pacific, had hired J&K to investigate. Certainly Braxton had good reason to feel vindictive toward the owners of the Southern Pacific, but right now it was hard for me to believe he could hate me enough to blow up an entire train just because Michael and I were on it.

I was not going to be satisfied until I could see him with my own eyes, and hear with my own ears whatever he had to say for himself. Not to mention that the foremost course of action must be to get Michael away from this big man, whether the latter proved to be Braxton Furnival or someone else.

I had followed the course of the others' discussion even while thinking my own thoughts, and now I interrupted Sandra in the midst of a sentence.

She was saying, "This whole town would come out in a heartbeat—"

"Meiling is right," I said.

Their three faces turned to me, and I was struck by what disparate examples of female beauty we had here. Sandra, who was equally comfortable in any article of clothing—or possibly without any at all, though I'd never had reason to test this out personally—was still in her robe and gown. Not even the heat of the woodstove could bring color to her pale skin, and her sharp but classic features were most definitely those of a "white woman." Bright Feather, who did not have red skin even though Indians were generally assumed to, nevertheless had a becoming pink flush on her dusky high cheekbones. Meiling, though dressed like a Chinese workman in a cotton tunic and trousers, quilted for warmth, with her long hair in a single braid down her back, was nevertheless the most exotically beautiful woman I'd ever known.

That striking impression took only an instant to register. They were all looking at me expectantly and I plunged ahead, sure now what I wanted to do. "Meiling is right because if this big man is indeed Braxton Furnival, then what he really most wants is me. He has good reason to hate me. I knew him well about a year ago. Let's just say he, well, he took a fancy to me. I used his interest to trick and humiliate him because I found out he was . . . dishonest." That was putting it mildly, but I did not even like to remember all the things I had found out about Braxton, much less to say them aloud.

I went on: "He has Michael for a hostage. That means our best chance of success will involve deception, and it is much easier to pull off a ruse when there are only a couple of people involved. The whole town, as grateful as I would be for so much help, could only succeed by overcoming him with force. In such a process, Michael might be killed."

Meiling nodded. "It is so."

Sandra looked doubtful, but Bright Feather said, "When you put it like that, I agree. Spell out your plan. We'll do what we can."

---

Half an hour later, just as the sun broke over the mountaintops, Meiling and I rode side by side out of Hiram, back the way she'd come. She rode her black horse, this time with a saddle borrowed from Feather. I drove a buggy that belonged to one of Sandra's regulars, since unfortunately my not-yet-entirely-healed legs would not allow me to ride, but I could sit easily enough.

We did not talk much, though I could not resist commenting that I'd been unaware Chinese women who'd grown up in San Francisco knew how to ride horses. Meiling replied, modestly, that such little skill as she possessed on horseback had been acquired during her time as a student at Stanford.

Our plan rested on an assumption that the big man and Michael would be on their way to Hiram, and that in her headlong flight last night, the horse had carried Meiling far enough down the road that she'd had a considerable head start. Still, we did not think we would have to ride far up the road before we came upon the men.

As indeed we did not. At first sight of horses in the distance, I went ahead more rapidly, while Meiling hung back and left the road. If these travelers should prove not to be the ones we sought, she would rejoin me.

It was critically important to our plan that I appear to be alone. Bright Feather and her husband Tom were to have left town ten minutes behind me and Meiling. That was some comfort, but of course a lot can happen in ten minutes.

I do not like guns, but I do know how to shoot and would not go into a situation like this unarmed. I had a shotgun on the seat beside me, borrowed from Tom, and I was prepared to use it. Closer and closer the two men on horseback approached. My heart was in my throat as I strained my eyes, seeking to identify Michael's contours, the so-familiar set of his head upon his neck. Perhaps these two men were not the two I sought, for where was the wagon Meiling had mentioned?

They must have left the wagon behind, for in another minute I had recognized Michael. The bulk of the man beside him could most certainly be Furnival. I took up the shotgun in my right hand, held the reins in my left, said a few reassuring words to the sturdy horse that pulled the buggy, and went on.

When we were about ten yards apart, I pulled back on the reins and said "Whoa!" And when the buggy came to a complete standstill, I placed the reins between my knees and raised the shotgun with both hands. I took aim.

"Stop where you are!" I called out in a loud voice.

They didn't stop. The big man had the reins of the second horse, and the man astride that second horse was my Michael, no longer a shadow of a doubt about that—certainly not after an involuntary "Fremont!" escaped his throat.

"Stop or I'll shoot!" I said.

They didn't, and I did. It is not the easiest thing in the world to aim an unfamiliar shotgun from a seated position, but in a crisis I am always surprised what one can do. My shot went wide, but that was what I had intended. I had made my point.

"I am coming closer," I said, and jacked another round into the chamber.

When I was within ten feet I was able to identify Braxton Furnival with certainty, although he had a wild look about him.

"Fremont Jones," he said. "It's true, you *are* alive. Where's the Chinese gal?"

"Yes, I'm alive. Meiling is at the hotel in Hiram. She fell off her horse and injured herself badly, but she came on nevertheless to tell me what had happened."

I cut my eyes quickly to Michael—I did not dare look away from Furnival for long, which I was sure Michael understood, even though he was trying to send me some message with his own eyes.

"Too bad." There was a trace of the old Braxton in the gaze he swept over me from head to foot. He'd been a connoisseur of women, and charming enough in a rather rough way. But either I looked too haggard now to be any longer appealing, or he just simply hated me, because the light of appreciation in his sweeping gaze soon turned to contempt. He said, "Just tell me one thing before I shoot you. Were you in your compartment when the train blew up?"

I blinked. For a moment my mind would not decipher his question. But then I saw it as an opportunity, and my brain began to function, this time at high speed. "No, I was not. I had been in the dining car and had not yet reached my compartment. I do not, actually, remember much about it yet. I had quite a blow on the head. Was that your doing? You dynamited the train?"

"He did it, all right," Michael said. "Last night he told me everything. He's a braggart, aren't you, Furnival?"

"Quiet, Kossoff. Now that I have her, you're no longer of any use to me. Make trouble, I'll just shoot you dead right here and now. Be a good fellow and maybe I'll give the two of you a little time together before I kill you both."

"You seem to forget," I said, "that I am armed. I will most certainly interfere with your plans. Answer the question, Braxton."

"I dynamited that train twice over. Once, with a timing mechanism on the trestle. Again with sticks of dynamite on a long fuse laid right outside your compartment. I didn't do the thing inside the train myself, of course, I paid somebody to do it. I wasn't on the train when it went. I'm not that stupid. That extra step with the dynamite in the train car was one I took after I recognized you and Kossoff getting on that particular train. I couldn't believe my luck. But that train was doomed anyway, even if you hadn't been on it."

"Just out of curiosity," I said, lowering the shotgun slightly as if dropping my guard, "was it you behind all those little episodes of railroad harassment that Michael and I were hired to investigate?"

"Of course it was me." Furnival preened, there was no other word for it, even though he was scarcely at the moment the peacock he used to be. More like a scraggly turkey.

He bragged for a bit. Every minute he talked was another minute for Meiling to get in place and make her move.

I raised the shotgun again and took aim. I had a bad moment when the horse decided we'd been sitting there long enough, as I was holding the reins between my knees and of course had no strength whatever in my legs. But the horse quieted, I didn't lose aim, and I said, "All right, that's enough. You're not really interested in Michael, Braxton. You know that, and I know it. Let him go, then toss away your gun, and I'll do the same. I'll come with you. My life for his."

"It's not his gun," Michael said grimly, "it's mine. He took it from me. And I don't want to trade."

"You have no say in this, Michael," I said. I sounded cold, and I felt that way too, entirely without emotion. I have observed several times now that I achieve this emotionless state when a true crisis is at hand. "Well, then, Braxton? What do you say?"

He never got a chance to say anything, because at that moment Meiling came running up behind him. In an astounding move she launched herself into the air with a great cry, and kicked Braxton Furnival two-footed with such force that she knocked him off his horse. Michael, although his hands were tied in front of him and I saw the pallor of sudden pain cross his face, slid off his black horse. The sling Meiling had told me he needed for a broken collarbone that he kept reinjuring hung empty from his neck, and he'd been riding without a saddle. With both hands still tied, he picked up the gun Braxton had dropped, but there was no need. Meiling was all over the man. Unarmed, he didn't stand a chance against her hands and feet.

It was all over by the time Tom and Feather rode up a few minutes later. We let the two of them do the honors of taking Braxton Furnival to Hiram's town jail.

———

We stayed on in Hiram, Utah, Michael and Meiling and I, as long as we dared. Until the snow threatened to lock us in for the winter, which was around the tenth of December. By the time of our leaving I had fully regained my strength and was beginning to walk again with the aid of only two canes.

I had purchased a small wire cage with a padded bottom for Hiram the Cat to ride in. Michael pretended not to approve of my pet, but I had caught him stroking the kitty a time or two when he thought my back was turned.

Hiram was in his cage, which was being carried by Meiling, and she had gone ahead to the wagon. I was making one last circuit of my room preparatory to turning it over to Sandra Hunter, saying my silent goodbyes and being sure I had not forgotten anything. I had asked to be left alone to say goodbye in privacy to this place that had been so very special to me, in ways I could not begin to put into words.

So I was startled when I heard Michael's voice.

"Fremont," he said, "may I come in?"

Distracted, I glanced over my shoulder, not sure I was ready yet to go. I felt as if I were leaving a haven. "I'll be out, there's no need for you to come in here."

"Oh, but there is," he said, "because I have something for you. Something very special that I've been saving for this moment. Something I had made in San Francisco, because—well, you'll see."

My curiosity overcame me. "Oh?"

Michael came into the room slowly, his hands behind his back.

"Turn around," he said, "so that your back is to me, and close your eyes."

"I don't know if I can trust you," I remarked lightly, but I did as I was told.

I heard a faint sound like a curtain falling, and then felt something soft on my shoulders, down my arms, against my neck—and Michael's arms enfolded me.

He, this man, was my real home, my true haven.

He said, "Don't look yet. No peeking. Just, um, move a step to your left, now half a step more . . . that's it. That's fine."

I teetered a little, for I was standing without the help of my two canes. But I scarcely noticed because my curiosity was overwhelming me.

"Now?" I asked.

"Now. Open your eyes and look into the mirror."

In Sandra Hunter's oval dressing table mirror I saw my reflection, and Michael's gift.

He had wrapped me in a new aubergine cape.

*If you enjoyed Fremont Jones's fifth adventure,*
*DEATH TRAIN TO BOSTON,*
*don't miss Dianne Day's sixth Fremont Jones*
*mystery,*
*BEACON STREET MOURNING,*
*available at your favorite bookstore in hardcover*
*from Doubleday in September 2000.*

In *Beacon Street Mourning* the normally intrepid Fremont Jones is thrust back into the world of her childhood—the proper Bostonian world from which she had escaped only a few short years. For the first time she must use her hard-won investigative skills to solve a case of a very personal nature.

Still not fully recovered from the two broken legs she suffered in *Death Train to Boston*, Fremont Jones learns that her father, Leonard Pembroke Jones, is gravely ill and hospitalized in Boston. Distressed, and always suspicious of her detested step-mother, Augusta, Fremont and her life-partner, Michael Archer, set out at once to be at her father's bedside.

When they arrive, he appears to be somewhat improved, although his longtime physician, Searles Cosgrove, is doubtful of a full recovery. Could Augusta have been complicit in his illness? Fremont, at least, is certain of it. When, once more at home, Leonard dies suddenly in the middle of the night, Fremont begins to look for poison. But then Augusta is shot to death, which would seem to exonerate her—or does it?

Determined to uncover the truth, Fremont and Michael begin an investigation of their own and discover potential enemies on all sides, and in the unlikeliest places.

### BEACON STREET MOURNING
*A Fremont Jones Mystery*
BY DIANNE DAY

## ABOUT THE AUTHOR

DIANNE DAY spent her early years in the Mississippi Delta before moving to San Francisco and the Bay Area. Fremont Jones has appeared in four previous mysteries: *The Strange Files of Fremont Jones*, which won the Macavity Award for Best First Novel, and three bestselling sequels. Day has now completed her sixth Fremont Jones mystery, *Beacon Street Mourning*, and is working on a novel of suspense based on the life of Clara Barton.

# -DIANNE DAY-

Brave, resourceful, adventurous Fremont Jones is a
woman ahead of her time...She's an investigator as
perspicacious as Sherlock Holmes and as
spirited as Kinsey Millhone.

## THE STRANGE FILES OF
## FREMONT JONES
_____ 56921-X  $5.99/$7.99 in Canada

## FIRE AND FOG
_____56922-8  $5.99/$7.99 in Canada

## THE BOHEMIAN MURDERS
_____57412-4  $5.99/$8.99 in Canada

## EMPEROR NORTON'S GHOST
_____58078-7  $5.99/$8.99 in Canada

---